I'll Be Your Dog

The book that bent the love triangle

Robbie McCallum

Cover Design by Andrew Marshall

A CIP Catalogue for this book is available from the British Library.

ISBN 978-1-907590-00-9

First Published in 2010 by Thinking Ink Limited

Thinking Ink Limited
Media House, Suite 32
Brighton BN2 3HB
United Kingdom

For Sue

Robbie McCallum was born in Glasgow, Scotland. He left school at 15 to become an apprentice in the Railway and subsequently studied at Nottingham University, University d'Orsay Paris, and the London College of Printing. He has won numerous awards for his writing and was nominated for a BAFTA for his film script RANK. Robbie is married with two children and divides his time between homes in Brighton, UK, and the City of Mindelo, on the island of São Vicente off the coast of West Africa.

CONTENTS

DOG   1
BITCH   5
VIXEN   7
BONE   9
BEG   12
HEAT   15
WOLF   17
KENNEL   20
TRICKS   25
CHOPS   32
PAW   34
PUP   42
SIT   47
BOWL   58
BARK   66
BITE   72
BITTEN   81
BASKET   94
ITCH   105
SCRATCH 110
DEAD   116
DOGHOUSE 127
ROLL   132
SNIFF   139
WAG   144
GROOM   151
PEDIGREE 164
BREED   171
SCENT   177
DOWN   183
LEASH   190
HOUND   195
STAY   200

DOG

S leeping with three women was never Easy's plan. If one of the drunks, bums or street jockeys had told him that within six months he would be having intimate, sexual relationships with three different women he'd have *thought* they'd flipped and gone crazy. If they'd told him these women would all be living in the same big, rambling house on Magazine he'd have been *sure* they were crazy. And if they'd told him he wouldn't be enjoying the sex half as much as any red-blooded heterosexual man thought he would, he would have rolled up his bedpack and gone found another tree to sleep under.

That said, Easy knew change was coming. He could feel the certainty of it deep inside, warming him like a good joke, a hot meal, or an unexpected hit of bourbon. He was 28, homeless, healthy, totally chilled, and he scudded along the New Orleans sidewalk to the upbeat, happy tune that had been playing inside his head ever since he could remember.

Kids roared in the yellow-hot streets—skipping in vast beehive huddles, hunting in wild banshee troupes and sending a bright, white baseball back and forth along the strip of hot asphalt with the beat of a giant metronome.

Easy caught the ball and took a big pretend bite—like it was a fresh green apple—with snap-crunch sound effects and all. The kids went pop-eyed, screamed and laughing—that one always worked on the little suckers.

Later, when the sun was closest and dead above and flattening the whole neighbourhood with a billion tons of photons, Easy helped an old lady onto her porch with her damp, sagging, paper-wrapped groceries. She was ancient with dark, dry, papery skin and although he knew she lived alone she'd bought food enough for a family of ten.

A waft of cat and urine rushed from her overcoat like heat from an oven as she fumbled for her keys.

Easy was trying to remember the last time he had a decent set-down at a proper table with a chair, when she stopped him on the threshold with the pale flat of her hand. His good Samaritan play was over and all he could do now was beg her for money.

The old woman thanked him and pinched his cheek like he was still some big, innocent kid. Then, she skipped inside like a teenage girl after her first date, and firmly shut the door.

Change was coming.

In the afternoon, under the shade of the old Magnolia trees, Easy passed a girl—the hot sunshine dapple sliding up over her body like liquid giraffe skin. He turned and watched her walking—she had it and within thirty seconds the street and the moment would be hers.

Her hair was held in a simple, high knot like the tail on a perky palomino pony, falling and swishing against the nape of her neck. Easy just soaked her all up and appreciated that beauty and gave thanks to Mother Earth. He hoped she'd turn and look back at him—share her moment. He found himself willing this beyond reason, forcing nature's hand—but she didn't turn around. Something else happened instead. Her little cloth purse fell from her shoulder bag and plopped silently onto the sidewalk like a dead lark.

In the whole shimmering, busy, black-baked summer street, with maybe two B-boys, the drug-store crew, and a Puerto Rican taxi driver checking out her lines, no-one spotted the purse fall but Easy.

It was a soft, comfortable, promising little weight on his fingertips. A precious thing; a gift from a spinster Aunt, ancient, with lace, fine trim, and sequins.

Easy didn't think too hard about the contents, pressing their weight into his palm, and stepped after the girl. As he approached he smelled her again - was wrapped in her vapour-trail freshness – and he suddenly didn't know what to say.

The girl just kept on walking. He could have stopped then, turned and walked away to a cooked breakfast, a pot of fresh coffee, and a good, hot bath. No one would have known but him. He saw himself—slinking off, head buried, shoulders hunched, hands thrust deeps in pockets—a different man forever.

'Ma'am,' he shouted, holding out the little purse so it was the first thing she saw when she turned. She smiled a beautiful smile and they stood there, just looking at each other. Easy couldn't speak and she grew shy right before his eyes. He suddenly felt acutely dirty in her glow. Her freshness and perfection were overpowering. She took her precious little cloth purse: 'Thanks,' she said softly and smiled again.

Easy was overcome—the way her lips drew back to expose that perfect band of teeth. To his horror, he winked! My God, he turned and walked off. Behind him he imagined the girl—still splashed in sunlight—now watching him go. He tried to walk smoothly, casually, like he returned precious cloth purses ten times a day—he couldn't quite affect the appropriately nonchalant gait, found his legs to be suddenly jerky, stiff, and rebellious.

He never looked back.

Later, when the sun was tired of bullying him and his thoughts were turning on hunger, he saw a quiet commotion at the end of the sidewalk and pushed through the warm, sweaty bodies to the centre of the crowd to see what was going on.

A little girl was crying. She wore blonde-pigtails, a cotton dress and patent shoes like she'd stepped from a 1950s Vermont postcard. An old guy, who turned out to be her grand daddy was down with on his knees on the oily road trying to calm her. The girl kept tearing free of his old arms and trying to hurl herself into the storm drain. Each time she got loose the old guy crumbled, looked overwhelmed and broken. Easy stepped forward, plucked the girl clear of the drain and put her back in the old man's frail, rangy embrace.

'Stay put, l'il sister.' He smiled at her then lay on his belly and peered into the hot, dark, stinking mouth of the culvert. The bright twin diamond eyes of the cutest kitten looked all the way back up at him.

Easy, now stripped down to his blue, busted jeans, emerged reeking and filthy out of the drain and presented the perfect little kitten to the perfect little girl. Hearty, joyous slaps rained down on his hot, sweaty back. He played modest, shuffled his feet, screwed the toe of his boot into the soft asphalt, repeated it was nothing and that anyone would have done the same—only somehow no-one had.

The girl came to him, clutching the little kitten like she'd never let it go again even if she lived to be a hundred. She spoke softly and when Easy bent down to hear her she planted the tenderest little whisperkiss on his smudged cheek. He felt the hot swell of pride flood over his chest and

3

climb up his neck—this was it, life, a moment well lived, a penny in the bank, suddenly every action was worthwhile and everything possible—just like we know it can be. He walked off, searching for a sunset.

That evening, Easy sprinted for the chain-boat as the ferrymen pulled the gangway and waved their thick, hairy dockwork arms. He ignored them and leapt from the quayside, grabbing the rusty handrail and swinging himself up and over to land solidly on the dew-wet deck. They cursed and threatened, closed him down and prodded stiff sausage fingers in his chest. He mugged and grinned and said nothing and let them get their pride and authority back in place. They rolled away to coil more rope.

As Easy stood looking across the water to New Orleans, he thought back over the day and felt complete. His Mind was silent, his Solar Plexus shone. He could feel the energy radiating from him, reaching out in all directions, huge tentacles, connecting him to the inevitable.

Change was coming.

BITCH

The Dead Pirate was a serious venue for pathological drinkers. The bare brick walls supported giant stuffed curves of fish and assortments of driftwood, munitions crates and vintage neon adverts for bygone brands of cigarettes and beer. The long, classic, dark wood bar was scarred and battered by shot-glass and time and BB King and his 'Lucille' ripped great holes in the thick smoke-filled air.

Beth, the owner, was a dark and sensuous creature. Sharp as a feral cat, ruthless, quick-limbed, and smutty. She helmed the bar with spirit and fire, stripped travelling salesmen of their profits, wedding bands, and sexual insecurities, and slugged it out with the most belligerent and alcohol-soaked dockworkers that she later mocked, screwed, then barred for life.

She rose from the cellar on that quiet, humid night and called out in her coarse, nonchalant voice for Crawford—the new Australian barman—to step in to the back office. To the remaining staff, her tone heralded the start of yet another routine sacking.

Crawford entered the room and found Beth leaning against the desk in a coil of blue smoke. She stubbed out her cigarette and fixed him with her low, level stare:

'Shut the door.'

He did so without taking his eyes off the woman, fearing she might pounce and poleaxe him with the angle-poise lamp or the heavy glass ashtray. She smiled, sensing his fear; her lips as ripe as a split plum.

'Do you know why I've asked to see you?'

He shook his head.

'Take a guess . . . '

He looked around the desktop and saw a roll of till receipts; evidence perhaps of his recent light-fingeredness. He shifted weight from one foot to the other then shrugged.

Beth put her hands on the desk slid back so that she was perched on the edge, dead in front of him. He could no longer see the till receipts, instead he noticed that Beth's skirt had hitched up to reveal she was not wearing underwear.

Crawford took in the tight mass of dark, dangerous curls, swallowed quietly and felt a familiar, sliding sensation in his gut.

Their eyes locked on to one another, reading, judging the moment. She was the more confident and smiled first—a menacing, playful smile.

'The moment I stepped in here, I knew I was screwed.'

He moved on her quickly, unbuckling his jeans. Beth conjured a condom from thin air, put the corner between her large, white, imperfect teeth and tore the foil.

They had sex.

Playful, energetic, physical sex.

Sex that was given meaning by their master-servant roles, the solidity of the office desk, and the proximity of the other staff. Finally, Beth's breath grew sharp, a groaning rose at the back of her throat, and she came.

Immediately, she dropped her legs, disengaging and shoving him away. He watched as she rounded the table, fixed herself a drink, straightened her skirt, sat, picked up the telephone and dialled:

'Donnie, it's me—put five hundred on Hound-Dog . . . no—you asshole—to win.'

She hung up and looked at Crawford, hanging there, his feet curled in slightly, his powerful arms hung low. She seemed genuinely surprised that he was still in the room.

'You're fired,' she said, reaching for her cigarettes. 'You can work out the weekend if you want but if I catch your hand in my till again I'll cut off your damn balls.'

VIXEN

The newsroom was a vast, orderly array of processed information. A massive, sanitized, dispassionate brain in a hardwired universe of happenings. It ran in real time and dealt with real events, spewed out real stories about real people but it itself was dead. It reported on life but life happened elsewhere, outside its sterile, smoked-glass enclosures, away from its Terabytes and Gigahertz, and deadlines, deliverables, and column inches.

Zoe was thirty-five and still screamingly fit. Today, she wore silk Cargo pants, a crocheted croptop from a thrift store in Irish Channel and that Rasta-hat she stole at the Superdome after her first assignment at the Comfortably Numb gig back in 1994. She came across as sexy and cool and unapproachable and *with it*. A prima-donna tank-girl. Punky, funky, and without the slightest suspicion of being a serial masturbator. The double page-layout for the new downtown parking zones was almost finished and she was feeling unjustifiably horny.

On the surface nothing ever fazed Zoe. If you were passing by her desk and glanced down you would assume she was concentrating hard on the mark-up, balancing the design, graphics, text and photo-imagery into one harmonious panoramic vista. But if you could trace her eye line with a laser-beam you would see she was only looking at the egg-timer icon, slowly emptying on her computer screen, as the latest image rendered out on the hard-drives in the dust-free, temperature-controlled, hermetically-sealed basements below.

Zoe hated waiting. Her clock was always tightly wound and ticked louder and faster than that of other women. She did more, achieved more,

7

lived more. That was her style, her method, her secret. She simply out-ran, out-jumped, out-worked the competition. Lately, however, she was beginning to feel, at her very core, a certain slowing up. Not a continuous recognizable sensation but a vague, sporadic slackening in tempo. Like a shift in gravity, like that specific sensation the body senses first when the fairground ride begins to come to an end.

She scanned the Newsroom and quickly found Chance, the thirty year-old, immaculately dressed black man, who was busy chatting up This Month's Conquest, a 20-year old Idiot from the temping agency to fill in over these last weeks. Chance had bought This Month's Conquest cappuccino and pastry from the coffee shop on Earhart. This was his tried and tested, and cost effective, routine, and was as sickeningly simple as it was successful.

He'd inform the Idiot, in his casual co-worker manner, that he was making the coffee run and ask her what she'd like. The question was delivered fait accompli—like a normal daily occurrence and time-honoured office ritual. She, being an Idiot and This Month's Conquest, wouldn't know what to order.

'Leave it to Chance,' he'd say and return 15 minutes later with a large cappuccino and an apple Danish.

The pastry was legendary at Vera's on Earhart—Chance was no fool. He would deliver the coffee and pastry and sit and chat with the Idiot until she had said 'Yes' at least half-a-dozen times, then he'd ask her out on a date. This would be his seventh question and she'd also say yes. He didn't have to work so hard; they always said yes.

He was over there right now asking the Idiot the seventh question. And she was blushing, and nodding her Idiot head, and saying 'yes'.

Zoe gagged—she had been asked the same seven questions and she had also answered yes—yes—yes—yes—yes—yes—yes!

Zoe's image-file rendered and was deemed 'acceptable' by the mainframe Gods. She filed and began to tidy her workstation and layout board. One last look over at Chance and the Idiot with the unmapped vagina. Oops. Steady.

From that angle, with This Month's Conquest sat straight-backed in her chair and Chance swaying and swaggering before her, Zoe could almost imaging him unzipping his pants, pulling out his thick black prick and slipping it into the Idiot's mouth as she laughed at one of his well worked jokes . . .

Zoe made her way to the restroom on the 1st floor. Cubicle 2. Her favorite.

BONE

Secretly Jane loved Hugo's study—the detail on the rich oak panelling, the endless chestnut shelves lined with slim, sombre, leather-bound volumes, the plumped davenports, the vast mahogany desk, and the generous views from the tall sash windows reaching out over Tulane's leafy campus.

'A bone, you say?' Hugo peered through his rimless, half-mooned spectacles, over the top of Jane's one page abstract, over the lip of the mahogany desk and down at Jane, who sat awkwardly, half-back, in the davenport with her feet every so slightly off the carpet. He was being deliberately melodramatic—the effect was considerable and calculated.

'A skull fragment,' she said, 'to be precise.'

'Well,' he sighed, letting her summary document float to the desk as he stood, 'There's been plenty of talk, I must say—Is it really everything I've been hearing?'

Jane thought long and hard before answering. Five years' Med School, a Master's in Osteology, a further MPhil in Archaeology, the three years' field work in Egypt . . . and then at last the *find*: It seemed her entire academic career had been heading inexorably towards this moment.

'Everything concerning "The Last Eunuch", Hugo—yes.'

Hugo had moved to the window and was now staring down at a freshman in a tight college sweater. She was bending over—straight legs locked, buttocks high, wide and flat—unchaining her bicycle from the

9

railings. He realised, after a moment's reverie, it was his turn to speak again.

'And you're determined to publish?'

Not the question, but the word caught Jane off balance. The rounded unattainable sound of it—*publish . . . publish . . . publish*—the lifeblood of Academia, the benchmark of career recognition, existence itself—to be *published*. Was she really this close? Was she really having the conversation with Hugo about being *published*? Was this, after everything, how it felt? How oddly vacuous. Then a sharp stab of emotion—that almost courageous swelling with just the hint of fear: Pride. In the event, all she could muster in response to his question was a slight, affected nod.

'What—just like that? What about Reese? And, Jesus Lord Almighty, what about Clements?'

'I didn't dig up the bone just to bury it, Hugo,' she replied without intending the pun or even, at that moment, realising it—but later, on the streetcar, when she re-ran the encounter over again and again in her head she would claim this moment as the turning point in the conversation.

'This is my turn,' she said, 'I've damn well earned it, Hugo, and I'm not to be passed over again.'

Hugo now turned to face her, then thought better of it and made for the drinks on the console. It was a little before six but it was, after all, a Friday and it was, after all, New Orleans.

'Jane,' he began as he sorted two tumblers and poured the liquor, 'these men are historians—academics like ourselves. They'll be ruined.'

He handed her the tumbler, moved on passed and, understanding the situation was going to require some careful, intimate negotiations, settled into the facing davenport.

'If they've been wrong all these years, Hugo, they were already ruined—Don't you think?'

He smiled, and took a little hit of bourbon, let it work across his tongue, then swallowed. 'Perhaps, but do we really need to go serving up our colleagues in quite such an obvious fashion?'

They were, Jane realised, getting down to the dirty business realities of academic existence. Money flowed downhill and only in well-worn channels. The faculty had to maintain its reputation—at all costs— everything, even her, it was clear, would ultimately be set in the balance and judged as either asset or liability.

'I'm not serving anybody up, Hugo, I'm simply asking for my work to be formally presented.' She'd wanted to say *published* but drew back at the very last—the mere thought of the word, again sending sharp tingles down her spine. 'I'm certainly not looking to go tearing reputations to shreds.'

'No.' Said Hugo, firmly. 'You'll just publish and let the critics do the dirty job for you.'

It now occurred to Jane that there was more under question than the validity of her work:

'You think I'm scared to take them on?'

'No, Jane, not at all—Just wondering why you need to.'

He was navigating his way back to that uncomfortable, well-mapped terrain again—her motives.

It was so unfair.

She wondered whether he'd ever questioned Clements about his desire to pursue a specific academic line. No, of course not, they were men, it was understood, good work needed to be done, money was available for research, papers were to be published. Jane got up, set the untouched bourbon on the desk and looked down at her professor. She'd felt certain she'd shaken the particular stigma of feminism some years ago and was in no mood to fight old battles. She'd made the *find*—this was no longer about her, it was about the facts—detailed research, painstaking archaeological technique and skilful precision—and if they pulled her on any of that, which was doubtful, there was still the carbon dating from a reputed neutral laboratory in Washington. No amount of 'penis-envy' mud slinging could dismiss that.

'Look, Hugo, my job's to tell the truth. I'll let you play politics.'

She picked up her bag and headed confidently for the door. Hugo, sensing he'd lost the initiative, tutted, and groaned in that precise boyish way of his. He was conscious that he still had a few seconds to chose his closing remarks as she made her way across the vast Moroccan tapis—Ah, the advantage of privilege . . .

'Fine,' he said in a low, projected voice, when he finally heard her hand settle on the antique door furniture, 'So, when can I see a draft?'

Jane's confidence suddenly evaporated as she remembered, with some indignity, the other reason she'd arranged to see Hugo that morning.

BEG

Easy waited patiently in line at the Employment Office. He lengthened his back and stood tall and erect, effecting as much physical distinction as possible between himself and the ragged straggle of drop-outs, deadbeats, prostitutes, and junkies strung out before him. He could feel the staff's eyes rest upon him fleetingly as they scanned the crowd and assessed the morning's workload. He kept his face calm, open, and serene and wondered just how different he really looked amidst the sea of time-wasters, wannabees, freaks, and hustlers.

The Officer who finally called his name was a gay cat from up river. He was slim with broad shoulders and narrow hips that went with power and stamina. Easy could imagine him out on the dancefloor at the All Ways Lounge on Men's Night. He had a cool, lyrical baritone to his voice and, whether affected or not, gave a concise poetic quality to the mundane, accusatory questioning he had to ladle out six hours a day. Easy called him the "Employment Dude", looked forward to their little spats and wondered if the latent sexual tension that he often sensed would show itself today.

'During the last thirty days have you sought and/or been offered and/or received any form of employment, whether payment and/or recompense was monetary and/or had defined cash value and/or was deemed payment in kind?'

12

'You get to say that *a lot*, don't cha?' Easy rubbed his palms on his thighs and whistled: 'You got it down, brother. It's the ding!'

'Please answer the question.'

There wasn't the slightest weariness or tension in his voice—Easy concluded Employment Dude was getting laid. He rarely made such observations or judgement about others but this made his fell happy for man.

'Well,' he began, 'about three weeks back I cut down a diseased sycamore tree from the front yard of a retired and/or disillusioned preacher man in Algiers.'

The Employment Dude smiled and wondered if Easy was toying with him: 'Did he pay you for this service?'

'He fixed me a crawdad po'boy and offered me a bottle of Czech Absinthe,' said Easy, raising his voice at the end of the sentence.

'But no money?'

'No money.' He shook his head. 'And he confessed the only reason he gave me Absinth was due to the Czech stuff didn't mix well in his Sazerac cocktails, which gotta be made with French and/or Swiss Absinthe and not the Bohemian brew.'

The Employment Dude gave Easy a meaningful stare. It could have meant 'don't fuck with me this morning' but Easy wasn't 100% sure.

'Anything else?'

'Yeah—apparently some folks fix their Sazeracs with Herbsaint, which is in fact a pastis—'

'Sir—' he interrupted, 'I meant anything else in the way of active employment?'

'Oh, right. No.' Easy lowered his eyes to study the bare, worn desk. They sprung back up with a recollection: 'Unless you count savin' this little girl's kitten that got stuck down a storm drain.'

The Employment Dude didn't see quite how that would qualify.

'Did you received any discernible benefits from undertaking the action?' He looked at Easy's wrinkling frown and decided to rephrase the question, 'Did you get paid for it?'

'Oh, I see.'

'Finally. So, moving on—'

'Her grandpappy slipped me a c-note. Does that count?'

The Dude became frustrated now and felt certain Easy was having him on. He looked at the office clock—it was eleven minutes past ten in the morning. He was due a refreshment break at half-passed and had to decide whether to drag this one out or cut it dry.

'The child's grandfather gave you a hundred dollars?' Easy nodded.

13

'For saving some kitten?' Easy shrugged and smiled. 'Can I ask what you did with the money?'

'Sure. I put a second toilet in the flophouse on Duke Street. There was like forty-three of us in there sharing the one can. *Hum-lah!*'

'You spent the hundred dollars putting a toilet in the government funded half-way house?'

'No, sir. The can only cost but forty-eight bucks—I plumbed it in there myself. With the rest, I bought some fried chicken and two gallons of lemonade for the guys down by the dockhouse.'

'You mean St. Lucien's shelter?

'No, not St. Lucien's, I'm talking about the guys that don't get in St. Lucien's. Yeah, those guys are like really . . . ' Easy recalled the men and thought for an appropriate word.

'Beyond our reach—' offered the Dude.

'Needin' our help,' said Easy at exactly the same time.

The Dude sat back in his seat, confused, humbled and mildly impressed. After a moment, he passed Easy a slip to sign and looked once again at his file.

'You know, most homeless people get their act sorted within the first six weeks. After that, chances of getting back into normal society get a lot less . . . statistically obvious.'

'Statistically obvious?'

'You start getting use to the chaos of the street. You deal with it. You have to, to survive—but pretty soon the chaos is all that's left.' He studied Easy's face to see if the words were having any effect at all. 'Wouldn't you like a place to call home?'

'Sure,' said Easy, coming alive, 'you kidding?'

'Then I'm gonna make it easier for you,' said the Dude, 'I'm gonna approve this month's payment but then I'm cutting you loose.' He looked at Easy to see how this was going over—his eyes were blank and accepting, neither frightened nor confused.

'You need to get yourself a job and a place to stay because, fun though these little encounters have been, I don't want to see you back here in front of me.' He closed the file and scraped his chair back to stand. Easy sat still.

'You have something to say?'

Easy looked up and fixed the Employment Dude with a laser beam stare. The Cat kept calm and rested his finger lightly on the security button under the desk. Easy's stare broke into a wide knowing smile.

'Well, ain't that the ding!'

Change was come.

14

HEAT

Approaching the elevator, Zoe saw the doors open and the shadow of a man fall across the yellow square of light on the lobby carpet. She hurried, weighed down with lens cases, hard-drives and a tangle of cables. She found herself making those little urgent noises that *other* people make when they can't— for whatever reason—simply call out: 'Hold the door.'

The occupant of the elevator could surely hear her and she now saw that the occupant of the elevator was Chance. A little scene unfolded in her imagination: He'd put his hand out and trip the door sensor. She'd rush in, laughing (no, not laughing, anybody laughing in a scenario was an idiot or a liar), she'd be breathless, and full of thanks. He'd be modest. They'd ride down together and make witty, esoteric small talk. It wouldn't be a big event, but it would be pertinent. It would be an ice-braker.

In the event, Chance saw her and looked briefly and directly into her eyes. He did not, however, hold the elevator. Instead, he held the look as the doors closed automatically between them.

*   *   *   *   *

Zoe ripped through the dead lines of traffic on her lightweight aluminum-alloy street hybrid—the humming, sticky treads, glued her to the soft tarry road, fixed her in place, and gave her something to fight against. If she didn't go up country this weekend, she'd swap out to the slick city

15

tyres. She'd go even faster but wouldn't get the same deep thigh workout—choices, choices.

Zoe stopped off at the gym in Fontainebleau. She ran five miles on her favoured treadmill waiting for the Tunturi 65 to free up. A Lost Cause—weighing well over 220 pound—was trying her best to smash the equipment to smithereens. She must have been 55 years of god-damned age—*why the fuck bother?*

When Zoe finally got on the machine she could palpably discern its recent abuse. The apparatus seemed shaken, traumatised, and grief-stricken; the seals and valves were stretched and tired, the hydraulic fluid hot, spongy and defeated. She gave up, feeling a creeping uselessness—which she attributed to the other woman—invading her, permeating her skin and flooding her body. She took a cool shower, went to the sauna, masturbated in the hot secret billows of steam as soon as she was alone, and came quickly but without any lingering satisfaction.

Cycling home, the slick speed saddle reaching high up between her thighs, she realised she may have done herself a little injury.

Crouching over the hand mirror on the bathroom floor she noticed her sex was a flushed and swollen. She also saw her small face, flanked by dreads, looking accusingly back up at her. She didn't seem to recognize herself at first.

She looked strange, almost alien.

So this was the face on which a guy like Chance lets elevator doors close.

WOLF

'Why not give it a go?' encouraged Hugo, tapping the cold ash from his pipe into the exquisite ebony bowl. Jane hesitated, waited for him to look up and register just how very serious she was.

'I'm not sharing this, Hugo.'

'No—no question, but let's broaden your camp a little—build an unassailable team around you.' He sensed she could see he was right, so he went about making a great fuss in scraping the bowl of his pipe with his penknife as he nonchalantly drove the sword home: 'Jules has a good brain.'

'Jules—are you kidding? He's Clements' lapdog. I'd be tipping my hand, no, no, it's completely out of the question.'

'Well, what about me? I'll edit the damn thing for you. You surely don't put me in their camp?'

This brought Jane up short—now he was testing her trust in him. She'd have to think fast or he'd get around her, the slippery old buzzard, filling her mind with doubts and strategies. 'You, Hugo,' she laughed, stalling, aiming for an affected humour, but it came out as a nervous, almost mocking shriek, 'You can't be serious. You're . . . anyway, you're far too busy.'

'It looks like I'm going to be busy either way,' he said with glum candour.

'No, Hugo, I need you to be free to look out for me. To take care of the politics.'

'But that's what I'm doing now, Jane, by asking you to bring in some help, some . . . ' he chose the word carefully, 'some balance.'

Jane thought for a moment. If she could have her pick of the faculty—who would she chose? No one. Her bar was just set too high. If, however, she imagined, she'd been involved in some car-crash and slipped into a coma—God forbid, and all that, but this type of thing happens—whom would she trust? Who would be that person to pick up her work and make sense of it?

'Wanda's a great editor—'

Hugo exploded. 'A man, damn it, Jane, don't make me have to spell this out. You leave yourself so wide open and it just makes it so easy for them.'

She understood at last; the determination in his voice revealed the scale of the task. It was also becoming concrete: it wasn't *her* but somehow her *her-ness* that was under question—it was ridiculous to pretend it wasn't personal but that was exactly the case Hugo was making. She felt her scalp suddenly crawl, the very follicles gather together and the hairs bristle. She counted to ten, slowly, in her mind and let out a long, low, silent breath and as she did, she realised Hugo had let something else slip through his intricate web of truths: now there was a *them*.

'Let me finish the first draft, okay. Then we'll see.'

Under the circumstances Hugo took this as a small but significant win and decided not to push the matter. 'Of course, of course. We'll get it written, then we'll get it right. So, how much longer do you need?'

'Oh, just two months, maybe three.'

Hugo sprung erect in his carved editor's chair like a little startled terrier. 'What? No, Jane, listen. This is already all over the faculty. I can hold them off maybe a month, six weeks, tops.'

'Six weeks is impossible. A work like this . . . '

'But you've been back six months. You come to me today,' he said, snatching the abstract from the desk, 'promising glory and bloodbaths and now it's "Oh, just two months, maybe three"—What's going on?'

'Look, Hugo, have I *ever* asked for an extension before—'

'No—which is precisely what worries me.'

They stood face to face, breathing hard, hoping they wouldn't go on like this all afternoon.

'Jane. Look, your life's your own and I've no right to ask but, if we're going to war, I need to hear it from you—just tell me this delay's something external?'

'External? What ever do you mean?'

'Tell me you're in debt, your house is being repossessed, anything. Tell me you've been diagnosed with cancer of the lymph gland, or joined a coven of black witches on Magazine, anything, anything but I need to know and get my head around it . . . '

'It's the house,' said Jane, 'If you must know, it's Zoe and Beth. They're a total nightmare and I can't get a damn word written.'

'Well—thank God for that.' Said Hugo, sitting finally and the looking for and lifting up his pipe. 'I thought for a horrible minute you might have met someone.' The minute the words left his lips he wished he hadn't spoken.

Jane flushed and wished the notion wasn't so obviously damned ridiculous.

KENNEL

J ane knew she should've got rid of Zoe and Beth and the start of the academic year—just handed them their month's notice, said she was selling up and going back to Egypt for good, any old thing. They would never have believed her but so what? At least then she could have found a couple of those Chinese MPhils when they first arrived on campus. "If you can stand that spitting they do in the mornings," Wanda had told her, "you hardly knew they were there." But she hadn't handed Zoe and Beth their notice—she'd done nothing and now living in the house was worse than ever.

'Why can't you just work out a rota, share the damned chores?' Advised Hugo.

'Share!' Jane replied. 'We couldn't share a cab out of the 9th Ward, Hugo—Zoe takes her own shower head into the bathroom and Beth thinks the dining table is for strip poker!'

It wasn't only how they lived together but how they treated the place. Since Jane's return she'd been at the house constantly, meticulously checking her field notes and writing up her thesis. And now because she was there most of the time, she was somehow expected to do the housework—like she came with the rent.

'Still no luck with the cleaner?' asked Hugo.

'No, but they're actually meant to be seeing people today.'

'Well, let's keep our fingers crossed, shall we?'

At that precise moment, over in the Garden District, in a large, run-down flat-board house, in a large, overgrown plot, Beth and Zoe were working frantically. The place was a pigsty, with personal junk, trinkets, and useless crap covering every available flat surface. Beth was trying to clear the mess but it was useless—this stuff needed to be sorted—she scooped huge armfuls into cheap black trashcan sacks which stretched, sagged, became translucent, burst and scattered the belongings in a fresh layer upon the old.

'Zoe! Get yo' skinny ass down here, sister—NOW!'

Upstairs, Zoe was in her bedroom working on her laptop. The space was crammed with teetering towers of slick, glossy magazines. Expensive flight-boxes were stacked full of cameras, filters and lens-kit, amongst various tripods, light stands, reflectors and flash-umbrellas.

'Be right down—just printing the names of who's coming?

'You already did that?' Beth screamed from below.

Zoe was in fact looking at a Health Website – The banner stripline read – *Ovulation Calendar - Download yours NOW*.

The egg-timer icon blinked . . . Zoe hated waiting.

Downstairs, the doorbell—an original relic—gave out its strange, choked clang.

Pandemonium!

Beth opened the under-stairs cupboard to hurl inside her great armfuls of rubbish bags but the cupboard was already full to toppling and great landslides of mess rushed out around her knees and ankles.

'ZOE!' She hollered, stuffing the slagheap of junk atop itself in an attempt to stem the flow.

The doorbell *r-r-rang* again.

Outside, a perfectly reasonable woman stood waiting and looking at the cracked and flaking paint on the door. She took her finger off the ancient ceramic doorbell button and examined its tip, it appeared clean but somehow felt greasy, sullied, and besmirched. She wiped it with a fresh handkerchief. From inside she heard someone crashing around violently. She took another opportunity to inspect the overgrown yard, sighed, and checked her watch.

Finally, Zoe came tumbling down the crowded stairs. Beth gave her a scowl and they traded barely whispered obscenities before they pasted on their public smiles and opened the door. The perfectly reasonable woman was gone.

*　　　*　　　*　　　*　　　*

21

At the same moment in Mama Lek's Vietnamese Laundromat, Easy was reading various postings for yard sales, missing pets, second hand trombones vendors and power yoga classes on the community board. One post caught his eye—a dog-eared JOB VACANCY with one perforated tab remaining. The advert was a full colour photocopy and written in bright glowing felt-tip pen and ran the semi-desperate call to arms: 'Can You Cure Our Chaos?'

Easy smiled and unpinned the whole advert.

Mama Lek, the 70 year-old Vietnamese owner, saw him and called out: 'Oh, Easy go look job-job?'

'You think I'm ready for it, Mama Lek?'

She came over and squeezed his biceps with a small iron like grip: 'Yee. Big muscle. Good for hard wuk.'

He smiled and began to read the advert again. Mama Lek cleared her throat and looked seriously up in his face: 'Easy got *lay-zoom-may*?'

Easy didn't understand

'No *lay-zoom-may*, no job-job. Come, come. Mama Lek, show Easy all it go about.'

They went thru to her tiny, perpetually damp office between the largest tumble dryers and she produced a well-thumbed manila file from an old bureau. Inside was a collection of *Résumés*—some neatly typed, some less formal.

'Oh,' said Easy, 'Those Lay-zoom-mays.'

*   *   *   *   *

The antique doorbell was being put through it paces that afternoon: *r-r-r . . . r-r-r . . . ring*. The door opened on a sequence of possible domestic saviours. They were all women in their 40s or 50s and were wary, suspicious, and variously disappointed that they'd made the effort and bothered to turn up.

Beth showed them the living room—where one woman found a bowl of putrid fruit on a dining chair. Zoe boldly led the way up the stairs, which were piled high with books, faded newspapers, china figurines and toilet-tissue—a mobile phone rang and when Zoe turned the domestic was scuttling back down the stairs and out into the bright, fresh air to take the call and never to be seen again.

22

I'LL BE YOUR DOG

Against Zoe's wishes, Beth dared show the bathroom—the prospective domestic screamed and ran, covering her nose and mouth like she'd found a long lost relative, dead on the toilet.

Zoe showed the yard to an elderly lady who readily agreed it was far too much work for a woman of her age, then bid them good day before hurdling the picket fence.

Beth walked a young, happy hippy girl around the kitchen. She had flowers in her hair and wore pink lipstick and matching eye-shadow. She touched the spice-rack which promptly fell into the sink.

'I'm ever so error prone.' She confessed.

'We don't mind,' pleaded Zoe.

'I've set fire to two houses—by accident, of course.'

'Right—?'

'Nobody died.'

'Good . . . good.'

'Except the dogs.'

That afternoon, Beth and Zoe opened the door to a series of extremely dubious Domestics—there was a punk girl with a bright blue Mohican—a huge, tattooed biker-chick and a very old Bag Lady who may have drifted in by accident.

They decided to hold brief informal interviews in the living room; Beth and Zoe sat together on the couch. Disaster reigned—a young Haitian woman dropped her pet python—a couple of semi-naked, gay Columbian twins wore nothing but bright orange rubber aprons. They could dance a fine *maranga* and sing in perfect harmony and shared four immaculate buttocks—a skinny Goth with deathly pale skin slipped into a coma and was taken away by a friend in a purple lacquered hearse.

For the most part Beth and Zoe sat hunched forward with their mouths agape as the doorbell *r-r-r-r-r-rang* its death knell on their hopes of domestic harmony . . .

Finally, when all hope was lost and the girls were only continuing out of a morbid curiosity, the door opened on a kindly looking, old-style Louisiana Mammy. She laughed deeply, admitted to being well over 60 but had a young attitude and a sprightly skip in her get-a-long. Beth and Zoe were hopeful.

The Mammy looked at the living room and rotting fruit and simply said "Uh-huh" in a kind, non-condescending Queen-like manner. Now out in the yard, stroking the dead plants and whispering to the withered trees, said turned and delivered a simple "Uh-huh"; and negotiating her considerable bulk up the avalanche primed stairs—"Uh-huh"; and finally,

23

when presented with the decrepit and unfathomable bathroom she simply replied: "Yep".

*   *   *   *   *

A few minutes ahead of time, Easy sauntered along the street and stopped outside the house. He looked the building over carefully, as if assessing the joint for a robbery, before stepping through the creaking, rotted gate.

The front door opened and the Mammy appeared buttoned in her best summer coat, Beth and Zoe were close behind her and wore expectant, needy looks on their faces.

'And you'll call us—promise?' asked Zoe but the Mammy said nothing.

'Look, you've got our number,' pressed Beth, 'just think it over and let us know—okay?'

The Mammy didn't speak until she had cleared the wooden steps. Back on terra firma, she finally turned to the girls:

'Ask me—y'all don't be needin' no house cleaner—y'all be needin' pest control, good lovin' and maybe li'l *tahp dollahr* psychiatry.'

She turned and left them—speechless and still and as the Mammy passed Easy—who'd heard the whole exchange clearly—she winked and whispered: 'Run a country mile, beau. Step in that place, there ain't no comin' out for a boy like you.'

She walked off—leaving them to it.

Easy looked up at Zoe and Beth and smiled. The girls composed themselves as best they could and stood looking down at the skinny, bedraggled guy. He had a certain something—was simultaneously handsome and downright quirky. Zoe suspected him of having a lisp, a clef-palate, a clubfoot, or—if he turned quickly to look at you—a boss-eye. Beth imagined he could play the devil banjo, and right off the bat, knew she'd probably end up nailing him.

Zoe had her heart set on the Mammy and—having already envisioned the warm kitchen table scenes, heard the soulful motherly advice, and tasted the chicken soup—she was disappointed in this new hopeful. It was an unjustifiable feeling, which quickly turned into a keen suspicion. Beth invited Easy to step inside and, with a little trepidation, he complied.

TRICKS

The title on his inexpertly typed résumé read—*Easy Does It!*—in an oversized, childish font. Beth led him through the clutter, with Zoe following tight behind, scrutinizing Easy's supposed history.

'So you worked on a fishing boat right outside Delacroix.'

'Yep—that was the ding. Tough work too—tossin' nets, haulin' nets, fixin' nets. Guttin' and freezin' the catch, you know?'

'And what—you got fired?'

'Nope—we ate up all the fishes. Tuna, Serra, big-eye, mackerel—there weren't nothing left but li'l biddy babies.

'Well, what have you been doing since?' asked Zoe.

'In a word—travelling.'

'What—around the world?' asked Beth.

'More like 'round Louisiana,' said Easy with a grin.

'And how did you make your living, travelling?'

'Oh, I got by. I can turn my hand to most things.' He looked at them and nodded to some unasked question: 'I guess I'm now 'bout ready to put down some roots.'

Beth and Zoe looked at him for a long moment. They seemed to be expecting some more information. Easy chose to shut up and did so until Beth finally suggested they continued on the tour.

Despite the mess and clutter, the living room impressed Easy. It had those generous colonial proportions and led on through to a spacious

25

open-plan kitchen. The sun streamed through the half pulled curtains and chopped the room into fat ribbons of sunshine and shade.

'Says here, cooking's one of your passions. Along with *Cleaning Up*, *Fixing what's broke* and *Silence . . .*'

Easy nodded simply and moved round the room, picking up a stiff dried out dishcloth and arranging old newspapers.

'Does silence qualify as a passion?' asked Beth, amused. Easy noticed she was wearing a permanent smile. Not on her mouth but in the eyes, like the whole thing was a sideshow they had to play at before they could get back to the more serious business of life.

'You know, I just put that down 'cos there was a box for it.'

Zoe turned to Beth: 'It's under *subjects pursued outside main vocation*'.

Easy smiled and shrugged his modest shrug. Zoe, he realised, would be the one he had to convince if he really wanted this job.

'Just how exactly do you pursue silence?' she continued as Easy tested a wobbly shelf and raised his eyebrows in mock concern.

'Well,' he began, 'for starters you gotta shut-up—quit the yadda-yadda—and just listen.' He paused a moment for effect. 'First thing you hear is all the electrical goods—washing machines, dryers, ice-boxes, freezers. You gotta switch 'em off or wrap 'em up. Next you hear your mind talking. You gotta quit that little voice too and that ain't so easy.'

'So,' Beth cut in, 'you meditate, right?'

'I guess some people would call it that, yeah.'

'But then what?' asked Zoe, exasperated, 'I mean, what do you do with yourself? Work stuff out? Plan your day? What?'

'No—', said Easy, 'It's kind of the opposite. I try to stop thinking an planning and working stuff out and just, like, kinda *be*.'

'He's a Zen master,' said Beth. 'That's cute.'

'Why don't you buy ear muffs?' mocked Zoe.

'Too much static,' replied Easy in a deadly serious tone, 'Neoprene plugs, however, are the ding!'

Easy had moved to the sink, which was rank and stacked full of dishes. He turned on the faucet, checked the water pressure and looked up to see the girls staring at him.

'It's only a box filler kind of hobby.'

A small laughed found its way out of Beth's throat and despite herself even Zoe managed a smile at this. Easy shrugged his shoulders and pointed out the doorway.

'Shall we?'

In the hallway, Easy moved up the narrow margin snaking between the piles of books and boxes that colonised every step. The girls followed—Beth right behind him, and checking out his ass, and making immature faces back at Zoe. Zoe was not terribly impressed but neither, when the moment arose, did she waste the opportunity to corroborate the evidence—it was a nice ass.

'Through checking me out?' Easy asked.

'Sorry? Yes,' said Zoe, her voice catching, 'I mean—No.'

His ass; the resume.

She got a quick grip on herself: 'One thing—it says here you've been in the service industry for ten years?'

'Yes, that's right.'

'But under *relevant experience* you've written *twelve months*. How does that work out?'

'Well, most people say they got ten years' experience when really they got one year's experience ten times over.' He rattled a loose stair rod and tutted.

'I learnt everything I've ever needed to know about how to serve people in the one year. I'm just being as honest as possible.'

'God—how refreshing,' said Beth, 'I'm always lying my ass off in interviews—and Hell—even when I'm not in interviews!'

'Trouble with lies is,' said Easy, interjecting, 'you gotta remember them. The truth, on the other hand, is like a purring cat—noble, easy-going, and takes care of itself.'

Zoe was warming to this man and she didn't like how this was making her feel. He was too much of a character to have around all the time. He'd drive you nuts, surely. What she wanted was the Mamma. Her heart was set and she wanted to get the conversation back to hard, basic facts. Facts upon which she could make straightforward decisions: 'Do you have any references?

'Nope. I never see the point—I mean, who's gonna hand out a bum reference?'

'I agree,' said Beth, 'its bullshit.'

'In personal services you gotta meet and get the vibe. See if there's a click. If you've got that you might be on you're way to something, don't you think?' He righted a pile of books that were going off at an acute angle. The girls swapped looks and Beth gave Zoe one of her looks. A look to give the guy a break, a look that encouraged her to realise he was their only option, a look that said *chill out*.

At the very top of the house the three of them gathered on the small, dark landing. The roof cut away sharply and the limited head room made the space unavoidably intimate. Easy opened the only door to reveal a tiny attic room, packed high with more junk.

'Wow, who does this lot own?'

'Actually, we can blame all this crap on Jane. It's hers, but obviously we'll clear it. I think the room itself could be lovely, don't you?'

As Easy pushed the door open again for a second look, a macabre figure suddenly lunged forward—the girls screamed—Easy grappled and rattled with the object for a moment, then stopped abruptly, and held it up by its neck to reveal a tired, age-browned medical skeleton.

'Ain't that the berries!'

'Damn thing,' screeched Beth, 'scared the livin' shit outta me.'

'It's Jane's—she's a—well she was a doctor. We'll throw it out.'

Easy stood the skeleton back up in the room: 'Nah, he's the ding - just needs a top hat for Mardi Gras.' He shook the skeleton's yellowed hand, formally and with some grace. 'Hey, brother, mind if I sneak-a-peek?' Easy looked past the skeleton and into the small stuffed room—it had rough sloped ceilings, exposed oak beams and was stacked high with chests, tea-crates, shoe boxes and box-files. The girls hoped he wouldn't be too put off.

'Yeah, that'd be perfect—it's been a while since I had my very own room.'

'Great—' said Beth, 'so, when could you start?'

But before Easy could answer, Zoe cut in and blurted out: 'If we decide—that is—after we talk it over and all.'

'I suppose you gotta give notice where you are?' Asked Beth.

'Nope, I'm at your disposable,' smiled Easy. 'Just say the word, or gimme the nod—If you decide to—that is—after you talk it over and all.'

'Three busy girls living together,' said Beth. 'You can guess what it's like?'

'I don't gotta guess, Lady, I can smell it!'

Beth's laugh broke loose again at Easy's casual, offbeat directness. It flowed naturally from him, with no judgement or malice.

Zoe, however, was less amused: 'Do you have much stuff?'

'No. Just the suitcase—I keep everything I own in that.'

'One case? I love it!' cried Beth. 'You are a Zen Master!'

'What's a guy need, anyway? Couple of T-shirts and a good toothbrush.'

'Neoprene earplugs,' added Zoe caustically.

'Yes, my earplugs, of course, and a pair of bluejeans. I don't believe in possessions, you know, they end up owning you.' His words hung there in the small headspace, framed by Jane's junk.

'Right, well,' said Zoe, 'I guess we'll, you know, talk it over and let you know.'

'You're thru with the interrogations?'

Zoe and Beth nodded.

'Because, if it's cool, I'd like to ask a few questions myself?'

'You wanna interview us?' Bawled Beth.

'Sure—I mean, let's be honest. We're creaking along here a little, ain't we? It's nice and polite and all, but I, for one, ain't 100 percent certain we got much of a click as yet, you know?'

'It's cool, said Beth, 'Whatever you want, but this girl needs some java.' She stood back and indicated that Easy should go down the stairs first, he did and both girls checked him out again.

Beth read Zoe's worried features and gave her another certain look not to mess this up.

*   *   *   *   *

In the living room, Easy whipped back the drapes, letting the sunshine flood into the room. Zoe discovered a pile of hitherto lost style magazines and began to gather them up. Beth picked her way through the detritus in the sink, trying to find clean coffee cups. As Easy talked, he moved about and just naturally and effortlessly began to clean up.

'So, Beth,' he began, 'you wanna tell me 'bout Zoe?' Zoe and Beth swapped looks. 'Oh, it's cool; trust me, and a hellovalot quicker. You tell me about Beth and she tells me about you. It beats having to go on and on, all day—justifying yourself.'

He filled the kettle, switched it on and drove his hand fearlessly into the filthy overgrown sink. He located and pulled the filthy swamp-mess of a plug—there was a slow, ominous gurgle, then nothing. He looked at them, waiting for his answer.

Beth was put neatly on the spot—and this amused her tremendously. Zoe, however, who was about to be talked about and discussed was once again on the defensive.

'Well, Zoe's a photographer at the Times Picayune in—you know—News. She works crazy hours, takes these great pictures, big campaigns, important issues, crime, homeless people, right Zoe?

'Yeah, I'm a freelancer. I pitch a story, work it up, smooch the editors—'

Easy who was now washing out the coffee cups, held up his wet sudsy hand: 'Sorry, Zoe. Can I stop you there? You'll get a turn in a moment.' He turned back to Beth. 'So, how'd you two guys meet?'

'New Year's Eve,' Beth recalled. 'Two, no—three years back. We throw a great party at the Dead Pirate—I run the joint, you know it, on Ursulines and Royal—'

'Oops,' Easy held his hand up again, 'now you're at it—I'll get all that off Zoe, if it's the ding. Did you both hit it right off?'

'Yeah. I think so—we had a lock-in. Zoe always takes the hi-stool where the bar swoops round by the jukebox. We just got to talking and as things slackened off we fell into conversation . . . I guess that's it.'

'Cool,' smiled Easy, 'Good detail.' He turned now to Zoe, who looked back at him with some trepidation. 'Your shout, sister. Spill the baked beans on Beth?'

'Well. Like the lady said, she runs The Dead Pirate on Ursulines—who do fantastic wines by the glass—which is why you'll find yours truly in there most weekends and afternoons if I'm working nights—'

As Easy held his hand—Zoe did the same. 'I'm on it. I'm on it,' she insisted. 'We first met New Year's Eve but we really became friends at that Valentine's party, remember?'

'Jesus, yeah. I'd totally wiped that.'

The kettle clicked off and Easy rinsed, examined, and filled the coffee pot.

'This guy was bugging me,' Zoe continued. 'He'd been a real pain in the ass all night so I blew him off—Not blew him, I didn't blow him—'

'I hear you,' smiled Easy.

'Anyway, I thought he'd left for good but later I saw him at the end of the bar—working his charm routine on Beth—so when he went to the restroom I sidled over and put her straight about him.'

'Sebastian!' Beth remembered.

'Right, Sebastian,' said Zoe, an almost vengeful look in her eye. 'Great looking guy—but a total moron.'

'He couldn't find his ass with both hands tied behind his back.'

Both girls laughed, recalling Sebastian and the night.

'Loving the same shit's no good—,' began Beth.

'You've got to hate the same shit to be *real* friends—,' finished Zoe.

They laughed and Easy wiped the coffee cups and set them on the counter.

'And how'd you come by living together?'

'Beth needed somewhere to stay; there was plenty of space here. I'd been renting off Jane, who owns the house but travels a lot. It just made sense.'

'And how do you find it living together?'

Zoe answered first, perhaps a little too quickly: 'Fine.'

Beth took a second longer: 'It has its moments.'

'Right, well that all sure helps—I've found talking about the small stuff just as important as talking about the big, important stuff.' He opened the fridge sniffed at the carton of milk—and jerked his head back like a cat had scratched his nose.

'*Hum-lah!*'

'Black's okay,' said the girls in familiar harmony.

'Have you given much thought,' asked Easy, disposing of the milk, 'about how you want this to work out?'

'Such as?' said Zoe, for the first real time believing that this man might actually come and work for them.

'Well, what sort of services you'd like me to provide, and which ones would you like me to make a priority?'

'Clearly,' Zoe began, 'we need someone to keep the place tidy.'

'And to fix up a few things here and there.'

'Yes. I feel like a dog in a deli—it's the ding to know where to start.'

'We need pretty much everything really,' concluded Zoe.

'You know,' said Beth, 'general looking after.'

'Yeah, I know,' said Easy with a genuine look around the room. 'So how you gonna let me know? Because you know I don't have a cell phone or anything.' He held up his hand, with his thumb and pinky extended, like he was holding a phone to his ear. The girls swapped a brief look then they both raised pretend phones to their ears . . .

'You're hired,' they announced together.

'Really? Great. I mean, you don't have to run it by Jane or anything?'

'Not at this juncture,' said Zoe.

'Go pack your case, boy,' said Beth, 'and be back here in the morning.'

Easy smiled. The thought of his very own attic room and the hours, days and weeks of meaningful work before him gave him a deep and lasting feeling of satisfaction.

CHOPS

Beth was telling a joke to the drunken group of travelling salesmen. They were on some annual haul and being losers with no sales figures to brag about, they were bored to death, hitting the liquor, and looking for amusement. The Dead Pirate was quiet but it was still early and these stiffs were the only trade. Beth hated these moments—when she was expected to turn it on, to entertain, to balance a ball on her nose like some circus seal. As she told the joke—a boisterous tale about Jimmy C. Newman lamming one into a Nashville Whore—the men looked at her with a general disgusted lustfulness. Although she'd never consider screwing any one of these gloomy, diminutive, shiny-assed pen-pushers individually, the image of some sordid episode where she fucked the Old Boy, Joe, whilst the rest of the team looked on filled her with a horrible, cold excitement.

'And Jimmy C. says, "Lady, the sex is *great* but why is it afterwards you make me put one hand on your titties and the other hand between you legs till the sun comes up?" And the whore says, "Last time I banged a Cajun, he stole my purse!"'

The businessmen roared loud and raucously but in the quick way the laughter died off she knew they were also appalled. They'd tell the joke later to other travelling salesmen at the conference but in their versions they'd take her—a mere waitress—out back and fuck her on the beer kegs. Beth grinned at them, held eye contract with one or two more than was wise, and slid away to join Zoe, who was on her cell-phone and wore a caring, pained look of worry.

'Don't tell me—,' she whispered to Zoe, 'the sperm bank cancelled your overdraft?'

Zoe covered the receiver and mouthed: 'Behave!' Then spoke into the phone in a clipped, professional manner. Beth knew immediately that the call was from Jane and they'd be talking about the interviews and specifically about Easy. She could imagine the gamut of questions Jane would be firing at Zoe and the impossible conditions she'd be imposing on such an appointment.

'No,' said Zoe, 'this cleaner's really different,' she winked at Beth. 'No, no. Certainly not at all like those other girls.' She rolled her eyes now—hopeful, she could continue to the end of the conversation without having technically lied. 'Well, they said they were very much looking forward to meeting you to, Jane. In fact,' she swallowed and got hold of herself, 'we're all looking forward to that . . . ' She couldn't look at Beth in the face now, one twinkle of the eye and it would be too much and she'd lose control. 'Beth? Yeah . . . ' she continued. 'I'd say Beth's *all over it*. Yeah, okay then. See you at the weekend. I'm sure it'll be a new start for us all.'

Beth was at the limit. Zoe hung up and looked at her: 'Well,' she announced, 'that all went rather better than expected.' They fell into one another. 'And I don't think I actually had to—you know—really lie too much of my ass off.'

'A few half truths, maybe?' joked Beth.

'Yes, and maybe even a white lie or three. But no dead fish, no barefaced, cold-hearted lies. And all for the girl's own good.'

'Exactly.'

'Exactly.'

'We've really—finally—got ourselves a cleaner.' Beth's voice was heavy with amusement but also a certain amount of pride. She was finally going to be able to live like a pig and still have a clean house. The girls embraced and kissed and slapped hands and bumped butts and got drunk and celebrated and did their little tribal routine.

PAW

Easy arrived bright and early next morning. He couldn't sleep and finally rose, dressed, paid his slop-house rent and caught the five-thirty chain ferry from Algiers. He hid his case under a rosebush in a garden along the street and waited on the corner of the block until an old uniformed deliveryman confirmed it was five-to-eight. He then collected the case, counted to three hundred as he made his way down the street and pressed the doorbell on his new life, occupation, and abode for the foreseeable. The bell made that horrible *choked* noise and he took his finger off the button quickly. He hesitated, wondering if anybody had heard him or would even be out of bed.

Just as he was about to give up and come back at eight-thirty, the door clicked and swung wide. Zoe was smiling out at him. Beth hung back in the shadows, looking dog rough. He held up his little suitcase and the girls smiled and ushered him inside.

The very first thing Easy did was make the girls some strong, hot coffee. They gave him a twenty-dollar bill to go to the store to buy milk and sugar.

He could have run for it right there and then and have been in gravy for the rest of the day. But he didn't. He knew good times where just around the corner. Things were changing.

He made a big point of giving Zoe every penny of change with the receipt. She didn't check it or seem at all bothered, as if she trusted him and it wasn't an issue. They were getting organised and making an effort

34

with a list of chores and errands and cleaning rotas and a thousand things for him to do and that was all sweet music and good.

Jane wasn't home so he couldn't meet her and tell her how glad he was to be working for them. Zoe said she'd be back at the weekend and later, with a sideways look in her eye, Beth confirmed the same. A definite tension came into the room whenever they spoke about Jane. Easy felt it but didn't have the right strategy to bring it about in conversation. What was clear was they all wanted this to work out and he for one certainly didn't want to give voice, thought, and energy to any other possibility.

For some good reason of their own, the girls had decided he should start by cleaning his own room, so they all marched to the top of the house. It proved a generous but impractical gesture—their being absolutely nowhere to put any of the boxes once they came out of the room.

Easy decided he should first clear the staircase—then he could move up and down freely with his arms loaded without falling head over tip and breaking his neck in a pile-drive. He was showing some initiative and the girls liked that—plus Easy knew another thing too—the clearing of the stairway would have an immediate effect right throughout the whole house.

On the bottom set of steps, Easy found a pile of old vinyl records and mix of 45s and 78s—bluegrass, blues, and some classic *zydeco*. He dusted them off and put a stack on the windup gramophone he found among the attic tea-chests. He worked quickly to rig this up, a little worried the girls would think he was goofing off but soon he had the stairwell filled with Joe Maphis' *Flop Eared Mule*, *Two More Bottles of Wine* by Emmilou Harris and the 1957 track by Ed Rush and George Cromerty—*Plastic Jesus*, which was one of his all time favourite songs. He took it as a sign of the good to come.

He worked quickly from step to step, sorting out the genuine rubbish from the obvious keepsakes. This was easy for him—as it always is when dealing with other people's junk. Thick expensive-looking Magazines were filed on the landing outside Zoe's room where she'd agreed—no promised—to go through them later. Old newspapers, yellow with age, were binned along with dusty receipts, utility bills, invoices, remittance advice slips and all manner of crumpled memos, dog-eared shopping lists, and ancient coffee ringed reminders for step-classes and deep thigh workouts. If a document wasn't to hand—Easy reasoned—in some easily accessible filing system, ready to be plucked free exactly when needed then there was no point keeping it at all. Whenever he asked the girls' advice they'd snatch the sheet from him, examine it with shame or contempt, frown and invariably hand it back with a puckered lower lip and a brief shake of the head. He was never any closer to a decision so he took it upon himself and decided not to bother them at all. A simple solution was found in the form of an oversize, durable trashcan liner. He'd fill it, store it in the shed for three or six months and if the girls still didn't require some vital scrap of paper from it dark reaches he'd then get rid.

More obvious items, which couldn't be thrown, were small brass statues, various broken but repairable antique lamps and three life-sized ceramic busts with the parts of the brain all laid out and written up like a street-map. The girls were equally at a loss as to where these should go, so Easy found space for them on the living room shelves, which he also cleared of assorted junk mail, post-its, and jottings with which they'd been fiendishly and inexplicably ram-packed.

By midday he'd cleared his way back up to the attic and was enjoying himself, scything a path, as it were, to his own little private part of the new jungle territory. He worked with enthusiasm and joy and upon finally reaching his door, gazed in happily at the task ahead. Before he could make a start though he heard Zoe calling up the stairwell for him to come down for lunch.

When he bounded across the lounge and began to scrub his hands under the faucet, he felt like a farmhand at the pump well and could sense something was wrong. Seeing the table bare—he had to hide his confusion, and of course, realise that he would be making lunch.

They gave him more money—Beth this time, and two scrunched twenty dollar bills—and he bought shellfish and po' boy bread from a deli on Magazine.

The sky was a heavy violet and deep with cloud and the air was thick but fresh. He wondered if the girls would eat take-out food for the rest of their days but over lunch they talked of the food they liked and wanted him to prepare. He loved to cook but said little, concentrating instead on the wonderful flavours bursting over his tongue from his po' boy sandwich. It was the best food he'd put in his mouth since a fair set down in May with the Sazerac Preacher. The criss-crossing fusion of flavours and the expectation of the task of clearing his own room was more than enough for a simple swamp rat like him to ponder.

*   *   *   *   *

The first item he removed from his room was Jane's medical skeleton: 'Keep smiling, *brother*, I'm your new room mate.'

I'LL BE YOUR DOG

The girls, who'd come up to lend a hand, watched on with interest as he climbed his way in, passing boxes and cartons back over his head. They dumped the stuff in the tiny hallway space until it was full then stood with a box a piece waiting for his next move. He directed them down to the lower hallway, thanked them for their help and went back up alone. The stuff in the boxes needed sorting and that was lonely, stranger work. If they hit an old box of photographs—anybody's photographs— you could lose two hours and he wanted to be in and settled by nightfall.

He searched the house for some temporary space but there was none. Mess and clutter still reigned. At last he came upon a brick built shed at the rear of the back yard. It was dry and had a solid wood door and clearly—due to the fact it wasn't rammed full of trash, litter and refuse— unknown to the girls.

Inside he found lubricating oil in a tin can with a long, spouted neck. He oiled the shed door padlock and set it on a rag to work through. A small, ancient toolbox held a basic toolkit, simple tools wrapped in separate leather cloths. He found pliers, cutters, a few wrenches and a set of screwdrivers—all flat ended with worn, red, wooden handles and a fine, thin coating of rust. There was a fine-point handsaw and a bow-saw for cutting branches, a claw-hammer, a wooden mallet and boxes of stamped nails and shiny brass screws in tiny unopened cardboard cartons. He cleared the workbench and returned with the boxes and tea-chests from the attic, stacking them neatly on the foot shelf to keep them off the floor and then when he'd used that space up, on the bench itself.

As he cleared his way through the attic he found a simple single cot bed—the type he imagined they used in the army. It creaked a lot but was firm and comfortable and the thin, blue-ticking mattress was in good condition and when unfolded, smelled of old books. He took his time to lay back and appreciate the moment. The sun was setting and casting watery shapes through the old glass in the window and up onto the attic ceiling. Motes of dust as big as Junebugs were caught in the light and floated in intricate patterns above his happy head.

Downstairs, he found himself alone. The girls were out or in there rooms so he began with fresh energy to tackle the living room. He brought down the gramophone and set it up on the breakfast counter. He danced around to the Zydeco music as he tidied up—working efficiently, filling yet more trash sacks with used tissues, takeaway leftovers, empty wine bottles and all the rest of what seemed like two years of laziness.

He swept, mopped and vacuumed, always moving to the music. He was so thoroughly absorbed in the work that he didn't notice Beth and

Zoe stood looking at him. From their overacted stance and the amused looks frozen on their faces, they'd been watching him dance and prance and clean now for some considerable time.

The gramophone was a big winner.

He cleaned the windows in the last of the fading light, his arms pumping to the beat. Already the house was looking perkier, and although there were still mountains of trash to deal with, lists of chores and repairs to draw up, prioritize and tackle, a definite start had begun. A datum of cleanliness and a benchmark for what could be achieved was being clearly set down and each large task began to define itself against the general mess and looked not only possible but instantly worth the effort.

When Easy had stacked the last of the days rubbish bags out in the street, Zoe was sure the refuse guys wouldn't take that much away in one hit. Beth suggested they bribe them but Easy waited till it was dark then calmly divided the bags evenly between the neighbours. In the morning, along with the thought of ever again living surrounded by so much garbage, scrap and languor, the trash was gone.

*   *   *   *   *

Stretching out against his warm cotton sheets, Easy yawned, woke then finally opened his eyes. His shoulders were stiff and he felt unusually at home. When he'd slipped into bed the night before, he'd not wanted to go to sleep right away and had enjoyed just lying there, listening to the safe sounding house, and watching how the street-lights played the branches of the sycamore trees across his ceiling. He felt like a kid again—was back in Pisgah, sleeping out under a million stars with his cousins Ed and Shim in Uncle Joe's hayrick.

He had finally slept and slept heavily and well, being woken by a black-throated warbler calling from the sycamore and the swish of morning traffic in the dark, wet streets below. Night rain, in a silent drizzle, had freshened the world. He was struck suddenly by how very different each day could be from its neighbor—and of how its many limitless and varied possibilities, came on the coattails of a good night's sleep.

Across town, he knew the bums and homeless would have already been dragged from their iron cots and sent out for a day's batting on the streets. Swiping the memories away like so many fat, noisy blue-bottles, he lay back, contented and rested, and contemplated the day's work ahead.

*   *   *   *   *

The house was quiet and peaceful. Once downstairs, he hesitated, not knowing if the girls were sleeping or at work. Despite the girls' approval, he decided to hold off with the music until later. He fetched an old hand brace from the shed, oiled its gearwheel, and drilled a small hole in the studwork wall. He tapped in a wall anchor, re-screwed the shelves, felt the teeth bite. It was level and sturdy and waiting to be filled.

He removed the books staggering in piles all over the dining table and stacked them alphabetically in the bookcases—his arms working at lightning speed.

At the market store on Magazine, he bought pancake mix and maple syrup with the change Zoe left on the kitchen counter—that would be breakfast, everyone liked pancakes. He also bought mangoes, because they looked good and were on offer and he couldn't remember how they tasted. On the way back he picked a great bunch of fresh gladioli poking through the fence from an overgrown and apparently abandoned garden. He trimmed the stems and dropped them into a sky blue vase in front of the fireplace—they fanned out, arranging themselves beautifully.

He tipped the bag of fresh mangoes into an earthenware bowl on the kitchen top—they were instantly perfect—a still life catching the morning sun . . . until Beth's hand plunged among them and plucked out the fattest and ripest. Her hair hung all over her face and her gown hung open showing a fair amount of her left breast.

'What's for breakfast?'

'Pancakes, with maple syrup.'

'Did I smell coffee?'

'I'll make you some—the bathroom's free if you want to go freshen—' he stopped himself and she looked at him and he rephrased his suggestion into a statement: 'I'm through with the bathroom.'

She plodded away, pulling the gown round her and tightening the belt. He watched her back and the belt drawing in at the waspish waste. She plopped down into a chair by the kitchen table, rubbed her eyes and sank her teeth right into the ripe fruit.

'Is Zoe at work?'

'I dunno,' she mumbled through mouthful of mango flesh.

'I was thinking about tackling your rooms today?'

Silence as he eyes moved about under the heavy lids.

'Is that alright? I mean, should I just get on with it?'

39

She thought for a second then shrugged: 'It's what you're here for.'
'Fine.'

Her fixed her coffee and pancakes, fetched more trash sacks from the shed and headed up the stairs.

Beth's room bore the pretensions of some erotic boudoir—a full-sized framed print by Gustave Klimt hung over the bed, the subject—half shrouded, her face in tortured ecstasy, reminded him of Beth. Glass lampshades and caned-bottomed chairs were draped with Indian silks and woven throws and cushions had been scattered about like giant rose petals. Stood along the dresser and mantle were little waxwork figurines of ghouls and skeletons and beautiful buxom women with voluptuous, long flowing hair. They were frozen in a graphic pornographic orgy—the maidens variously being taken from behind, their arms pinned back, breast jutting out, their heads hung low in shame, exhaustion or defeat, their faces distorted masks of horror, surprise, and agony. Behind them, the ghouls and skeletons grinned, cracked mouthed, their wicked faces leering, set in deep delight, their oversized waxy sexes luminous, poised or penetrating.

He found packets of exotic condoms in a large, deep, pewter bowl—coloured, flavoured, ribbed, barbed and even ones with strange grotesque animal heads on the tip. He dusted them and moved on . . .

Zoe's room was a different story: artfully full of stylish clutter, sixty-dollar photo magazines, enormous coffee table books, choreographed wallets of black and white 10 x 8s. Each piece of furniture was a composition, draped, swagged, backlit, and art directed. Easy steadily cleared and tidied, sorting the various camera equipment back into its protective cases, clearing dusty wineglasses and dinner plates from under the bed.

The room soon acquired a spacious, comfortable and Zen-like aura. Flipping the mattress, Easy found an oversize hardback - *Getting to Know Your Menstrual Cycle*. He went to shelve it, thought, and then slipped it back under the mattress where he found it.

Jane's room was the largest in the house with a sweeping bay window that gave out over the garden. The walls were lined with a faded beige pattern-paper that took on the effect of parchment as it span between the hung African masks and tribal shields. Great stacks of volumes covered the floor and gave shade and shelter to little settlements of dusty notes on the carpet. Some had toppled, slipping across the rugs and entombing their studies like huge cryptic playing cards.

Sat squarely upon the desk was an outdated computer—the keyboard buried in half filled jotters, the screen plastered in sticker-notes. The bed was a single, brass-framed affair with its old-fashioned quilts and simple, lace-trimmed pillows. It was shoved over into the room's most shadowed corner, uninviting, cold, and forgotten.

On the desk, Easy found a sealed glass Petri dish, which he picked up and examined. Inside was a small brownish fragment of wood or stone or bone, perhaps an inch in length. Easy was puzzled why anyone would keep the horrid thing but sensed enough to merit its importance. He put it up on the overhang of the shelf, safe above the threat of avalanche from the competing mounds of texts, literature, and research.

He stripped all the beds and washed and hung out the sheets, duvet covers and pillow cases. The plastic-coated clothesline—dried out and perished—snapped, about mid-way, and half way through the task, sending the wet sheets into the fallen leaves and dirt. He shook them out but knew they'd needed washing again. He replaced the line with a waxed sash cord he found in the drawer in the shed and carried on.

He stood in the afternoon air and thought about the yard itself. This was next, he thought, then he could start on the outside of the house proper; clean the windows, fix up the flat boards, maybe even repaint the whole front, right up to the eaves. But that would cost money for primer, filler, scratch-paper and paint, and, of course, a decent 14-treat ladder.

He decided he'd talk to the girls about it when Jane arrived—when they'd all had the opportunity to be properly introduced and the chance to see how they all got along.

PUP

'What's *he* doing here?' boomed Jane in her overly dramatic way. Normally, Zoe would have dismissed her tone as matron-like and irritating but today was different, today she had to deal with it, today had to work out.

They were standing in the spotless, gleaming, freshly spiced and fragranced living room, looking at Jane's old medical skeleton, which had been mended, waxed, and polished, and now proudly occupied one corner.

'We didn't know what to do with it—then we just got used to it there and thought it would be a bit of fun, you know?' She was speaking too quickly and a little too much and it was making her nervous. 'We couldn't just throw him out, could we now? After all—it's yours.'

Jane remembered her Med School days and one particular afternoon when the skeleton, en route to some presentation, had stood temporarily in the living room, just a few feet from where it stood now. She was preparing herself and was squeezing in one last rehearsal. The skeleton seemed strangely familiar and she was transported back through the years and heard distinctly, each and every time she passed it, how her mother had gasped and tutted. But it also looked different now, aged of course, but somehow detached, like a prop in some French Quarter theme bar.

'Well, I'm not sure about him but the place looks totally wonderful. It reminds me . . . of how it was when I was growing up.' She ran her hand along the top of the sofa made a little turn and sat down. 'We really must make an effort to keep it this way.'

'Hello,' said Zoe, 'that's why we got the cleaner.'

Jane looked around again and drew in the whole atmosphere. It was genuine, authentic, convincing at first contact; not the usual cover up, sweepings under the rug and the cupboards groaning with refuse. This was a surprise, the girls had made the effort and found a cleaner—and a cleaner who could clearly clean. She saw herself writing up the thesis, working productively at her desk through the morning, and then drifting down for a cup of tea and walking silently through the ordered, tidy room. It felt acutely grown up and in some proper, dignified way, like she was finally exerting some small measure of control over this significant part of her life.

She felt the first slow pull of the desk, that familiar excitement, knowing that you were required and capable of vital, imperative work and, although she couldn't wait to begin, the feeling was so exquisite that she resolved to savour every beat.

Zoe watched her, closely and with hope. Jane's first day back in the house after two weeks certainly seemed to get off to a good start. Zoe knew they had some difficult moments ahead; the first meeting between Jane and Laurie was bound to be tricky but so far so go, so she decided to press on.

'We bought that Earl Grey you like?'

'Oh, how thoughtful.'

'The old box had dried out. Beth's idea, actually.'

Jane smiled, surprised—Beth! Thinking of others? Would wonders ever cease? This was certainly turning into a homecoming she'd remember. She was just about to ask after the cleaner when the doorbell *r-r-r-rang*, cutting the air with that jagged rasp.

'I'll go,' said Zoe, knowing this was the moment. This was it—a scene she had played over in her mind all morning: She'd let Beth and Easy in and follow them down the hallway and through to the living room. Jane would see Beth first then Easy—Zoe would be at the back, still in the hallway or even as far back as the door, she'd miss the whole horrible look of realisation in Jane's eyes. That, she realised, she couldn't stand. The rest of it—the justifications and explanations about Easy employment and all its detail she could cope with. She'd be rational, forceful, and pragmatic and play all Jane's concerns out into the small acceptable margins. At all costs, however, she'd avoid that first look.

43

'No,' said Jane, jumping up and skipping out into the hallway, 'I'll get it.'

Zoe froze, watched Jane's girlish calf disappear round the doorframe. She saw the scene now play out again only she was the one alone in the living room when the others came in. Her face, and those first reactions, caught, exposed, in no-man's land. In a snap decision she followed Jane out to play the whole scene in the hallway, her face at Jane's shoulder.

The bell sounded again as Jane opened the big front door, swinging it wide on the cordial, smiling face of Easy. He stood there, peeping over several bags of groceries and just beamed:

'I'll name that tune in one!'

'Sorry?' Whispered Jane, confused.

'The doorbell—It's a good tune played properly.' He laughed, a little too intimately for Jane's liking. 'Don't worry—I'll get round to fixing that today, it's on my list.'

'Your list?' She repeated, her voice now a shallow breath.

'You must be Jane,' he beamed, 'I'm Easy.' And he set the groceries down and shook her hand busily. Jane's face drained away into this opaque mask of horror. This was it—the moment . . .

'Let me take these,' said Zoe, snatching up the grocery bags, positioning herself carefully to avoid eye contact with anyone.

Beth arrived, clumping up the steps with more bags. Jane eyes shone out from her pale face like those on a dying fish. Beth, in contrast to Zoe, seemed to embrace all Jane's discomfort. She got right on in there, staring at her like some blind specimen in a glass jar.

'Oh, Jane, you looked around already? Isn't it just marvellous what Easy's done to this old pile?'

Jane still couldn't respond. Easy stopped pumping her hand like a well handle. Zoe slipped away down the hall, to the safety of the kitchen, calling back in a light, affected, carefree voice:

'Jane was just saying the house hasn't looked like this since she was a girl.'

Jane remained frozen. Easy was expecting some type of reaction from her but this certainly wasn't it. He'd never met anyone like Jane before. Not as an adult. She was a brainbox type for sure, he could tell that right off, but she also had a presence. A definite core strength that seemed almost to hold her erect. He noticed she had a long, slender nose which drew your eye up towards a smooth, high forehead that was bisected by a pale blue but very distinguishing vein. He realised Jane was the sort of person who had genuine detachment, the sort who could take herself off somewhere, right in the middle of a crowd, and have a good hard think, even though she was being stared at. She was taller than he'd imagined, and for some reason he'd expected her to have a little more of the School Marm about her. In truth, she struck him somewhere between a Preacher's wife and a lanky librarian.

Beth squeezed by, a smile on her lips, but smart enough to hold her tongue. Easy picked up the remaining groceries and followed, leaving Jane stood holding the open door and staring off down the street.

He unpacked the groceries and began to put away. No one spoke, but he could see Beth and Zoe swapping little furtive looks. They continued like this, pretending in their movements that everything was normal but the air was hostile and supercharged—like the inside of a shining, over-pumped party balloon.

He put on more coffee and washed out some cups. The reek of drains rushed at him like an oven blast. He saw Jane was in the room now and stood in the middle of the rug, stock still, and staring at him. She seemed poised to speak but no sound would come. The seconds ticked slowly by. Finally, Easy held his arms out to the sides and did a full, slow turn.

'I dance too,' he said, 'if you flip me nickels.'

She was suddenly awake and with them and embarrassed. She turned away, and stepped right into Zoe, their eyes met and Zoe asked in a voice which was quiet and steady and playful: 'What's going on?'

'Don't, Zoe, please,' Jane hissed. 'This sort of thing—', she waived an arm back of herself, 'From Beth, I expect it . . . but not from you.'

The balloon was bursting in stop-motion . . . Zoe's mouth formed a silent O. Jane's words hung frozen in the air like shrapnel from a grenade . . . Beth was looking over from the fridge, her eyebrows arched in glee, enjoying every second . . .

'*Hum-a-hum-lah*,' said Easy, interrupting, 'this sink's all backed up. That's the stink I've been talking 'bout.'

Time began again slowly, like an old 45 on the turntable after a power cut.

'Can you fix it?' Asked Beth, never for a second taking her eyes off Jane.

'Sure—it's a five minute job.'

'Then get after it, mister.'

Easy opened the pearl-rimmed buttons of his denim shirt, *pop, pop, pop*, momentarily revealing a broad, hairless chest before he disappeared beneath the sink.

Jane and Zoe were still locked together, like mime-wrestlers, in the middle of the room.

'You have references, I presume?'

45

'What—You think we'd just dragged some guy in off the street?'

'And please, for the love of God, tell me he's on some probationary period.'

'Four weeks,' said Zoe—not missing a heartbeat.

'Then it's not a total galloping mess, is it?'

There was a loud *glooping* from under the sink and Easy moaned and stood up to reveal his chest and hands are covered in gunk from the drain trap.

'Oh, my—,' he said, drawing his head away from the pungent, acidic reek, 'That's got to be months' worth. Pass me that rag, Beth.'

Beth fetched the old tea towel and took it over to Easy. She considered wiping his chest but thought better of it and slapped the towel in his sticky, wet hand.

Easy began to wipe off his chest and neck. A short seismic span of time elapsed whilst all three women looked at him and took in the vision of his hard arms working over the lean, tanned body.

Jane turned and walked crisply from the room. Beth was first to speak. She caught Zoe's look, smiled, and said in her low, even drawl: 'Yeah, yeah, yeah, but can he cook?'

SIT

Jane stomped up the stairs. Her mind was racing and getting nowhere. How could they? They had spoken about this very thing, right at the beginning of the search—a male cleaner was out, out, *out*. Damn them, she thought. Damn them and their little game all to hell.

As she climbed the steps, she became aware of something—something new. It was in the light—this change—and not altogether unpleasant. Damn them, damn them, *damn them*.

She was too angry to immediately pinpoint the change but by the second staircase she began to realise—something about the walls and surfaces had been modified—they exhibited a particular brightness, a specific sun-filled quality. The hallways and stairs seemed wider and more generous and passage through them was now quick and strangely effortless—then it hit her—the *stuff* was gone—the *stuff*. But when she thought about what the stuff actually was she couldn't bring it to mind clearly. It was books, yes, *books*—wasn't it? Or research—yes, no—yes, it was research and cuttings and articles and essential *information*—wasn't it? Whatever it was that was gone had left no imprint of shadow—it had simply been removed and in its removal the space had been brought back into useful service.

Slamming her bedroom door with sufficient force that the vibration made a glass rattle on the kitchen shelf, Jane turned and was so struck by the order before her, she assumed she was in the wrong room. She paused, collected herself and looked again. She saw acres of polished

47

boards. They reflected the light back up into the room and shone off the walls and ceiling so that the air itself seemed to glow. She saw the neatly arranged desk and ordered shelves—they were unrecognisable yet familiar, it was as if, in some parallel world, this was how they should be.

She then panicked, rushed to her desk and checked her work. The notebooks were there but she could not see the bone. She shoved books aside, sending them to the floor, but it was still no good.

The idiots. The idiots. *The idiots.*

Leaning up, a bright shaft of sunlight flashed across her face and she saw it—the Petri dish—safely placed out of harm's way on the shelf where Easy has put it. Her relief was profound but also, she realised, tinged with the regret that she no longer had an unassailable excuse to get rid of the man.

Calming now, she took in the books on the shelves—seeing them all in alphabetical order—an idea seized her and she ran her finger along the row and pulled free a slim, leather bound volume—*Tongues Of Fire*. She knew it—she'd had it all along—she hadn't lost the book—or rather, she now admitted, she had lost it but only amidst the other volumes strewn throughout her bedroom.

A small cluster of daffodils shone from the vase on her bedside table. She smelled them, sat on the freshly made bed with the book and Petri dish in her lap and considered the whole situation.

Across town, in Mama-Lek's Laundromat, Easy folded the girls' clothes and drank tea with the patron. She asked him a hundred questions about his new job but never stopped moving long enough for Easy to give her a proper answer.

'So, Easy big-shot, big-shot now, wash prity-tings for prity woman,' she joked seeing him folding one of Beth's blouses.

'Three women' he smiled.

'Fee-woman! *Weee-eee.* Sound like could be lotta fun-fun to Mama-Lek. Lotta fun-fun or bigtam boo-hoo,' she boomed, 'Easy gotto be clebber-boy, clebber-boy. Don't go scoo-ing up bigtam opp-toon-tee.'

'Don't worry, Mama-Lek,' said Easy, heeding her words of wisdom, 'I aim to keep it real simple.'

*   *   *   *   *

Beth waited by her car on the side of the highway. She'd lost a nail getting the hood up and now steam rose in great clouds from the engine. Her interest in automobiles started and ended with mechanics. Not the inner workings of combustion engines but those sweaty, oily, muscle rippling Neanderthals, with torn overalls, greasy baseball caps and calloused hands. That said, Beth knew she'd screwed up—the last time she'd had the car serviced there were three inches of snow on the ground.

Through the steam, she could make out the defined, compact, confusing blocks of the engine and wondered why she'd even bothered to lift the hood. People always did that—like that was something they knew they could do—lift the lid. Big deal. After that, it might as well have been brain surgery. What did people expect? They'd see something that clearly didn't belong—like a dead cat, or a melted skateboard—and by pulling it out and tossing it down the bank the car would be fine and they could carry on with their lives?

She was going to miss a meeting and would have to call ahead and cancel. That was the professional thing to do—call ahead and lie.

Only that wasn't going to happen.

Beth had overcome her technophobia but only to a point. She weakened and bought a cell phone—fine—but there was no way she was going in for the extras. The extras, for Beth, meant the use of the in-built camera, video messaging, and even basic texts. The address book she liked. The thought of having all your contacts in the palm of your hand gave her the appropriate sense of power. But alas, as this accomplishment depended on the ability to type in your contacts names, it was useless.

Predictive text—the very breakthrough designed for the Luddites and laggards like Beth—proved to be a technological step too far. If she'd learned how to disable the feature sooner it may have saved her address book but she didn't and so had rendered most of her entries in absolute jibberish.

Removed from her office Rolodex, she was limited to making calls to numbers she knew by heart and those last ten numbers stored in her call log. Today's meeting, having been made last month and confirmed two days ago, had been shunted off into the ether. She had, however, called home and spoke to Easy, although she wasn't at all sure he'd completely understood her predicament as he'd simply acknowledged the situation and abruptly hung up.

She knew one thing—she should stay in her car because this was one of those dangerous situations where any freak could see her and pull over at any minute. Sitting in the car however, she felt even more like a sitting duck so she abandoned that idea and instead paced up and down the hard shoulder, holding her cell phone to her ear, laughing and tossing her head back just so—calm and relaxed and assured giving off the serious, super-confident, unmistakable vibe that the cavalry were just over the hill.

A taxi blasted its horn as it sped passed and pulled in up ahead. The reverse lights came on and it made its way back to her. As it approached she could see Easy smiling through the back window and the relief, that was unexpected, suddenly flooded through her.

He hopped out, walked over and waited for her to finish her fake call and whispered, 'You alright?'

'Yeah, yeah.' She looked at the cell then put it away, 'I'm fine. What a drag.'

'Sorry I took so long. You didn't call the garage?'

'No. That's right?'

'I know. I called them to check they knew where you were and they hadn't heard from you.'

'Right. Thanks. I'm a complete airhead today.'

'No problem.'

Beth lit up a cigarette, leaned against the car and contemplated her ruined day. Easy however had already started transferring her liquor samples to the taxi. When he saw her standing looking at him with a confused look on her face, he stopped—

'You take the cab on to your meeting, yeah? I'll wait here for the grease-monkey.'

'Oh—' she said, flicking the cigarette in a high arc over the crash barrier, 'you total star!' She gave him a little peck on the cheek and helped him clear the rest of her stuff from the back seat. Her day was back on track and she was instantly on form and dealing with it—telling the driver where she wanted to go in District 13 and to avoid the *damn* road works on Pontchartrain Drive.

Easy waved her off, and kept waving till the taxi was a dot in his scrunched-up left eyeball. He then felt the little spot on his cheek where her wide, soft lips had landed. He wondered how the little scenario would have looked like from the fast lane, zipping by at 90. Easy enjoyed thinking about that for a full twenty-two minutes until the recovery truck turned up.

*   *   *   *   *

Alone, Zoe stood in the newsroom kitchen area, waiting for the kettle to boil up and click off—she hated waiting and looked out across the office. Today, there was some genuine activity taking place—not a Stop-Press, not a City Hall Foundation Shaker, not a Pulitzer Prize winning Scoop—

but the retirement of a senile, senior sub-editor in 'advertorial'. The kettle plumed steam and waited for some manual interjection.

Zoe made a cup of 'herbal decaf', working the teabag against the side of the cup with her spoon to hurry the process. She wondered whether it really affected the taste but couldn't remember a time when she let the tea infuse properly. The instruction on the back of the box specifically said—Bring fresh water to a Rolling Boil, then steep for 5-8 minutes. Five to eight minutes—*who were they kidding*? Where did they think we were, anyway—Shaanxi Province?

She scooped out the teabag and dropped it in the pedal bin. Someone was behind her, silent and watching and she couldn't tell how long they been standing there.

It was Chance, and when she turned to look at him it was clear he'd been checking out her ass and was not trying ever so hard to cover it up. He smiled, reached passed her and opened the fridge. The light popped off his spotless white shirt and Zoe caught the fresh zing of his deodorant. It was a smell she remembered but this seemed stronger, like maybe he'd just sprayed himself before coming over.

Zoe suddenly became self-conscious, watching him pluck out and crack open a slim tube of high-energy drink. They stood very close together with him turned a little to the side and as he tipped his head back took a deep slug, she watched his Adam's Apple raking up and down.

'That stuff's hell on your sperm count.' She heard herself say. He stopped drinking and looked at her so steadily she could make out little twin flashes of the refrigerator light in his irises.

'I'll bear that in mind,' he said and drained off the can in another long but less satisfying guzzle. This was it—he crushed the can and dropped it in the pedal bin that she was still holding open with her foot—he was going—the moment was over—slipping into history—past . . .

'Who's retiring?'

'What?' He now seemed irritated by the question.

'Who is that—getting their gold watch?' she joked.

'Hooberman—I think.' He looked over at the little geriatric crowd. 'It could be anyone of them—everyone's ancient in Adver-T.'

'Are they going to give him a send off?'

'God—I don't know. Do they still party at that age?' They both laughed, but Zoe realised he was laughing inwardly, at his own joke, and didn't need her audience.

She'd thought once or twice that morning of asking him if he was going to the 'Hooberman' thing, but now it seemed pretty redundant. Chance straightened and looked again at the little team of old-timers—

there was something in his look—almost an arrogance—like he was looking at something very foreign and a little alien—a toddler with a nest of ants. He grunted and made a move to leave.

'So,' she said, stepping into the zone, 'Got anything planned for the weekend?'

He turned and dipped his head. The same detached, alien look was now directed at her. 'Staying clear of crazy, single white Venus flytraps.' He took another step, then turned to address her: 'How 'bout you?'

But he didn't wait for her answer and just swaggered out. Zoe, totally floored, cursed herself. Blood rushed to her face and she felt it boil in tiny prickles under her hair. She held a mock gun to her temple, cocked her thumb, and pulled the trigger.

*   *   *   *   *

Jane chopped away at her keyboard. She worked quickly but had a clumsy, staccato, six-fingered style—battering the keys in a random, haphazard flurry.

A stubby pencil, well chewed and working from one side of her mouth to the other, was occasionally plucked free and made to jot or tick in her dog-eared notepad. Progress was being made and her desk was again a triumphant mess—open books scattered in a tide, lapping right up to the sill on the bay window.

After a gentle knock on the door, Jane called, 'Come in,' spitting the pencil out, where it bounced on the thick rug and hopped under the desk.

Easy entered slowly with a pot of tea, china cup, a little jug of milk and sugar in a cut-glass bowl all set out on a colonial style wickerwork tray. He looked at Jane bent under the desk in search of her pencil, and then at the progress on the screen.

'You writing a book?'

She straightened up and gave him a certain look: 'Thesis.'

'Bless you!' he said but kerbed it when he clocked she was not in the least bit amused. 'It's 'bout that biddy spec of bone, ain't it?'

'Yes. Now, if you'd kindly set the tray down. I'm right in the middle of it all and I really must, must get on.'

He looked for a place to rest the tray and finally moved to the bed and set it down on the soft mattress. The typing began behind him and he turned to see her pounding away enthusiastically. Her hair was tied up atop her head like a pineapple sprout where the sprigs danced about, shuddering to the click-clacking rhythm. It mesmerised him for a second

52

or so and he stood waiting until she stopped and made another jotting: 'You find that bone on one of your round the world trips?'

'Er, Yes—in Egypt, now please, I really must work—'

'Sure,' he said, heading out. 'Sorry—I just don't see what's so impo'tant about a little crumb of bone that it makes someone forget their manners.'

She watched him walk to the door, the color rising in her cheeks. As he stepped out she spoke in a flurry: 'It's from a eunuch's skull!'

He popped his head back in, 'Wow.'

'I'm sorry, it really is most rude of me but I'm just under quite a bit of pressure—most of it self-imposed.'

He smiled and nodded that he understood. 'A real eunuch, huh? What, like, you know . . . ' Easy did a comical chopping action with his hand across his groin. Jane frowned and nodded and before she could begin again Easy asked: 'How could you tell he was a real eunuch? I mean, wasn't he all . . . decomposin'?'

'Of course, yes, yes—completely, thousands of years ago.' She hesitated, looking at him, wondering whether it was worth explaining any of this. 'It's the way the body was arranged, you see?'

He nodded.

Clueless, she thought.

'They used to bury servants along with the Pharaohs.'

'Yeah, I remember reading that somewheres. Sugar?'

'What? Yes, no—no sugar, thank you.'

He stirred her tea anyway and stood holding the cup: 'Go on.'

'Sorry?'

'You were talking about burying Pharaohs.'

'Yes, well—Only this particular Pharaoh was a fake.'

'A phony Pharaoh?' he said smiling and she didn't know if he was genuinely interested, or just pulling her leg, or even if they were talking on the same level at all. He was like a kid at Christmas, unwrapping a train set and playing with the wrapping paper.

'This individual was just a wealthy landowner who lived like a Pharaoh. There were clues in the eunuch's uniform too. Buckles, parts of a breast-plate and an ornamental knife.'

'Wow, suddenly you're, like, the female Indiana Jones.'

Jane frowned, unsure if this was meant to be a compliment. Easy set the teacup on the desk, easing a little more space beside her notebook.

'Thank you.'

'No problem. Hey, I'll read it for you, if you like.'

'Sorry?'

53

'Your book—I'll give it the once over when you're ready. My spelling's always been purty spot on.'

She now looked at him like he'd completely lost the plot but he just smiled confidently back.

'Well,' she said, 'we'll see, shall we?'

He then crossed the room and opened the window a little, winked at her like they were both in on some joke and left.

Jane sipped the tea—it was hot and just right and strangely delicious. She went to shut the far window but saw the daffodils on the sill gently flutter in its breeze. She went back and sat down again, took another sip of the fresh perfect tea, and went back to work.

*   *   *   *   *

Beth wiped down the bartop—speaking into her cell, discreet but angry: 'Screw you, Donnie. I'm good for it. A grand on *Begin-Again*. No, to place. What do you think I am, crazy?' She hung up and headed back down the bar, where the Licence Inspector from City Hall was finishing up his paperwork.

'So, we all in order?'

'Sure,' he smiled, 'You just gotta sign here and here and I'll get this processed for you, right away.'

She signed and offered her hand for him to shake. 'So, we're set?'

'It's a formality,' he assured her, his oily palm lingering in hers just a second too long. 'You've already got the 3am licence—the extension's a shoo-in.' He finally let her go and she reached for a bottle of Wild Turkey, cracked the neck and poured celebratory measures into the two waiting tumblers. He made the grunts and gestures that he shouldn't really be drinking on the good Citizens' clock but she batted him down with a slight shake of the head and poured him a full 12-month DUI measure.

Business was done—almost—and she snuck a look and caught the old familiar look in his eye. Like a hunger. He wanted it, this time. Sometimes he didn't, and that was good but always left her a little anxious—until the licence came through. But this time he'd collect—right on the office desk.

They smiled insincerely at each other and she prayed they'd soon promote some younger guy, who still had all his hair, kept himself in shape, and knew a thing or two about where to buy deodorant.

*   *   *   *   *

Zoe was at her workstation when she'd had the unusually strong urge to call him and now, due to some interruption at his end, she was effectively on hold.

Zoe hated to wait.

On her computer was an empty Skype window showing a little snug library room somewhere up country.

'Dad?' she called again, impatience rising in her voice.

Zoe's Dad, seventy-three, ex-army, finally sat back down into the frame. 'Sorry, Chicken,' he said, 'Prostate. So—what were you gonna tell me?'

'Nothing—I just wanted to see when you could come up to the city. Pay me a visit.'

'What—you short of money?'

'I haven't borrowed money off you in, like, ten years.'

'What's up then?'

'Nothing. I just never get to see you anymore. You gotta be more pro-active, Dad. Who's organizing your weekends now?'

'I am,' he said proudly. 'I got the club and my fishing. I'm fine, really,' he pulled a body-builder pose flexing his biceps, holding his breath in and grinning, then he suddenly thought of something and frowned at her playfully: 'Hey—You gotta boyfriend?'

'What?' Zoe laughed mechanically; she was floored, stalling for time.

'I thought maybe that's why you were ringing. To tell me about some guy you'd met.'

'No. That's not why I was ringing, dad. I was thinking about you,' she lied, because he was right and he got her every time.

'Well, if there *is* a guy you wanna tell me about then go right ahead.'

'There isn't, dad, so drop it.'

'Fine—if it's still early days—you know best. You know where I am when you want to go public.'

'Jesus! Dad.' She was about to get angry with him, or with herself, for being so obvious when she heard the sound of another call come through on his Skpye—

'Look, honey, I got to take this. You wanna hold?'

'No. I do not.'

'Sure—I'll call you back in half an hour.' He hung up and Zoe looked as the window collapsed on the screen to reveal her own flat reflection. She glanced around the office, suddenly lost.

*   *   *   *   *

Jane was not alone in the house. She could hear the others downstairs—their conversation drifting up the stairwell.

She'd completed three chapters in as many days and was calculating the date when she'd finish if she could keep up this rate when she tripped over Easy's beat up cowboy boots in the hallway. She picked them up with her fingertips like a couple of dead racoons, carried them downstairs and put them outside with the trash.

The house was immaculate but Easy, the man himself, was another curious thing. He had to go and go quickly before he got too settled and began making attachments. His personal smell was beginning to permeate the place. He didn't seem to use a deodorant and smelled strongly of carbolic soap and washing detergent—but that was just a mask. His own oily odour lingered underneath, persistent, latent, and manly, and that worried Jane.

She checked the bathroom again, running her finger along the surfaces and even the top of the mirror but it was yet again dust-free - and the whole room was spotless.

Turning to leave, she saw that the toilet seat has been left up and she walked over to it slowly then slammed it down and headed in for the fight!

In the kitchen, Easy cooked breakfast. Zoe and Beth both sat at the table drinking coffee and making a list of things they hated.

'Fat women who exercise'

'Young guys with beards,' said Beth.

'Women who drink too much,' added Zoe.

'Men who don't drink enough, added Beth and they laughed. Zoe got suddenly serious.

'I know—Guys who toot the car horn when they pick you up for a date.'

They both groaned and agreed. 'That's just so disrespectful. A man's got to be something special between the sheets to get away with that shit.'

Jane entered and took in the scene. Her little tirade was directed at anyone who'd care to listen but fell principally in Easy's direction.

'Someone left the toilet seat up!' she declared. 'If there's one thing I can't abide it's a toilet with the seat up. The seat should be down. Down, not up!'

'Shall I put that on the list?' suggested Zoe, trying to lighten the mood. Easy wiped his hands and began to tip-toe round to Jane in an exaggerated fashion and make his apology. Beth saw him, realized what he was going to do and took action—

'Sorry, Jane, that was me,' said Beth, taking the words out of Easy's mouth. 'I was feeling lousy earlier, thought I was going to be sick. Sorry.'

Jane stood there, deflated, having nowhere to go. 'Oh, right,' she began. 'Because if there is one thing I simply will not tolerate it's—'

Beth interrupted, without crawling or backing down: 'Yes, we know. Down, not up. I said I'm sorry. I forgot, alright?'

'Right.'

There was a long uneasy silence.

'Hey, cher,' said Easy softly to Jane, 'If you like, I'll keep an eye on that sort of thing. Just let me know any customs and foibles you have in the sanitation department and I'll make sure it don't happen again.'

Jane's eyes sprung open like she'd been tweaked on both ears. 'Right,' she said. 'Okay. Good. You make sure you do!'

She turned to leave—

'Vittles in five,' said Easy. 'Or if that don't fit with your timetable, I can fix you something later once I been to the store.'

'No, yes. I'll be right down,' said Jane, then she paused shut her eyes and continued, 'and please—don't ever call me *cher*.'

Easy gave her a big smile and the double the thumbs up before he knew it he'd started humming his little tune again.

Jane left. Beth waited to hear her footsteps on the stairs then winked at Zoe. Jane suddenly shouted—'And stop humming that dreadful tune!'

Easy shut up and they all looked at each other like naughty school children.

*   *   *   *   *

Jane reached her room, closed the door, and composed herself. They could always make her feel like an idiot—now he was in on it with them.

Her desk had been tidied again and she saw a jar of orange HB pencils on the shelf. She took a pencil—noticed it had been freshly sharpened—realised they all had.

Jane looked at the growing thickness of the manuscript—she was making progress, good progress, but she was still at a critical stage, where the various evidence was established but no overall argument had yet been proved. She needed more than ever the time to think and to concentrate. A typo suddenly leapt from the text and she noted the error. In doing so she scanned a phrase and felt it could be trimmed, clarified. She sat and continued to work.

BOWL

The girls sat quietly at the table, cutting thick slices of fresh homemade bread and dunking them deep in Easy's spicy vegetable soup. It was the first of many such meals that they would enjoy and as they ate they contemplated what future dishes lay in store. Easy kept back in the kitchen area, keeping an eye on the proceedings over the breakfast bar. He shook the frying pan and sprinkled the devilled kidneys with the miniature bottle of Tabasco sauce that he kept on a keychain.

Zoe was keen for this first big meal to work out and observed Jane closely, hoping for early clues to her precise mood, in the hope of steering the conversation safely along civil lines.

'This is delicious. Beth, Jane, don't you think?'

Beth moaned in carnal satisfaction. She was one of God's creatures who had no inhibitions about being spoiled, pampered, and catered for and was enjoying every moment.

Jane remained silent. She was fully aware of Zoe's thin plan and had realised before taking her seat that if Easy proved himself tonight he would only be harder to get rid of in the days to come.

'Where did you learn to cook like this?' said Zoe, trying to casually bring Easy into the conversation.

'We all had mothers once,' said Easy, 'we ought to remember.' Then he chuckled and clucked and appeared at the side of the table where he

wiped his hands on his kitchen apron. 'Actually,' he said. 'I'm self taught—
'
'What, from library books?' said Jane, not quite to herself.
'Yep—and a two-ring hotplate!' he shot back.
'Well, you're a fabulous cook.'
'Thank you, Zoe. Polite of you to say so.'
Beth finished, plonked down the spoon and pushed her bowl forward. She smacked her lips, yawned, and then, as if remembering, reached for her glass and took a big slug of wine.
'Well, pluck a duck and call it Thanksgiving—that was heaven. Did you say you got desert?'
'You still got your entrée yet. And if you eat it all up then maybe there's a little Bayou surprise.'
She yawned again, satisfied: 'I love surprises.'
'Food's the second most primitive comfort—' he began.
'I know the first,' Beth cut in, flashing her eyes at Zoe—
'I guess you do. That's why you're all worn out.'
He drew the bottle from the ice bucket and poured them more wine. When he got to Jane, she covered her glass with the flat of her hand and cast her eyes away to some spot on the rug. It was mighty fine acting, thought Easy, straight out of some French chamber piece, or a Texan cat house.
'Do you have a favorite dish, Easy?' continued Zoe.
'Sure—My speciality's Cajun Gourmet.'
'Bluh,' said Beth. 'Chicken fried gator!'
'Not Creole, Betty, I'm talking proper *Cajun*.' He twisted the bottle back into the ice in the bucket. A moment passed where Beth or someone else could have commented on this new name and it would have ended there. The second-hand ticked on by and to Easy at least from that moment on she became Betty: 'Roux darker than the reverse light on a witch's cat, *tasso* so fresh he's still squealing, gumbo *feelay* with all the mudbugs. That's what I'm talking about. *Haat* sauces, McIlhenny Tabasco. Hey, you know they even got one now with Habaneros? *Phew-wee* them spices sure thin the blood. Help a young boy think in a straight line.'
Easy cleared the soup bowls, leaving the women to look at each other, while he went to the kitchen.
'Ain't this the *ding*? Said Beth enjoying the effect it had on Jane.
'I think we're making a big mistake,' said Jane in something like a venomous whisper. Zoe put her fingers in ears, like a schoolgirl:
'La-la-la. I'm not listening.'

59

'Loosen up, sister. You've got a swinging brick in your chest, instead of a heart.'

'Who do you think you're speaking to?'

'God, Jane—would you just listen to yourself. You should be in Charlotte, running a reformatory for wayward girls.'

Easy returned with the main courses placed neatly along his arm and stood poised to serve. Zoe was thankful; his presence seemed to quieten Jane, like she was too scared or dignified to bring up his presence whilst he was present. That suited her fine, anything to put some time on the clock.

'You really like this work, don't you?' asked Zoe.

'I've come to accept over the years that I'm the type of guy who's gotta be busy or be kept busy,' he smiled, 'Too much iron in the blood, I guess.' He flashed his eyes, manically, 'I git the Cabin Fever just by sitting still.'

'Don't worry,' said Beth, 'We'll keep you occupied. You can be our kitchen bitch—'

Zoe kicked Beth under the table and she took it and the message. Easy placed the entrées—taking pride in his work, turning the plates an inch or so, to present the food just so. He didn't over-do it; kept a comfortable feel to proceedings but put real care into it, pure concentration. Jane was working hard to remain unimpressed and communicating it with every fibre of her being.

'Have you,' asked Jane in a deliberately measured tone, 'got any . . . friends, Mr. Easy?'

'It's just Easy—there ain't no Mister. And, no, I've lost all my close friends eventually.'

'Really,' quizzed Jane, finally getting the scent of something, 'And why was that, do you think?'

'Oh, some of 'em died and some of 'em married up and some I just never got round to calling back.' He smiled, without irony, then added, 'I've got acquaintances, but we're not close—not like the way you girls are.'

Beth nearly brought up a whole piece of kidney. Zoe and finally Jane reached for their wine and drank as they considered this remark.

'What about—you know, *girlfriends*?' The word jammed in her gullet and came out strangled and wrong.

Beth rolled her eyes.

'Oh, I see. Well, no. Not now,' he said, taking the soup terrine from the dresser through to the kitchen. 'So, you needn't worry about me bringing the ladies home,' he called back, 'If that's what's tying your panty-hoes in a Spanish knot.'

Jane flushed. If Easy hadn't exited just then she might have thrown her chair back and stormed out. But the exit was taken and she sat in a quiet rage. Zoe sensed the whole evening was coming apart.

'I've been engaged mind you,' continued Easy, obliviously calling out from the kitchen, 'A couple of times—'

'A couple?' said Zoe.

'Yeah, it ain't so difficult to get snared up a couple of times if you're the sort of guy like me.'

'And what sort of guy would that be exactly?' pressed Jane, sensing blood.

'Oh, you know,' said Easy in a low contented voice as he stepped into the room, 'happy-go-lucky.' He then set the big bowl of salad down, mixed the leaves with the wooden tossers and stood back from the table: 'Voila! Bon appetite.'

As the women began, Easy returned to the kitchen area and began, as quietly as possible, to clean up. They ate for a moment or two then Jane placed her knife and fork by her plate and cleared her throat.

'What happened?' she called through to the kitchen, 'To these girls you were engaged to?'

So here we were, thought Easy, the old life story again. He wondered briefly why it always seemed like he had to go first. He came through and looked at the girls wondering how his tale would go down.

'You really wanna know?'

'Yes,' said Jane, 'if you don't mind the question?'

'It ain't pretty,' began Easy, 'and it probably ain't table talk—'

'Well,' interrupted Zoe, 'if you'd rather not—'

'I can clean it up a little as I go,' said Easy, and jumped up on one of the breakfast barstools. 'First girl I was engaged to marry died in tragic accident. A Mack Truck reversed over her in the parking lot back of Pete's Crab 'N' Gumbo out on highway 10. She was one *helluva* sweet girl. Dorota Wanda Cecilia Wadjakovska, of Polish extraction, but we all called her Dot.'

'My God,' said Zoe, 'I read about that.'

Beth thought it was horseshit but intriguing enough. Jane kept silent, hoping he was digging himself a hole big enough to trip up and fall into. Easy just nodded, leaned back and reminisced.

'She always wore these sunshades and a polka-dot beret, you know? I didn't deserve that girl. Really. She was too kind hearted. We were trying for a child and I remember the moment she told me she was in the family way,' he smiled. 'Just said it right out over breakfast the morning of the

61

day she died. I'm just cutting into my strawberry pancake and she tells me she's missed her monthlies. Funny how some images stick, ain't it?'

The girls were silent—Beth couldn't decide whether to laugh out loud. Was he pulling their leg?

'She wasn't pregnant though—Thank God. They found out in the post-mortem. The Doctor sat me down with the Hospital Padre and showed me the report so as I could get the thought out of my mind for once and all. That was eating me up pretty bad, as I remember.' He fell silent and looked from Jane to Beth to Zoe. 'Funny how we got to be saved from our self at times, ain't it?'

Beth was fit to pop. Zoe looked at Jane who was, it seemed, unexpectedly moved. Easy hopped off the stool, strolled round the breakfast bar to the kitchen and began to wash up and dry the dishes.

'Nicolette McClusky was the second girl I got engaged to marry. She was Dot's best friend and that started out as a big mistake.' He nodded adding emphasis where none was needed. 'I gave her a ride back from the crematorium. She was crying, I was crying. Next thing we were kissing.' He looked slightly bashful now, not embarrassed but like a teenager caught kissing his date at the door. 'That happens, you know. It's this death and sex thing. Powerful crazy stuff.'

The girls were now speechless. Beth stared straight ahead of her, Jane had her hands folded in her lap and Zoe was passed caring as to where all this was going.

'The mortuary had given me this see-through plastic bag containing all Dot's belongings. For some reason, it was still sitting there on the back seat. We were twisted round crying and kissing and I could just see the broken sun-shades and that polka-dot beret.'

The growing swell of nervous laughter that was building inside Beth's chest suddenly overtook her and she emitted a short, involuntarily chortle. Both Zoe and Jane gave her scalding looks but Easy just nodded and continued as if he completely knew where Beth was coming from. 'Yeah, you don't see them around much these days, do you? Anyways, Nicolette fell pregnant straight away. I was so happy. With Dot I've got to admit but I'd been worrying I couldn't have kids, y'know, *shooting blanks*, having doubts, thought my end game was nothing more than a puff of talcum powder.'

Beth who had got hold of herself, now sprayed a half-mouthful of wine across the table. Easy fetched a tea towel and began to wipe it up as he pushed on.

'I rushed out and bought a buggy and baby clothes and cartoon wallpaper, all in blue. I felt sure it was a boy but Nicolette said it was a li'l girl inside her. You'd think a mom would know, huh?'

He nodded at Zoe for no particular reason and she nodded right back.

'When we found out it was twins I skipped out and bought the whole same lot all over again, but this time in pink! Seemed to make some crazy sense at the time . . .' He laughed, slapping his forehead, as the memories flooded back in around him.

'On the Sunday she took clean off with our upstairs neighbour. He was a good buddy of mine—name of Jimmy Lee Bujeau. A keen horticulturist—or so I believed up until that Sunday. Always tending our window boxes, anyhow.' He shrugged, shook off a faraway look. 'I guess I should've clicked what was going on between Jimmy Lee and Nicollete but you never think that kinda thing is ever going to happen to you, do you? It turned out they were his twins, see? They'd been carrying on together all along, even before the funeral—even before the tragic accident with the Mack Truck in the parking lot out back of Pete's Crab 'N' Gumbo down on highway 10.'

'How do you know the kids were his?' asked Zoe.

'Well, that bit was easy—the twins were real pretty and of course jet-black just like Jimmy-Lee.'

Again Beth laughed out loud and held her hands up to apologize.

'Good Lord, Beth,' Jane scolded, 'Have you no feelings?'

Her eyes had a power that Zoe had never seen before. It almost outshone the fact that Jane had, for the very first time since he arrived, actually said a word in Easy's defence.

'I'm sorry, I'm sorry,' said Beth, her whole body still convulsed in pleasure, 'but this is like Oprah on acid.'

'I know,' Easy threw up his hands in agreement, 'you couldn't make it up if you tried, huh? There's a happy ending though. My wife's Mexican!'

'Your *wife*!' said Jane. She was on the hook now and striking hard against the line. She'd never before heard a story so charmingly ridiculous but at the same time so brutally endearing. For the second time since he'd arrived she really didn't know what to think.

'Yeah, a purty li'l senorita name of Malinalxochi. But we all called her Lina, for short. Married her so she could get the residency. You know the deal? We had a Civil Ceremony over City Park. It was the *ding*. A lovely sunny day, you know—right between Christmas and New Years when the sun stays real low and always shines in your eyes.'

'A Winter Sun,' said Jane.

63

'Is that what they call it?' he smiled. 'We got cool shots from her cousin who worked in the one-hour-photo and had a grande *soiree* in that old Louie's Crawdad overlooking Lake Pontchartrain. There was a Zydeco band, gallons of free beer, and lots and lots of dancing.'

Easy had a big smile on his face, remembering the day, you could almost hear the music.

'What happened to her?' asked Zoe, a little fearful for the Mexican girl.

'Well, after the wedding we moved in to a warehouse in Teche Street overlooking the toll road—'

'You moved into a warehouse!' said Jane.

'In Algiers!' said Beth.

'Yeah, it was the *boudoir*. The Bacchus Krewe kept their float there in secret. Lina's uncle was into that big-time. Mardi Gras and scrap metal were his two great passions.'

Beth was now in hysterics—slapping her thigh and pounding the table—it was a gig, a put on, a *goddamned* stand-up routine—it had to be.

'We had a lotta fun, Lina and me,' Easy went on. 'You know, in the street, you see these kids and you just see they're in love, they're in like this bubble, all protected and nothing can touch them? Well, that was us. Her parents owned a scrap-metal dealership down in Chihuahua and they sent money over every month. That was the *ding*, 'cos as you know, it's usually the other way round with the Mexicans. Anyhow, we put some of the money by each month and pretty soon we'd saved up a little fighting fund and we spent it on bus tickets to go down there to Chihuahua and pay her folks a flying visit. They were a blast, especially her pop—not some big shot asshole like I'd expected with his own scrap dealership and all. They lived right on the river—'

'The Chuviscar,' Jane said.

'Yeah, you know it? They had this lovely old stone bridge, like a big arch reflecting in the water. Only it wasn't there anymore. It'd been blown up in some revolution. Lina's mom showed me an old picture-postcard of how it once looked—which was real nice. Now it looked kinda stupid—just these two stumps going nowhere slow.'

Easy stood there with his two hands held up like the two halves of the bridge.

'When we got back to Algiers, Lina split and decided to go it alone.'

'What? Just like that?' asked Jane.

'Sure. That's how it is with Mexican chicks.'

'Do you know what happened to her?' asked Zoe.

'Nope. I haven't had sight nor sound of her in like five years so I guess she must have made out.'

'But you're still married to her?' asked Jane.

'Hell, I reckon I still am—least on paper.' He smiled and thought of the possibilities.

'Look—excuse me,' said Beth, in a sudden serious tone, 'but how in the hell is that a happy ending?'

'Well, Dot got killed by a Mack Truck, Nicolette skipped out with Jimmy Lee, marrying Lina really helped her out, gave her a bit of stability when she needed it most.'

'But she had to marry you else she'd have got deported. Seems to me she dumped you first chance she got—what's so happy about that?'

'I mean to say it ain't tragic like the first two. Sometimes when you just don't let things fall apart it can turn into a real result.'

Beth remained unconvinced: 'I don't know if he's Buddha or Homer Simpson.'

Zoe tutted. She was rocked by the story but didn't know what any of it meant, especially to Easy's prospects of continued employment.

'No. I think it's great,' said Beth. 'I'm happy even. Me, Nicolette and Lina would have got on like peas in the pod. I'm holding judgement on the other chick 'cos I am not a fan of polka-dots.'

Jane scraped her chair back and stood abruptly as if she was about to begin some after dinner speech. Beth half expected she'd tap the side of her wineglass with her spoon to get everyone's attention.

'Well, I really don't know what to say,' she began. 'It's—well, it's amazing that you can talk like that—so openly, about your private affairs.'

'Well, you can't keep stuff like that inside, huh?' said Easy, 'You'd come apart at the stitching.'

A silence followed and Easy decided it was time to start clearing the dishes to the sink.

'Bet you wish you hadn't asked now, eh?'

'No, no,' said Jane, 'I'm glad I asked. I admire such honesty. I do.' Jane made her way to the door—she needed time alone, time to think about this person.

'Well, where you going?' he smiled, 'I ain't finished yet.'

There followed a horrible moment when they all looked at him and each other like they'd actually have to endure another fateful turn to his story—but Easy returned with a large, exquisite chocolate cake.

'The Bayou surprise, remember?' he said, 'Fresh chocolate gateaux!' and he beamed them all a smile.

BARK

Beth shoved the young man down the stairs. He tripped and stumbled, half-dressed, completely hung-over and trying to get his pants up around his ass. 'Okay—hold on, lady, give me a *goddamned* minute,' he pleaded in vain. In the hallway, Beth opened the front door and guided him out. He finally got his pants fastened and turned—his zipper wide open and his shirt undone, showing off that flat, hard stomach.

'Where's the fire, lady?'

'I never, ever, ever do mornings,' she stated calmly and closed the door in his face.

*   *   *   *   *

'I don't believe I'm hearing this!' said Zoe. She was in her bedroom talking to her dad on her laptop. He busied himself, expertly cleaning a handgun, while she packed her camera kit, cleaned her lenses with a chamois. He'd just delivered the news—he was seeing someone, a woman he'd met at the singles' club.

'Take it easy, honey. I'm a big guy.'

'Are you *sleeping* with her? I mean, do you still do that?'

'You kiddin'? Sure we do. Right up until the end, your mom and I had a fantastic sex life—'

Zoe stuck her fingers in her ears: 'La-La-la—I can't hear you—la-la-la.'

66

Dad laughed, looking at her down the hundred miles of fibre optics as Zoe continued to 'la-la-la'.

'You still do that? You were like sixteen when I last saw you do that.' He smiled, then it suddenly hit him and he said to himself: 'Jesus, where does it all go?' and fell so silent and still that Zoe stopped and looked at him.

'Have you stopped talking about your sex life? Dad, are you okay?'

'Zoe. I'm great—really, I am,' he said, perking up a bit, 'but if I'm totally honest, my only one problem is *you*!'

'Me?'

'You could tell me, couldn't you?' He was suddenly deadly serious, 'If you were in some kind of trouble?'

'Jesus, Dad. What brought this on?'

'You were always such a happy kid. Took all the knocks, full of life and confidence, and always smiling. I don't know, maybe it just this thing—' he meant the computer, 'It's not virtual. It's almost *more* than real. You know, when I think of you now, I don't think when you last came home. I think of our last video-call. And when I remember your face it this face on the computer screen, and honey, you just never seem that happy anymore?'

Zoe had nothing to say to that. Dad sat, looking at her, aching.

'If some clever dick invents a cuddles option with this contraption, they'd clean up.'

*   *   *   *   *

Jane stood at the window looking out across the roofs at the cloudless sky. The printer hummed noisily on her desk—printing the latest edit and filling the room with the hot smell of carbon.

Down below, in the garden, Easy was potting the Fetterbush and Joepeye they had bought at the garden centre. He watered the plants and set them in the shade, then loaded all the potting tools in the wheelbarrow and walked it across to the shed. He worked like someone still new at the job and still fascinated and eager to try out all the tools. He reappeared, working the freshly-oiled shears in the air—*snip snip snip*— and set about the marshland that had once been a manicured lawn.

She noticed the sweat soaking through in tiny patches down the back of his T-shirt. He suddenly stopped working, straightened, and looked up at the house as if he could sense he was being watched. Jane stepped clear of the window. When, after a moment, she looked down again, Easy had his arms above his head and was stripping off the T-shirt. He wiped his armpits with the shirt, tossed it over the arm of the wheelbarrow and continued to clear the long grass.

Jane looked at his muscles ripple and flex, smooth under the skin. He had several small, dark moles and was practically hairless, with just a few telltale tufts of hair leading down from his navel. After a moment of so, when her awareness returned to the room, she noticed the printer was out of paper and its tiny amber light was flashing.

*   *   *   *   *

'Too much, too much! Easy stop-stop.' Mama-Lek was in full throw this afternoon and letting Easy have it right between the eyes.

'But they asked me. What—you want me to lie to them?'

'You say ebery-ting?'

He nodded.

'Indian wife?'

He nodded.

'Jelly-Lee babies?'

Of course, he nodded.

'Pokah-do-bellay?'

Easy . . . just . . . nodded.

'Oh, Easy bad boy. What's your problem—you no like job-job?'

'What do you mean? I love my job, they just asked me, is all.'

Mama-Lek hopped off her battered wooden stool and shuffled over to the big industrial dryers. She opened one of the big heavy doors and swung it back and forth on its hinges.

'Come here minit.'

'What?'

'Come here for Mamma-Lek.'

Confused, he came over and looked at her. She leaned forward and put her head in the mouth of the dryer, then gestured for him to do the same. Even more confused he began to bend forward to look inside. As he did, Mama-Lek grabbed hold of the door with both hands and held it steady. Her knuckles shone white and a funny look danced in her eyes. She was braced—like a baseball player—ready to let loose with the door and slam a home run.

'No stop-stop. Easy put head in. Go on.'

'You're gonna slam the door on my head!'

'Sure I am—*yes*. But I just ask you, is all.'

68

He took the point. She swung the door closed and it *clanged* and rattled the big shiny drum.

*   *   *   *   *

Zoe was running late—and she was *never* late. Something about that conversation with her dad had got her all mixed up. Lately, he'd developed that ability to land those bombshells on her. He wasn't malicious—he was just getting old and his time was more precious and good form was *out the window*. If it needed saying—he just came out with it, unformed and raw.

She'd grabbed the 28-50mm lens instead of the 35-80mm and only realised when she'd cycled half way to the shoot. The assignment was a routine *plight of the homeless* gig. She'd find her photo down by the waterfront. She knew just the spot. Along between *Huey P. Long* and the container depots. There was a little patch of wood where the homeless had got in and set up a *tramp-camp* among the shadows.

Billie—the office gossip and a fully paid up, flag-waving lesbian—was also Zoe's part-time assistant and occasional minder. She was not impressed by Zoe's tardiness. The plan had been to catch the homeless at the mobile soup kitchen, which set up at just after 9am. Now, it was gone 10 and the crowd of hobos had come, looked suitably forlorn, bedraggled, and photogenic, but had since dispersed. They could still salvage the assignment but now they'd have to get down and dirty, in amongst the stink and heat of cardboard city, and that was what was pissing Billie off.

They climbed through the broken chain-link fencing and got into the sycamores and acacias. The shade took the edge off the heat but the air was thick with sharp, foul surprises and the mugginess was feral and oppressive.

'You can't shoot him,' hissed Billie as Zoe snapped off a few frames of an old man. He was wasted away and practically naked: 'He's dead. They won't run it.'

'He's not dead. He's breathing.'

'He's not breathing. I can't get a dead man to sign the release.'

'If he's dead we don't need a release. Over-riding interest—it's public domain.'

'My god—you're a machine. What about his family? Do you ever think about that?'

'More than you think—and more than they thought about him, apparently.'

69

Zoe got in close and took some rough, angry angles. She ended with the flashlight 'BAM' and it froze the whole thing tight, bright and dirty—like a 1940s crime scene. The man stirred and came round, lost, groaning and calling for help.

'Give him some water—and a release form.'

'But probably not in that order, huh?' hissed Billie.

The flash proved to be a smart move—more homeless, all men, literally crawled out of the woodwork. They were in a terrible state and Zoe knew the series was going to be shocking. She had to work hard to get in close and frame them up. Standing back they looked, if anything, like a set up, a travelling freak show, some old Michael Jackson dance troupe tribute.

Billie kept her cool in the truck on the way back whilst Zoe's bike bounced around in back, scratching the paintwork. They were chasing the midday deadline so there wasn't time to argue about it. It wasn't until they were a few blocks from the paper that the pressure eased off and Billie finally got it off her chest.

'So—what the hell happened to you this morning, anyway?'

Zoe remembered the mad rush after her dad's call. The thoughts of him with some *ancient* new woman—his old papery hands touching her body. Jesus. When did all that *stop*?

She was forming her story carefully, knowing that whatever she told Billie, the story would quickly be spiced up and let slip in the newsroom. Zoe ran a pretty tight ship when it came to office gossip but Billie was going to spread something about her that afternoon, that was obvious, just to get the morning's frustration off her back.

'Don't tell me—they finally found you a sperm match?'

This kind of remark would normally have gotten under Zoe's skin but today all she could do was smile and say—

'Screw you, Billie.'

'I wish, honey. I haven't gotten laid since Thanksgiving—*two thousand five*!'

She shrieked at her own joke and Zoe thought they were done with the questions and onto new territory but when she stole a quick look she found Billie staring over at her intently, trying to read her mood. The traffic moved off but Billie held her ground and maintained the look—

'What? You holdin' out on me now?'

She had nothing to say but Zoe knew that wasn't somehow going to be acceptable. Billie needed something—a *tidbit*—a *tattle-tale*. So, Zoe did what she often did in these circumstances—she just pulled her lips into a thin line, smiled out her eyes, and stalled.

'Oh, you whore, you strumpet and lady-*jezebel*. You got laid! Don't tell me. Don't tell me. Chance right? Right? Yes. No. Okay, not Chance, then. Someone else? You tell me—I'll shut up and you tell me. And I promise, Zoe, I won't say a goddamned word to another living soul.'

Zoe knew this was bullshit. She knew what ever she said was going to go round and round that dead, sterile office like a bag of frosted donuts and within a few short days would be the one and only full-blown topic of conversation.

'Promise?' said Zoe, an idea suddenly forming out of the ether and growing each second with clarity.

Billie made a big show of crossing her heart and hoping to die.

'I've met a guy.'

BITE

Easy knocked on Jane's door and entered. She was sat reading in the big plantation chair by the window overlooking the garden. She looked tired and at first, with her eyes downcast as the book in her lap, he thought she was sneaking forty winks.

'You got a minute?'

'Not really—' said Jane looking up sharply, but he was in the room now and bouncing around in the middle of the rug.

'I been thinking—you know this Eunuch dude—the one you're writing your story on?'

'Mmm?'

'You reckon he *knew* the Pharaoh was a fake?'

'Er, oh—er, probably yes.'

'He did?'

'We can't know, of course, but on the evidence we have it's safe to say it's probable.'

'So, how come he let himself get fooled into an early grave by this old rake?'

'We can't begin to understand what his options were—'

'Yeah, but let's be honest. Being buried alive was, like—definitely the wrong decision.'

'Evidently.'

'And that's what I just don't get. See, if this Eunuch dude's so dumb, how come there's a brain-box like you, with diplomas and degrees in

72

professions you ain't even using, writing a thesis 'bout the dude—three thousand years after he's dead?'

Jane placed a bookmark in the book and put it to the side. She got up and stretched.

'The importance of this Eunuch '*dude*'—as you put it—is that he was probably *The Last Eunuch*.'

'Oh, what—the last one ever?'

'No—The Last Eunuch—the one who's cited for having penned the famous proverb.' It was clear to Jane from the open, honest look on Easy's face that he didn't understand what she's talking about. 'There was a proverb written by the very last of the Egyptian eunuchs. It's an ode to male servitude.'

'You mean—like a poem?'

Jane nodded.

'How's it go?' he asked excited.

'Well, it's written in Middle Egyptian—you know—*hieroglyphics*?'

'Bless you,' he smiled and this time and found the way he delivered the joke to be quite amusing.

She crossed to the desk, pulled out a few oversized tomes from the pile and opened them up to reveal pages of intricate symbols with complicated phonetics and translations.

'These are hieroglyphics—the Egyptians wrote in pictures, you see?'

Easy nodded—he had never seen such a detailed and complicated text and was going to say—*It's all Greek to me*—but thought better of it.

'Is there an English version?'

'Of the ode? Oh, yes—many versions—but my favourite was written by Sir Ranulph Saxonby, the historian.'

'Do you know it?'

'Yes. It goes something like "*Dogs don't flee if hit with bones, So every hound will find his home.*" She looked at him and smiled.

'Hey, that's the *ding*. Maybe this guy wasn't such a *wingbat* after all.'

'Historians built theories on the proverb's origin—right here at Tulane. Sir Ranulph was one of the founders of our department. The theories caused quite a stir when they were first published but now they're pretty well accepted. Those involved practically wrote themselves a whole aisle at the library—did quite well out of it too,' she said rubbing her thumbs and fingers together. 'Scholarships, research grants, bursaries, professorships, lecture circuits, speaking engagements.'

'The old ker-*ching*, huh?'

She nooded: 'Problem is—they got their dates wrong,' she grinned like this was the worst possible type of professional error and being as they were talking history Easy kind of agreed. 'And my paper's going to ride a coach and horses right through the whole sorry mess.' She shot her eyebrows up high for effect.

Easy was impressed and eager to learn more. They stood grinning and nodding at each other like toy dogs on a dashboard.

'So,' said Easy, 'You think you're 'bout ready to let me sneak-a-peek?'

Jane suddenly clamped up. She stopped nodding, half turned away and made her way back to the chair by the window. 'Well,' she began, 'You know, I'm not really sure how I feel about that, just now.'

'Hey, what have you got to lose? I'm pretty interested in what you've been saying about this guy and like I said, spelling was always my strong suit.'

'Yes, yes, quite. I appreciate your offer. And your interest. Really I do. It's just that . . . well, there's no polite way to put this, so—'

'Oh,' he said, flatly, the penny dropping.

'But maybe,' she said backtracking, 'You know—when I'm ready. You know, fresh pair of eyes and all that.'

He nodded but the brief excitement they had shared just moments ago was totally gone.

'Fine,' he said, hurt and unable to keep the knowledge of it off his face, 'you let me know.'

*   *   *   *   *

Beth was vomiting down the toilet bowl. She'd been at it most of the morning but the nausea was still there and strong.

She was hot and sweating and had yanked dressing gown up through the knot so it hung wide open to the waist. She stared down at her breasts, hanging, pendulous, and the folds and creases of her stomach. It felt massive and angry and vindictive and seemed set on exacting due revenge for the previous night's binge.

She spat, cleared her mouth and shuffled on her knees over to get a drink from the basin faucet. The water was cool, then turned cold. It hit her stomach and *bounced*—she vomited again.

There was a gentle knock on the door and she heard Easy's voice, calm and caring: 'Hey, Betty . . . ?'

Oh, God, she thought. She prayed for him to say something dumb-ass stupid, something she could throw back at him—something like 'Are you okay in there?' She was just waiting for the words. 'Yeah, I'm fine,' she'd say, 'I always make this much fucking noise in the can!'

74

'Open up,' he whispered, 'I fixed you something. You need to keep your fluids up.'

She shuffled over and unlocked the door. He slipped in, looking cool and clean and the very picture of health. He passed her a glass, fizzing over with salts. Tiny bubbles shot up her nose as she took a sip.

'Baby sips, okay—otherwise you won't keep it down.'

Later, when he'd helped her up onto her feet and shouldered her down the corridor and into her bed, she slept again and didn't wake until the late afternoon. Her guts were calm but she felt drained and desperately needed to pee. She padded down the corridor, the air chilling the sweat on the backs of her legs. She shivered, vowed never to drink again then, with her hand turning the doorknob, remembered the mess she'd left in the bathroom.

What a state to get into. She really had to get a grip on it. Business had been good since the new licence came through but she could not go on like this. There were enough fucked up lady bar managers in New Orleans as it was—she didn't need to join their ranks in AA, NA, Townsend House, Grace Recovery or Ochsner Med. She wouldn't give it up—*no*—she just had to calm it down—maybe even go in an hour or two later—that was the trick—if she could get one of her bitch-lazy staff to get responsible and open up . . .

She held her breath, pinched her nose and turned the handle—one whiff of stale vomit and she'd back at square one, knees on the cold tiles, head in the bowl. But Easy had cleaned up—the whole room was spotless. She stood there, thinking of him—mopping out after her, wiping away her little flecks of sick, spraying away her smell.

Hell—even the toilet seat was down.

* * * * *

Zoe was working at her huge digital layout screen—sorting shots for her article. The homeless piece had grown—as she knew it would—but now it was going to be a campaign. The Paper was behind it all of a sudden and she had two junior hacks, one who she knew to be a decent reporter, working up the latest story to meet the late edition.

Across the sea of desks and partitions she watched Billie delivering copy—and gossip—to the pressroom. There was nothing subtle about it any more. She'd been rubbing sticks for two whole days now and several little boomerang whispers had landed within earshot back around her desk.

I'LL BE YOUR DOG

Zoe's met some new guy—soon became—*Zoe's fucking some guy*—grew into—*Zoe's fucking some homeless guy*—which this morning became—*Zoe's fucking Billie.*

By tomorrow she mused, it would be—*Zoe and Billie are fucking a dead homeless guy.*

Strangely, the chit-chat didn't bug her one bit. It was *their* gossip but *her* limelight and the two seemed only to benefit her. She alone was immune to it because she alone knew it was bullshit. It might of mattered if there was any truth to it. But no—it was 100% bull, which made it hilarious and idiotic and almost harmless and she suddenly wished she'd started a lot more rumours a long time ago.

As Billie circulated, colleagues would look over at Zoe, who'd pretend to be flat-out-working-her-ass-off but always with this subtle, yet unmistakable self-satisfied tweak at the corners of her smile. The scandal was working wonders and brought a whole new dimension to the dull, sterile office.

The breakthrough came the following day, when Zoe was walking back through the main room, winding that *I'm getting plenty body* of hers between the desks, pretending not to look about but hoping to catch sight of Chance. She returned to her private area and was surprised to see the man himself sitting casually on her desk. He wore a fresh white shirt, slim dark slacks and penny loafers. On the desk by his side sat two pastries and two large cappuccinos.

'So,' he began in the calm polite almost humble voice, 'this comes as a big surprise to me too but I've got this huge, huge favour to ask of you.'

Zoe was unable to speak—she felt her throat constrict and catch. She kept calm and just looked at him . . .

'Please—*please* tell me you like the theatre?'

This was it—it was happening right here and right now, at her desk. There was the Cappuccino and the Apple Danish. The wait was over. She pretended to put some paperwork down and finally, when she felt sure she could deliver the line without making a complete mess of it she said:

'Sure, I like the theatre.'

They smiled at each other.

*   *   *   *   *

Jane had finally finished her first draft and felt tired, numb, and elated. It wasn't over—it was never *over* until it was *published*—but she was close. Very close. She'd thought about Easy's offer and, although it was clearly

76

ridiculous and academically pointless, decided it would be good for her nerves. She had plenty of time and who knew—he might pick up a few typos if his spelling really was *"purty spot on"*.

She took the last sheaf of warm pages from the printer and added them neatly to the new manuscript on the desk.

She selected a freshly sharpened HB pencil, set it on top and turned and presented the lot to Easy like a birthday present. He took up the manuscript excitedly, moved across to the bay window, got comfortable in the plantation chair and immediately began to read.

'Well, I'll be . . . you know, downstairs if you need to—well—you know?' But by now Easy wasn't even listening—and had already, to Jane's chagrin, scribbled a little something on the front page. Jane leaned over to see the correction but Easy clutched the papers to his chest and shoo-shooed her away.

She left nervously—instantly doubting the whole exercise.

*   *   *   *   *

'You bite mo-big than you bell-*ee*,' said Mama-Lek, seeing Easy across the Laundromat, reading the manuscript. He was sat cross-legged on an economy washtub with the mass of papers in his lap and he was frowning in concentration, and being made to think, and being made to decide, and make furious little scribblings as he went.

Mama-Lek walked by with a service wash and peeked at the growing pile of marked-up sheets . . .

'Wha? You go back college? Im-*proovin*' you ass,' she teased.

'Just doing a favour for Jane.'

'Oh,' she said, 'Jus do faber fo Jay*ing*.' She thumped his foot to get his attention: 'Jus mek sure is all you do big-shot two-job bad-boy.'

He looked up—hardly hearing her. Mama Lek nodded and kept on walking.

'It's cool,' he called after her. 'I got it covered.'

*   *   *   *   *

He was in the garden watering a Silverbell and checking on the Virginia Willow when it happened. Both plants had taken well and were looking very much at home. The garden itself still needed work but was beginning to take on a cared-for, satisfied shape.

77

He'd needed to get out in the fresh air after so much bookwork—his eyes hurt, his mouth tasted of pencil wood—he'd gone through two whole HB pencils—and he'd worn a little ridge along his finger from all the scribbling. It was a blast though—reading something like that—and he was trying to remember when he's last enjoyed thinking about something so important and so complicated for so hard and so long when a cool shadow fell across him and his planting.

He turned to see Jane, stood squarely on both feet and holding the manuscript down to one side like a stunned goose by its feet.

'What do you mean—it's boring?' She was angry and little patches of it were erupting like fire all over her face. 'What did you expect—"The Mummy Returns"? It's a *goddam* academic paper.'

She stood there, over him, as he rose up and balanced the rake against the wheelbarrow. His voice was quiet and deliberate: 'I bet Einstein wasn't boring.'

'Einstein!' she exploded, 'Albert Einstein?' She waved the manuscript in a wide, exasperated arc. 'What the hell do *you* know about Einstein?' A brief silence followed, then Jane bellowed: 'Well?'

He spoke quietly and non-confrontationally. 'I know he flunked grade school in Austria, had bad hair, and figured out *E equals M C squared*.' Easy now brought his gaze up and their eyes locked for the first time: 'What else do *you* know about him?'

Jane was momentarily stumped. Was he for real this guy? And what a fool she'd been to let him read her work—her confidence was shattered and now here she was arguing with the damn hillbilly *houseman* out in the garden.

'It don't got to be dull,' he added in the same quiet voice, 'just because it's academic. Give it some pep!'

'Pep!' she spat.

'Yeah, the truth always got *pep*, you know that. E equals m c squared doesn't hang about.' He wiped the dirt from his hands and let her think about that for a minute. 'And one other thing—I made some of those cuts in there because you tend to repeat yourself a bit.'

'Repeat myself?'

'And you could maybe rethink some of those sideswipes at *what's-his-name*—the big flunky—Clements? The way you got it now, it comes over like . . . what's the word, like . . .

'Like he's a talentless, egocentric, bigoted, son-of-a-bitch?' she exploded.

'No—like you envy him,' Easy corrected, calmly.

Jane was floored. She couldn't get her legs to work to turn and walk away. She just stood there and let it all in. A new anger caught in her, starting low in the pit of her stomach, and anger born from humiliation but also a deeper revelation—he was right, this *yardman* with his gumbo drawl and swamp-rat smile. She hurled the manuscript right in his face— it exploded, scattering pages all over the yard like confetti at a giant's wedding.

She stormed off through the paper cloud.

Easy watched her go, then started to gather up the pages. He rearranged the manuscript and took it up to her room. They needed to talk this out. Maybe his comments were a little too abrupt, too brutal— but he wasn't practiced in the art, and, to be honest, he thought she'd take it well, more like an adult.

He knocked the door but she didn't answer.

'I'll just leave it out here,' he said.

He knocked again, more impatiently this time, and then tried the handle. The door swung open and he saw that she wasn't there. He picked the manuscript up and left it on her desk, and put the Petri dish on top to stop the pages blowing off in the breeze.

*   *   *   *   *

Downstairs, Beth was on the telephone, smirking with insolence and her voice had a mocking hardness. 'Listen, Donnie, I play odds not luck,' she said. 'And you don't need to tell me everything comes in cycles—I'm a woman.' She poured herself a large measure of Vodka, chilling it over a tall column of ice. 'Just put the full two-four on *Do it or Die* to win.'

She hung up, took the cranberry juice from the refrigerator and added a splash of colour to her drink. It seemed hardly worth it, thought Easy, as she then drank the whole thing down in three long satisfying gulps, and immediately began to fix another.

'No objections, I hope?' she said, seeing the look on his face. Easy shook his head. 'Good—because now I don't have to tell you to mind your own damn business.'

'Been there, sister. Wipe that slate—whatever it takes to move on right along.'

She looked at him a moment: 'What, you mean last night? That guy? That guy's history.' She flicked her hand across her forehead like the memory's wiped. Easy copied the action as he cleaned, agreeing with her. 'Ancient history,' she added.

'Jurassic.' He agreed and she smiled. She thought to thank him for clearing up the bathroom and was just about to say something along those lines when he did the little *wipe your mind* action again in his mildly infuriating way.

'You know,' she said, getting an idea, 'I got a confession to make.'

'You want me to call up the Padre.'

'I said you were my husband.'

Easy stopped plumping the cushions and looked at her. She smiled back; glad to have his full attention at last.

'That guy? Why'd you tell him a thing like that?'

'I thought it would get him all fired up, you know.'

'Did it?'

'Actually, no. It made him impotent.' She laughed and took a drink, really enjoying herself. 'The thought of you,' she said, 'in the same house, creeping about full of rage, ready to bust in any second and catch his lily-white ass in the moonlight.'

Easy thought about this, then grabbed up his duster and began to clean. 'I'd have said that would have done the other—you know?

'I was banking on it. But no, he went *flaccid*,' she dragged the word out and her top lip curled up showing a row of wet, slippery teeth.

'No *ding* . . . ' said Easy, trying not to swallow too hard.

'Damn skippy,' teased Beth, 'He was limp and loose, brother. Slack, lax, and danglin' . . . '

Easy felt a little shiver run down his back. Beth enjoyed the effect she was having on him. 'Still,' he said, 'You can't always have pepper in your gumbo.'

Beth laughed, picked up her drink and pursued him around the room as he pretended to clean. 'Oh, I didn't give up. He weren't *spent*.' She flashed her eyes. 'No, sir—so, I talked him round. Lured him out. Coaxed him back up?' She had her hand turned palm up and her long fingernails tickled the air, beckoning: 'You guys are one big E-zone,' she grinned: 'Ears, lips, neck, stomach, thighs . . . underbelly . . . *tip*!' She now had Easy backed up and trapped in the kitchen area. He really couldn't look her in the eye. She enjoyed the power she had over him for a few seconds, then stepped back and giggled playfully like life was all a big game. 'Well, strap me to the hog and roll me in the mud—I do believe you're fresh out of comeback.' She flashed her eyes, turned and walked away.

BITTEN

J ane couldn't stay mad at Easy for long, it was impossible and, of course, there was no avoiding him. He was everywhere, all over the house, and with perfectly good reason. She couldn't sustain the pretence: she was hiding—shut away in her room, or scurrying in and out for long walks through the district. As the hours turned into days, she found herself dwelling upon his remarks. He'd put these little fragments in her head, these soundbites, critical shrapnel that she had to work through. Over time, however, she came to realise that his advice hadn't been cruel or mocking—he was just unskilled in giving criticism, and she was forced to conclude that she was just as unskilled at receiving it.

More astoundingly, she'd had to concede, when she'd finally dragged up the courage to re-read the manuscript—that the great lummox was right. Point by point, in his barely legible spider crawl, he noted each error, inconsistency, and repetition in her argument.

It seems, he'd written in the margin after savaging a particular favorite chapter of hers, *you got the tendency to dance around the chair a-while before sitting to sing.*

It was bitter medicine but once she'd finally let go of defending her position and the realisation that he was correct took hold, it was a revelation. Never before had she gained such swift critical distance.

She apologized to him one quiet Saturday morning. He simply nodded and carried on with his chores. She'd hoped to clear the air at one swipe, get back to that understanding they had, but it was clearly going to take time. Still, she'd made the first move and said her piece and later that evening, whilst she was working through the manuscript with the piercing clarity she previously only achieved with others' work, he brought her a cup of Earl Grey.

'Friends?'

'Friends,' she replied and invited him to stay.

*   *   *   *   *

Easy now sat across in the plantation chair, watching Jane work. He was wearing one of her African masks that he'd fetched from its hook on the wall. He'd been trying to be make an effort and be serious but watching someone read was the hardest work he'd ever done. He dozed off and woke with a snort and an eraser bouncing off his shoulder.

'You're snoring,' she said, and her tone made him understand they were okay again and all was forgiven.

She was still only half way through the manuscript but now worked with passion, furiously cutting whole sections and making her own frenzied notes—the discarded pages, spilled off her lap and spread over the floor. It reminded him of an oak tree he once saw that had been struck by a bolt of lightning and was frantically shedding all its acorns before it died. She was muttering to herself too, not caring that he could hear or that it made her sound half crazy.

'Ugh,' she went, sounding physically winded, 'there I go again . . . ' and she made a savage cut.

'You want some more tea?' he said finally, unable to tolerate anymore and dragging himself upright.

'Shshsh—*what*? No. Damn. Uh . . . I don't believe—' and on it went. Easy left, closing the door quietly.

Downstairs he tidied a little and prepared tonight's dinners. Zoe was working late and Beth had left him a not saying she wanted something light—

'How 'bout some beef and apple bites?' he'd suggested.

'What in the hell is that when it's at home?'

'Rye-bread, lightly buttered, thin layer of horseradish and mayo, slice of deli-beef, slice of fresh apple, a sprinkle of shredded Swiss cheese then two minutes under the grill?'

'Perfect.'

So he set to it. He'd ask Jane later; maybe make her a little *bayou salad* or a *baked kibbie*. He couldn't somehow picture Beth and Jane sitting together at the table, making small talk—

'*So, Beth—how is the alcoholism business?*'

'*Great. How's it going with your dead bone deal?*'

He washed off some cracked wheat and put it to soak while he ground up the rest of the beef—*baked kibbie* it was.

*   *   *   *   *

Jane knocked on Easy's door. It was slightly open but she couldn't see the one small part of the room that contained the bed. She imagined he was sitting there, meditating, or cleaning his toenails or. She heard no sound and she knocked again in such a way that the door swung open. The room was empty.

He'd kept it simple and somehow she knew he would and she liked that. As a girl, the room had been her den and she knew every inch of it but in an intricate, fragmented childhood scale—a crack in the plaster was the Orinoco river, vast and raging; a tiny, ancient patch of damp, cratered and watermarked, was the whole dark side of some mysterious planet. She remembered giving tea parties below the window and holding class to obedient rows of dolls and teddy-bears with her miniature blackboard.

His bed, the single army style cot, was where her dolls-house had been. Apart from the chair, which doubled as a bedside table, it was the only piece of furniture. His suitcase lay open on the blankets and she found herself poking around inside almost without thinking. Easy was using it as a wardrobe and closet and kept it in the space under the bed. She saw a pair of worn blue jeans, boxer shorts, and two little bottles of hot sauce.

Jane suddenly heard Easy's footsteps bounding up the stairs and she panicked, stepped back from the suitcase and struck her head on a beam. She froze, her head crooked, her body half turned towards the door and couldn't think of what to do next. She has no good excuse to be in his room and was caught red-handed.

Easy swished in with a fluffy white bath-towel over his head. Jane braced herself for a collision but it did not come. Easy had stopped two foot from her and had began to dry his hair, rubbing his fingers through the towel vigorously, the whole of him *shuddering* in the action.. Jane just stood and watched. She had the impression she was in the presence of a

83

big, overgrown puppy—a golden retriever at nine-months—not quite fully-grown with oversized paws and jaws, shaking the river from his fur. He was holding his breath and she could smell him, clean and spicy, fresh from the shower.

As Easy shook away under the towel, the other, smaller towel that was fastened tight around his waist loosened itself. Jane saw the corner peel back like a flag in the breeze . . . then it stopped and just hung there, hitched, pinched by its own weight . . . and finally unravelled and slipped to the carpet.

Jane turned her head away but her eyes were drawn magnetically to the dark gathering of slick, black hair in his crotch. She was transfixed, watching him jiggle away—the skin on penis was smooth and a shade darker than his loins— a single pattern of pale blue veins mapped its length. He wasn't circumcised and his foreskin drew around his glans and formed a cute, puckered nipple. The penis wiggled and shook to its own design—attached to the juddering body but less rigorous—somehow of itself—autonomous.

Easy abruptly removed the towel and saw Jane standing there right in front of him—horrified. He was feeling so invigorated and full of energy that the surprise hardly registered, and just bounced off his solar plexus—he didn't flinch or draw back or make any attempt to cover himself.

They stared at each other for a full, eternal three seconds. Jane felt the pulse *whomp* in her throat—

'Well, butter my biscuits!' said Easy, finally breaking the silence, 'New curtains?'

'Sorry?' was all Jane could manage.

Easy fixed the big-towel around his waist and smiled.

'That's very pretty frock.'

Jane realised he was referring to her floral print summer dress. It was a 50s cut, with a fitted bodice, gathered waist and swing skirt. It had huge, red, cabbage-sized, roses and she always wore it when she needed to make herself feel happy.

'Thank you,' she said. 'Look, sorry, I came to speak to you—I wasn't snooping.'

'That's alright.'

'I've finished reading your notes and I've made some changes—'

'Good.' He said noticing the thick wad of pages clutched in her fist.

'Well, actually, quite a few changes.'

'Oh, that's cool.'

'And I came up to ask. Would you do me a favour and read it again?'

'Sure.'

He reached for the pages and Jane feared the towel would slip again—
.

'NO! No, *Ohmygod*, no. This isn't it—this is what I've cut. I . . . it's downstairs. You can just read it when you've next got time.'

'Okay. Whatever.'

She left, having to step around him in the small room and knocking her head again on the ceiling between the beams. Easy smiled, watching her go and grabbed his jeans.

*   *   *   *   *

Zoe was on the massage slab, being pulverized by the new German girl. It was late and all the good masseurs had finished or were out earning real dough on client calls. This girl was clearly from the East.

'All over me like a cheap suit,' said Zoe, into her mobile.

Across town, in the Quarter, Beth was working. It was hot and sticky and the bar was quiet: 'You know what they say. Telephone, telegraph, *tell-a-dyke*.' She heard Zoe's laughter coming down the line—forced, metallic.

'So when's the big conception—I mean *date*?'

'Up yours, girl. Saturday, if you must know. Up town. He's taking me to the Mahalia Jackson.'

'The theatre!' said Beth concentrating on a couple who were deep into some melodramatic argument. The girl was pretty and blond and needy and emotional. The guy was an all American jock—big and beefy and kind of perfect, but with just the right amount of Mississippi mud in his mix.

Zoe remembered Chance at her workstation, how he'd asked her out, the way he phrased it. She'd not agreed straight away, had enjoyed keeping him waiting for just a few moments—with everything frozen, undecided and full of possibility.

He'd followed her out to the lobby and had called the elevator. 'Until Friday night then,' he said, as the doors opened. It was almost a statement, a foregone conclusion, and overly cool.

'Sure—' she replied, 'I'll check my calendar and let you know.' And she left him there, stepping into the elevator and timing her turn just as the doors between them.

On the ride down, she saw herself, alone in the lift, falling away from him and into the darkness of the shaft. Two floors down, she'd suddenly gone wild and celebrated, punching the air, slam dancing off the sides of

85

the elevator and funking up and back like James Brown. She'd composed herself just as the doors opened, and glided out into the lobby on a cushion of air.

'What you going to see?'

'What? Oh—it's a new piece called *His Black Ass Is Mine.*' Zoe heard Beth laugh—that deep, knowing crackle in her throat. The masseur began to beat along Zoe's back as she spoke, making her voice jump.

'Oh, and he's in such *ri-di-cu-lous-ly* good condition right now. It's like you can see his genome.'

'Is it a nice genome?' asked Beth looking at the all American couple and their gargantuan little break-up. She was probably a week late, terrified of being pregnant and asking him to commit. He was scared, numb, innocent. It would be something, she thought, to fuck someone in that state.

'*Y-e-e-e-s.*' stuttered Zoe, under the East German's cleansing blows.

'I should hope—you spent so long *grooming* this guy.'

Zoe took her ear off the phone and spoke to the masseur.

'Hey, ease up Helga. I *b-r-u-i-s-e* easy.'

'What *are* you doing there?' Asked Beth, finally intrigued.

'Preparing the drop-zone.'

Beth grunted—she could see Zoe in the Gym and envied her determination and, if she was honest, her body. One thing was sure though, if she had a waistline, ass and thighs like that, she wouldn't be blowing them all on some baby lust.

Beth now saw the blonde girl snap emotionally and slap her useless beefcake boyfriend across the face. She left, yanking her jacket free and sending the chair crashing to the floor. It was quiet an exit and, thought Beth, almost certainly planned. The guy sat dejected, casting off ashamed and apologetic glances at those around him. He stood the chair back up and Beth got a good look at him—young, square-jawed, ever so slightly drunk.

'Zoe, look, my date just turned up.'

'I thought you were working?'

'I'm always working.'

'Tart!'

'Kettle, pot, black. Don't over till the field, Zoe—see you later.'

'No, you won't—I'll be in bed with a Nelsons *Formula H* face pack.'

*   *   *   *   *

I'LL BE YOUR DOG

Easy lay completely still on the living room floor. It was still and humid and he could hear the crickets in the yard through the fly screen. He was wearing his earplugs and they felt neat and snug. There was a light skein of sweat on his calm, content face and subtle enlightenments fluctuated across his features.

He loved that feeling when the plugs grew to fill up his ear canals—like a gradual tuning out of the world—never knowing when the silence would level out—how deep it would take you. And that pressure—a growing, swelling force, the weight of inner peace, like a presence.

As he sank into trance, he thought of Jane and her Thesis—or what had she called it? . . . A draft—that was it—a *draft*—like it was now a small, temporary thing that had less importance, and could be viewed, modified, improved, and even ignored if necessary. But by calling it a draft its power had ironically grown—it was now a serious read, punchy and arrogant—rough and raw and uncompromising.

He recalled the scene: He sat in her room, finished the conclusions and looked up to find her stood against the wall with her hands behind her back and that look on her face. Whatever he had to say this time she wanted it fresh and undiluted and straight off the top of his head. He held her gaze a second then saw how much it meant to her and quickly nodded. 'I think you really nailed it.'

'*We* nailed it, you mean.' Then: 'You really think so?'

'Sure.'

'I think so too.'

'If I was Clements, I'd be checking the Craigslist or signing up for a Katrina Clean-Up Krewe.'

'Thank you, thank you, thank you.' She'd rushed at him and he thought she was going to plant a kiss on his cheek like the way Betty had done out on the expressway. But she took the manuscript off his lap, gave his hand a little squeeze and left.

He sank, and sank, deeper and deeper—letting go, and feeling good and light.

One last weird image—as he dropped—Zoe's room, the door flung wide and her pregnancy book and ovulation chart spread out across the bed. These were caught—along with a thermometer in a glass of water on the bedside console—in the yellow cone of light from the angle poise. Some small-scale military operation was being meticulously planned out—the taking of a hilltop machinegun nest in Tripoli, perhaps, or the sinking of some dark, stealthy submarine in Southern France.

Then Zoe—zipping out of the bathroom and heading straight at him down the hallway—she never saw him till the last minute and when she looked up they both shrieked. She, because he was just suddenly there and so silent. He, because she'd had some wild, white-blue voodoo mask painted on her face. The image finally faded and he slipped away and under and floated off into himself.

*   *   *   *   *

Beth was giving the young Jock a blowjob. They were crammed into the back seat of a towncar—leatherette, fake smell of pine covering the reek of strong tobacco, crumbs and lint and *God knows what* down the crease of the seat.

The guy was drunk and confused—if he'd been the more sensitive type you might have described him as upset—yet he still couldn't believe his luck and apparent good change of fortune: one minute he was enduring monumental grief from his long standing cheerleader prick-tease girlfriend:

'Why can't you commit?' 'What is it you want?' 'You don't love me.' The next he was getting his balls sucked up through his dick by this weird, hot, sexy, barmaid. She was old—not ancient—but like 30 or something. She was soft and stacked and all trussed into an expensive satiny dress. This was not a girl his mom would meet. This was a girl the boys would hear about.

She gave head like a porn star—plenty of lubrication—literally spat all over him—constant movement—twisting the wrist—rolling the neck—flicking and licking and biting and teasing so he didn't know where the next tingle of pleasure would land.

She bobbed up suddenly and grabbed two big fistfuls of the his thick curly hair—

'Your turn,' she said, forcing his head down between her legs.

Her knickers were gone—he certainly hadn't taken them off—and she was hot and ready and so very different from his cheerleader. He suddenly felt uneasy, even a little out of control, scared, and wanted to slow things down a bit.

'Hey, hey, at least tell me your name?'

She rammed his head back in place and held him with her thighs. She could hear him protesting but his lips worked into her and it was good.

'Didn't your momma tell you—don't speak with your mouth full.'

He gave in and was soon playing the hungry calf. She rubbed his crotch with her foot and felt a warm, healthy erection reaching down the leg is his pants. She'd get off first, she thought, right on top of him, then get down to business.

There was a knock on the window and Beth looked out through the condensation at the Taxi Driver—he was wearing a vest and a leather cap—like an old-fashioned truck driver. He tapped his watch and shrugged at her—but she could tell he was only wanting to catch a little of the action.

'Back off, asshole, we're on the meter.'

*   *   *   *   *

Hugo feared bad news when she called him at home. The minute he heard her voice—not its urgency, that he could deal with, but its new and unmistakable confidence.

He turned off the radio, cleared his dinner tray to the kitchen and fetched some whisky tumblers and a bottle of bourbon—a Jefferson Reserve 15 year. He set them out with some soda and ice on the silver-set on the study console, pulled a couple of Wingback library chairs round into the pool of light and turned off the central pendant. He poured himself a measure, added a single cube of ice, sat back and began to plan his strategy.

She arrived 20 minutes later in a flurry of apologies, the self-assurance he'd picked-up over the phone had evaporated and she was her old clumsy, uncomfortable, flustered self. He was almost tempted to postpone the meeting but she suddenly got herself together, remembered why she was there and thrust the manuscript at him.

She refused a drink. He poured himself another then sat and began to read.

*   *   *   *   *

They were both drunk and the keys wouldn't fit in the lock. Beth let the Jock try and he got it to open first time—she shoved him at the door and it swung wide and hit the wall and he fell into the darkness and crashed onto the floor.

They giggled, a lot. And they *shooshed* each other until Beth said: 'What are *you* shooshing for?'

'I dunno.' And they giggled again.

She dragged him down the hallway and into the vast, empty living room. It was cosy and lit with little pools of lamplight. She could see he was impressed and imagined him in some scummy, bullshit frat house with a slogan over the door like: "Men of talent, temperament and conviction, dedicated to friendship, justice and learning" . . . or such other utter bollox. Bring it on thought Beth—I'll screw them all.

She headed straight for the refrigerator and the Vodka. The bottle was practically empty—just enough for two neat shots. She drank it off and looked at the Jock.

'Oops—sorry.' She hoped she looked like a brunette Marilyn Monroe, cute beyond reason, voluptuous, instantly forgivable. The Jock stood looking at her—not knowing what this wild creature would do next.

'Don't move,' she said. 'Stay put.' She ran out and up the stairs to find another bottle.

The Jock looked around the room, thinking this could work out after all—he'd get seriously laid, slip away Scot-free and satiated in the early morning and allow himself to wallow in remorse and feel suitably guilty. He'd go crawling back to the cheerleader—beg, conform, and submit— enjoy her body for all its perfection and never again take it for granted. It would be a watershed for them and he could see now that he just needed this one wild night of sex and abandon before he could fully give himself to her, properly commit. And all these thoughts of his future happiness and the immediate prospect of some down and dirty no strings sex seemed suddenly so correct that it took him a few seconds to realise he was looking at a pair of naked size-10 feet sticking out from around the back of the sofa.

He came closer and looked down at Easy—earplugs, asleep, beatific smile.

'Fuck this!' Said the Jock in a whisper so loud that Easy suddenly woke and opened his eyes—

'Hey—what's the ding?' He said, sitting up.

'Who the hell are you?' asked the Jock.

'Who the *hell* you think?'

He Jock was backing out now—running back to his cheerleader as fast as he could. 'Shit man, I'm sorry—your old lady's one crazy individual.'

Easy got up and although he was four inches shorter and sixty pounds lighter, dominated the Jock, all the way across the room.

'Pull up a chair, bro,' he grinned, 'We'll open a bottle and all get properly acquainted.'

'Uh-uh,' said the Jock—finding himself suddenly in some David Lynch moment: 'This is too much like a Sunday morning for a Friday night.' And he then left, quickly and quietly.

Easy waited till he heard the front door click and then allowed himself a smile. He sat and pondered the event, then heard Beth's footsteps on the stairs and looked on as she rushed in brandishing a fresh bottle of Vodka. 'Got it!' she growled heading for the fridge, addressing Easy, and realising the Jock was gone all in the same instant.

'Where is he?'

'Who?'

But Beth was already turned around and heading out. She rushed down the hallway, threw the door open and toppled out to the sidewalk—

'CHICKEN SHIT!' she roared into the empty street, then came back and slammed the door.

She found Easy sitting calmly—rubbing his eyes.

'Spineless—crustacean—a mollusc . . .'

Easy realised it was probably a good time to be going off to his bed. He stretched, tried to act real natural and began to exit. He was so nearly out the door when she spoke—

'Pour me a drink.' She collapsed on the sofa, her legs spread like a prizefighter on the stool after 14 of a 15-round knock-down-drag-out winner takes all slugging match.

Easy hesitated.

'Pour me a damn drink—*please.*'

Against his better judgement he stepped back into the room, fetched a clean glass and took the Vodka bottle to crack it open—

'This is warm, Betty!'

'Pour it!'

'Let me get you some ice—'

'Pour the damn drink!'

He poured a neat measure and handed her the highball. She threw it back before he could set the bottle down and thrust the glass up at him.

'Again . . . *please.*' Easy hesitated then poured a dangerously, large measure—*glug, glug, glug, glug, glug, glug*—right up and over the rim so that a splash or so ran down the back of her hand. Beth gave him a look, then brought the glass of warm vodka to her mouth and drank. She made her way sickeningly through the measure but then gagged and couldn't finish it off. He was glad. She coughed and heaved, dropped the glass on the carpet and sprawled back into the sofa.

Easy decided it was now time to go. He'd let her calm down, then come check on her in ten minutes. Fetch her a pillow and that favourite throw from her bed. That was a good plan and that's what he decided he would do.

'Stay.' She said. 'Don't leave just now.'

91

'I'll just go fetch some bedding.'

'*Stay.*'

There was a long beat—he didn't understand the command—a sheep dog on a windy hillside with a new owner.

'What do you want, Beth?'

'Get outta here then, you coward.'

She bent forward, found the glass and poured her own measure—but steadily, with renewed purpose and without spilling a drop. She began to drink again, slowly, like there was no stopping her.

Easy stared at her. He came and sat on the arm of the sofa. She knew he was there and looking at her: 'What?'

His voice was relaxed and definite: 'You're a mess when you're this drunk.'

'What's it to you?'

'Look at yourself, Betty, your face is all caved in.'

She laughed at his honesty: 'You weird, freaky bastard.'

She turned to him and Easy reached over and brushed a lock of loose hair behind from her face. His fingers touched her cheek and they felt cool and steady. Beth set the glass down and faced him. She put on her best pout, gathered up all her reserves and looked him right in the eye.

He was strangely handsome, the quirkiness she'd always seen at a distance was gone and he was in proportion and right. His forehead was smooth, wide and strong. His eyes were clear and light brown, with a honeyed, hazel fleck. If you'd asked her yesterday she'd have sworn on the bible they were blue.

She kissed him, softly on the mouth. It was a minor moment—his own lips didn't move—and afterwards she wondered whether she'd kissed him at all or just thought about it. Then his face came alive in a smile and she saw the full-bloodied man in there with his needs and wants and she felt back on safe ground and smiled. He came for her now and kissed her fully. She met him then drew back and gave him a little something to chase. He moved tight against her and kissed her again, this time more fully and she let her tongue run over his teeth. His breath was cool and neutral. He grinned.

'Keep your pants on, boy. You're not in the Garden of Eden yet.'

They slowly came together in a full, passionate kiss.

*   *   *   *   *

Once upstairs, they flopped onto her bed. He'd made it fresh that morning and the sheets were clean and stiff and he suddenly realised what they were doing. She pulled off his clothes and he in turn lifted her skirt and ran his hands into her warm curves.

'This is bad,' he said.

'I know—isn't it good?'

'We shouldn't be doing this.'

'Exactly.'

Beth moved down quickly and got him into her mouth.

'Beth!' he said, but it was no use now—the talking was over—what could she possibly want to hear at this stage.

'I've got to tell you, please.'

It was too late—she worked her head—he didn't stand a chance.

'I haven't been with a woman in a long time.'

Oh—she thought—this is different. 'How long?'

'Very long.'

'Over 12 months?'

'Yeah.'

She laughed, wickedly and flashed him her look. 'Then I really am the fuck-of-the-year.'

BASKET

Hugo read the manuscript in a single intense sitting and then simply stood and left the room. He said nothing and had a trouble meeting her hungry gaze. Jane had watched him read with mounting dread. The further he progressed, calmly turning each page without any comment of acknowledgement of her presence, the more she felt *stretched*. The tension between great hope and greater despair. This was not a moment casually passing. No, this was seismic, and there was going to be fallout, and consequences for her.

Finally, he returned to the room. He'd removed his waistcoat and looked pale and solemn and he stopped in the middle ground and spoke quietly.

'I shall read it again,' he said. 'Please, I've made up the guest room, you should stay.'

'No. No,' Jane jumped up, sensing a chance to flee. 'I'll call a taxi.'

'Please,' he said, definitively, 'stay—we need to talk but I must read it again.' He started for the manuscript on the table, then stopped. 'But first,' he said, 'first—I must pee.'

He left the room again and after a few moments Jane couldn't bear being alone and gravitated out to the corridor and stood waiting in the dark. The light poured from the study doorway and she could see her shadow on the hallway boards. She felt very lonely and suddenly had the urge to run back into the room, snatch up the manuscript and run, and run, and run.

The toilet flushed somewhere along the corridor and she heard Hugo's footsteps. He stopped, seeing her in the hallway and beckoned her along to the guest room.

The room was small but exquisitely furnished. The antiques and framed photographs were perfect and polished—a yesteryear capsule, a step back in time. A silk nightgown lay across the bed. It smelled clean and faintly of Hugo—vetiver, pipe tobacco, and leathery notes. The bed was piled thick with blankets—plaid and tartan, with rope-stitch round the edge. It was the sort of blanket John Garfield had in the back of his Buick in the *Postman Always Rings Twice*. But it was so hot, there was no need, and she stacked them onto the little Queen Ann bedside chair, and pulled back the thick, brushed cotton bed sheets.

She couldn't sleep—picturing Hugo rereading the work—making his own notes. And thinking about the conversation they'd have in the morning. It would be over a cooked breakfast—Hugo breaking eggs one-handed into the frying pan as he shattered her dreams of ever being published, outlining precisely why her argument was all an utter nonsense and convincing her—finally—to let the matter drop. She sat up impulsively, wanting to flee again, to run down the corridor, to crash into the study and tell him to stop!

The feeling passed almost immediately, leaving a fuzzy numbness across her stomach. She saw a small shelf of reading books and automatically scanned the spines—*Enid Blyton* and the *Famous Five, the Hardy Boys Adventures*—she had imagined they would be philosophical texts—Hugo's private joke on a little light reading but these were books for others, his nieces and nephews perhaps. Her eyes continued until she found what she hoped for, yes—some *Malory Towers*. She took the book, plumped the pillows and escaped to her childhood.

She read a couple of chapters, realising she was more tired than she thought then woke with a start as the book fell across her chest. She was lost for a moment, taking in the room absently before it all came rushing back. She didn't know how long she'd been asleep. It was still dark outside and very quiet and all she could hear was the ticking of a wind-up bedside clock.

Her mind drifted down the corridor again to the study and she wondered if Hugo was still in there reading or whether he had now finished. It suddenly occurred to her that there was a telephone in the study—a black antique Bakelite 'dog-and-bone' with a twisted flex. She imagined Hugo on the phone now, calling up Clements and his cronies and tipping them off that their game was up. She saw Clements making his dark, silent way over to Hugo's house—where he had her held captive—to finish her off and burry her body in a shallow grave before dawn.

The idea was ridiculous.

She threw the sheets back and climbed out of bed. She needed to see if the study light was on—if progress was being made. The door handle turned but did nothing and she suddenly realised she'd been locked in. Part of her panicked, the other part of her twisted the lock the other way. But now she could feel the handle move by itself—there was a hand on the other side. There was then a knock at the door.

'Jane?' It was Hugo. He opened the door a crack. 'Are you decent—I saw the light on?'

She drew back from the door and he opened it a little further. She sat back down on the bed, and then pulled the sheet over her thighs.

He stood there looking paler than before and tired but somehow with a new attitude of resignation.

'You still reading?'

'No—I've just finished.'

They looked at each other.

'And . . . ?'

'And it's wonderful.' He smiled, and the relief coursed through her, but there was still something wrong.

'You're going to publish me?'

'Of course, Jane, no question.' He looked round for somewhere to sit and registered the blankets on the chair.

'Do you mind?'

He moved the blankets to the floor, where they toppled over a second after he sat down and yawned.

'I had thought you'd make a mess of it,' he said, scratching the back of his head, 'but it's marvellous—your best work yet.'

He looked older and frail and in decline and his praise was somehow worthless—like he was her grandfather, looking at her schoolwork. The lines around his eyes and mouth were deep and all seemed to point down.

'They will come for us, you know,' he said grimly. 'This is their whole life we're talking about—their wives *work* on campus—some of their kids come here.' He put his hands on his knees and his shoulders sagged. 'They can't just clear their desks and walk, you know.'

Jane thought about this. 'No,' she said, 'and neither can we.'

That self-assurance had returned to her voice and he nodded. They looked at the middle ground, contemplating what had to be done. He rose, finally, with some stiffness and made his way to the door.

'You know what else?' he said, but brightly as if on a completely different subject. 'It's a damn good read—a page turner.'

'You think it lacks credibility?'

'No, no.' He realised she'd got the completely wrong end of the stick. 'The case is complete. It's just,' he stopped and chose carefully, 'you've never written like that before. It's so direct, so balanced and so . . . *raw*.'

She smiled, relieved and had a sudden thought to rush home and tell Easy everything.

'Anything I should know about there?' asked Hugo.

'Sorry—like what?'

'I don't know,' he laughed, 'some change in prescribed medication perhaps, or you've joined a cult, or found yourself a nice Freshman?'

'No, no and . . . *no*.' She wanted to be away from him now, alone, at home and couldn't think why. She hated that he couldn't accept she'd just done this herself. And of course, she hadn't, but he didn't know that for sure.

She got up and began dressing.

'You're not going?'

'I can't sleep here, Hugo, I need my bed.'

'Look, don't rush off—I'll call you a cab.'

He went, moving slowly down the hall. Jane dressed, went to the bathroom and threw water on her face.

As they waited for the taxi, they agreed to meet tomorrow on campus, to formally discuss the Thesis and its publication. The word didn't resonate with her now—like its value had been reduced or perhaps just more clearly understood.

The taxi driver was a lonely man at the start of a long shift who wanted to make small talk. Jane couldn't. He sulked a bit but she didn't care and, for once, didn't mind that she didn't care. He dropped her off and charged her fourteen dollars. She didn't complain but she didn't tip him ether.

As she climbed the stairs she heard guttural, earthy sounds and they forced her to stop and listen. It was the sound of a tree branch sheared and moaning, or a gas boiler drawing its last breath. Then it came into focus—it was Beth having sex.

It was almost the last straw.

There was something in the sheer animal abandonment of the sounds that knotted up her guts in a sickening way. She carried on up the stairs as her ears began to decipher and translate the groans into words.

'Yes. Do it. Yes. Don't. No. There. There. Yes. Yes.'

Where was 'There' exactly? Jane covered her ears and ran passed Beth's door.

She changed for bed and put on some Debussy to centre her nerves and drown out the noises from below. Each time she lowered the volume she could make out the low, brutal wailing—equally exciting and disgusting. She both envied and hated Beth and found her only way forward and out of it was to drum up a great weight of pity for the girl.

She climbed into bed and lay there and let the music soak into her tired muscles and run down her spine. Her mind went back to Hugo's house and his perfect miniature study and forward to their meeting tomorrow . . . she suddenly wanted to tell Easy all about it, hear what he had to say. She bolted upright, thought seriously about it—realised he too might be awake with all this racket going on.

She got out of bed, crept along the corridor, passed Beth's room and then climbed the steps to the attic. Easy's door creaked open and Jane stuck her head in. In the darkness, she could see his shape, long and still under the bed sheets. Beth was still howling from her bedroom, below.

'Easy?' she whispered, then, 'Easy—are you wake?'

She crept in, crouching for some reason, and touched his foot through the blankets. He didn't stir, was fast asleep, and Jane suddenly felt very awkward and retreated.

*   *   *   *   *

Easy woke with a start—Beth's slack, hung-over face not three inches from his own—was not a pretty sight. They had woken at first light and fell into each other again—without thinking. It had been slow and soft and incredibly intense. He was sore but numb and he was hard and took a long time to come. She clung to him, sleepy and warm and shuddering in deep, pithy spasms.

Her breath was sharp now on his face, hot and laced with ethanol. Easy took in the situation—he was wrapped and trapped, entwined in her dead arms and legs and the sun was already slanting through the gaps in the blinds.

This was not good—they'd heard Zoe come home at around 3am from her night shoot. He'd hid in the closet, Beth lay under the sheets giggling and they'd listened to her crashing her camera cases down into a pile in the hallway and stomp off to bed. She would sleep late but he couldn't tell what time it was now.

He began to extricate himself, slowly, freeing himself from her drugged octopus arms. She moaned, threw an arm back across his neck and buried her head into his chest. He let her settle, then tried again, slip-sliding inch by inch towards the edge of the bed and freedom.

Once downstairs, he began to clean up. He drew the curtains and threw open the windows. The cool air felt fresh and good on his skin. He set up the ironing board and fetched the basket of clothes and sheets.

Work was good. He could switch off his mind, stop thinking and just *do*. He turned on the iron and took a quick shower. He could smell Beth on his fingers and taste her on his breath. He scrubbed away the images, lathering himself in spicy, lemon suds.

Her stomach; soft, full, and voluptuous.

Her breasts, swinging and rolling—those dark, surprisingly dry nipples—cool on his lips. The sweat in the creases of her neck. Her sex, hotter and hungrier than either of them.

He ironed—the clothes first then began on the sheets. Hanging the ironing on the back of the chairs, his foot rolled over something and he looked down to see a sock—his sock from the previous night—on the floor. A flashback of Beth, on her knees, sucking his toes, hit him with full force. What had they done? What had *he* done? He slipped into a panic, began to rush the sheets, rucking them and ironing in the creases . . . and then he stopped and remembered his breathing and let out the tension, little by little, with each out-breath until it was just what it was—a *thing* that had *happened*.

He decided to make a pot of coffee—then decided against caffeine and poured himself a fruit juice. He calmed, and was almost about to smile when he heard footsteps coming down the stairs. He glanced around the room and saw—Jane's bag, nestled behind the door—and at the last possible second, Beth's bra caught on the door handle!

*   *   *   *   *

Jane found Easy ironing in the front room. He was struggling with a black bra, and using the very tip of the iron. He looked up and smiled but she could tell he didn't look altogether pleased to see her.

'Well hey, *cher*, when did you get back?'

'Last night, for all the good *that* did me.' She observed him for some collusive gesture: 'What—you didn't *hear* that? You're telling me you really slept through *that* din?'

He was conscious of two things—one, that she clearly didn't suspect him and two, that he didn't want to lie to her. What had happened had happened and lying about it was keeping it alive—feeding it, and bringing it into the here and now. On the other hand, he wasn't just going to fess up and lay it all out on Jane at this hour of the morning.

'I grabbed an hour or so—when I could.'

'Well, did you see him? She normally tosses them out at dawn like mangy dogs but I never heard him leave yet?'

'Oh, he's long gone.'

'Really?'

'Yep. Heard him leave at the crack of dawn.'

Easy grabbed up a pair of leggings from across the back of a chair. He shook them out and laid them across the ironing board.

'Are those mine?' asked Jane.

'Sure,'

'They look brand new. What ever have you done to them?'

'I washed them by hand and gave them an iron on low temp. You know with vinegar paper?'

'Vinegar paper?'

'Sure—brings them right on. And I'm afraid they were a bit worn up the crotch. What do they call it? Bobbly! So I shaved them.'

'You shaved the crotch of my leggings!'

'With a Bic Razor. It's the *ding*. It's the only way I know to deal with bobbles; I don't care what the commercials tell you. You'll notice the difference soon as you slip them on.'

Jane stood, incredulous, examining the leggings.

'Good Lord.'

'Hey, don't mention it—It's what I'm here for.'

'You know,' she said, unable to really look at him in the face and sound convincing, 'you really should ask before you . . . you know—' she realised she was in a corner but kept painting, 'Go fiddling around, in the crotches,' paint, dip, paint, 'of other people's trousers.'

'I'll try to bear that in mind.' He smiled; glad they had got off the subject of Beth for a moment.

'So—' said Jane, 'What was he like?'

He swallowed, cleared his throat and decided whatever happened he would not to tell a lie.

100

I'LL BE YOUR DOG

*   *   *   *   *

Zoe and Jane strolled along the sidewalk, arm in arm. It was a rare moment for them, this intimacy, and brought about by their gossip of Beth. Easy, laden down with groceries, tried to keep pace and eavesdrop.

'Nope, I was exhausted,' Zoe said, 'Slept like a log.'

'This was something else. I'd never heard anything like it—not even in Egypt.' She saw Easy, hovering and frowned. He moved away, casually. 'I was dreaming about the Lesser Pied Kingfisher,' she began as if it made perfect sense to Zoe, 'I spotted a nesting pair on the Nile Valley. They make this beautiful *kweek-kweek* sound when they're building a nest.' Zoe looked at her like she'd gone out to lunch. 'The *kweek-kweeking* turned into their yelps and sighs and pants and groans and the bedsprings grinding away and the headboard slapping the wall.'

Zoe couldn't help but laugh at Jane's description: 'Good old Beth.'

'Don't, Zoe—that girl doesn't need any encouragement.' She continued with her tale. 'When I thought it was all over, you know, after the theatrics of the great climactic onslaught—they'd be this brief, welcome silence, then these great, plodding footsteps like the iceman making his rounds, then it would start all over again in a different part of the room.'

'What time did she kick him out?'

'That's the thing,' Jane's eyes flashed. 'They had another go at it this morning—which is very unlike Beth.'

'Did you see this guy?'

'No—but Easy did.' They both looked at Easy, who smiled, modestly burdened with such privileged information.

'Well?' said Zoe.

'Well, what?' said Easy.

'Spill the beans—'

'Uh-huh. You wanna know more, you better ask Beth.'

'You told me he was a funny little guy with checked pants and a pipe.'

'A pipe!' shrieked Zoe.

'I said that as a joke. So you'd quit bugging me.'

'She'd have a gate post on a summer's day if someone hung his jacket on it.'

They walked on. Easy wished he hadn't said anything. One lie begets another . . .

*   *   *   *   *

Later, out in the garden, Jane—now wearing her leggings—was working through her stretches. She was in limbo—caught between last night and the looming meeting with Hugo.

As part of her routine she put her hands between her legs—and brought herself up short. It was a powerful, quiet moment, her fingertips running over the smoothness of the fabric, her skin beneath, Easy with his little Bic Razor, working away, intently, his strong, diligent, fingers pushing and pulling at the material.

A wind blew through the shrubs and Jane stood amidst all this, frozen in sudden strange realisation that she wouldn't meet Hugo at all.

It was window day and up in the bathroom Easy was cleaning the shower glass, the mirror and the little side opener at the foot of the bathtub. He'd stopped and was looking down on Jane, still frozen like a photograph.

* * * * *

Zoe was in her room—naked from the waist down, her Dead Kennedys T-shirt rolled up passed the navel, applying *bikini line* when her cell-phone rang. She saw Chance's name, fought back a spike of excitement and answered.

'Hello . . . '

'It's Chance,' he said, letting this hang there like it was important enough information all by itself. In truth, she found it a turn on. She'd realised early on she was drawn to those people who thought a lot of themselves.

'Everything okay?' She was trying hard to keep the growing anxiety from her voice.

'Not really—' here it comes, she thought. 'What are you doing right now?'

'Oh, prep. Are we still on for Friday night?'

There was along silence.

'This is going to sound lame, but my Gran Izzy took ill.'

'Your Gran Izzy?'

'Yeah. She lives up in Solitude and they rushed her in to hospital last night—it doesn't look good.'

'Right.'

'I'm driving up with my brother this weekend—'

'You have a brother?'

'Er, yeah—the whole family's been called home.'

102

'Oh. Right. Well, I'm sorry to hear that. Was she old? Is she old, I mean?'

'Er, yeah—she's eighty, eighty-three.'

'Well, I guess that happens when you get old.' What was she talking about? There was another silence.

'I hope she gets better.'

'Yeah. Look, sorry to let you down like this.'

Like what? She thought—at such short notice, over the phone, when she's doing her bikini line, *what*?

'Hey, no problem. Call me when you get back and maybe we can reschedule.'

'For sure, yeah, I mean we're still going on a date, right?'

'Give me a call next week.'

'Sure, sure. I'll be back at work Monday.'

'Okay—safe journey.'

She cut the call and breathed deeply. She thought she had handled it quite well—considering—and he did seem genuine. She stood there half naked and smothered in this useless cream that was beginning to irritate. Suddenly, she brought her knee up like a baseball player and pitched her cell-phone clean out the open window.

'And screw you too!'

*   *   *   *   *

That night, Easy was coming out the shower when he heard Zoe's voice:

'Easy! *Easy!*' She was irritated, angry and unfocused.

'What's the *ding-a-ling*?' He called down the stairs but she appeared behind him on the hallway and seeing his naked torso and the towel neatly wrapped around his waist and was momentarily distracted.

'My dress, my dry cleaning—where'd you put it?'

Easy realised he'd completely forgot to pick it up. He pulled a face: 'Oops!'

'It's one thing I asked you to do.'

'I'm sorry—they'll be closed now. I can get it first thing.'

'No, don't bother, that's no good. Just pick it up by tomorrow night and please don't let this happen again.'

'No, *cher*, I'm sorry, I won't.'

Her gym bag was slung over her shoulder and she was heading out. He realised he was blocking her way, so he carried on down the stairs and

103

she followed him, looking at his muscular back and neat, square shoulders.

Jane was waiting by the front door as Easy and Zoe came down the stairs. She was watching his stomach muscles and neat little crotch jiggling away beneath the towel and was braced—half-expecting another revealing glimpse.

'I'm really sorry,' he repeated.

'Okay—just don't do it again and don't forget tomorrow, okay?'

'Sure.'

But she hadn't really got whatever it was off her chest and turned to him by the doorway.

'And put some damn clothes on, will you?'

'Okay, sure, sorry.'

'And stop saying sorry.'

'Okay, sorry . . . I mean, righto.'

Zoe turned, looked at Jane and they both stepped into the night.

He stood there for a moment, wondering what had got into her, then went back up the stairs. He hadn't seen Zoe like that before and it troubled him.

As he passed Beth's door it clicked and opened showing an inch or two of darkness. He stopped and waited. A narrow strip of her appeared—tight to the door, a pink dagger of thigh, a filet of breast, half her mouth giving no clue to her mood and one eye, staring at him, flat and black.

She slid away, letting the door swing open. Easy thought about the long list of chores he still had to get through, then joined her.

ITCH

T he health Club was busy that night. Menace laced the heavy sweat-laden air, fuelled by a quiet, ferocious competition for the machines. Zoe seemed to enjoy it, saw it as an opportunity to hone her skills, to practice in a microcosm of the real life war being raged out in the bars, restaurants, and clubland—paintballing for the single woman.

'She'll be in bed the rest of the week now,' Jane said coolly, 'savouring her wounds.' They sat opposite each other in the steam room. Zoe couldn't quite make out Jane's face through the hot plumes of vapour.

'Least she's getting some. I say live and let live.'

'Live! With her it's an ambush, slaughter, total annihilation. I just can't see the point in what she does. I mean, where's the thrill of courtship? The slow fever of romance?'

Zoe now shifted to afford a good look at Jane, without making it too obvious. She was wiping down her arms and studying her own small, pale breasts. She felt totally at ease with her nudity around other women, cloaked in a boarding-school-girl aura—like a hard-earned shroud of purity.

'She's just going through that phase,' said Zoe. 'We've all—' she was going to say *done it* but realized Jane probably hadn't and probably never would, '—thought about it.'

'Perhaps—though not quite with Beth's *devotion*,' concluded Jane. She got up, doused the coals with cold water and was lost in a fresh, hot cloud of steam. She emerged, tendrils of mist wrapping round her shoulders and sat again.

'What bothers me is she's not looking for anything—nothing permanent at all. She's just *doing it*. She's not the least bit interested in romance or love or commitment.'

Zoe laughed, suddenly seeing Beth in a ridiculous white wedding dress, swaying drunkenly down the aisle to where some clean-shaven, longshoreman stood petrified before the Altar.

'Somehow, I don't think Beth's got her sights on commitment.'

'But that's what we live for, isn't it? A true sign. It's the only way you can be sure of someone. You're not left guessing, straightening your petticoat.'

Zoe laughed again, this time at the thought of Jane and her ludicrously brief and tragic sexual history. She'd confessed all to Zoe one night not long after she'd moved in and when they'd both drank far too much Sancerre. It had involved a Future Farmer of America, cask beer, hay-bails, splinters and a split condom. It wasn't pretty and certainly void of commitment.

'Falling in love doesn't just happen, Jane, not in real life. In real life, you have to work the shit out and take care of business. In real life you have to do the groundwork. Make your nest. Prepare the trap.'

'Prepare the trap?'

'Sure. Look at Mother Nature—that's how she does it.'

'God,' said Jane, wiping her arms down again, 'that's so incredibly cynical.'

'And so incredibly practical.'

'But really—where's the romance? You live like that and you're so completely doomed. No-one can ever stroll out of the sunset and whisk you away.'

Zoe snorted. It amused her to hear Jane talk like this—she felt, sophisticated, mature, and worldly-wise by comparison—and it also took her mind off Chance and his presumably dying Grandmother.

'Jane,' she said, calming and turning serious for a moment, 'When did that last remotely happen to anyone you remotely know?'

Jane couldn't reply—Snap-shots of Doris Day, Audrey Hepburn, and Grace Kelly flashed through her mind but she wasn't going to shoot herself in the foot or give up on her ideal that easily.

'Exactly. Not much whiskin' going on down N'Orlins this year.'

'But how would *you* know? You're too busy doing all this *groundwork* to see it. What a way to go on. You're almost as bad as Beth—worse in

106

some ways. I mean—neither of you will ever turn round one day and go *Bam—you got me.*'

Jane now had her hands clasped over her heart, with her elbows sticking out like an opera singer. She had a curious, prim, half crazed look in her eye and it took all of Zoe's resolve to refrain from saying: 'And you will?'

Later, when Zoe had demonstrated superiority on the light weights and they were warming down on the exercise bikes, Jane's words wormed themselves back in to Zoe's thinking. Okay, maybe she *was* a bit predetermined, premeditated, and mechanical, but that was how she was built. If she was being over-prepared—*so what*? She could always rein back a bit if needed—couldn't she, *couldn't she*?

She stole little looks at Jane's reflection in the full-length mirrors and tried to focus in on what had gotten into her. Sure, she'd finished her Thesis and she was entitled to be pretty wired after pulling that whole deal together. She recalled her own senior year—assignments, essays, deadlines, the self-imposed pressure, the intensity of the final exams and then, suddenly, it was over. Waking up in the morning to stillness and silence, afternoons a hundred miles deep, nights a vacuum, into which she poured alcohol and boys.

She remembered waking one night in a fevered panic about not handing in some mid-term project. An Ansel Adams Study, a tribute to a photographer she hated, and she'd never missed a deadline her whole life. She'd rushed about for a full two minutes, scattering albums and presentation wallets across the apartment until she realised she'd left college almost two years ago and it was all just some concluding shockwave of that intense final year. Jane needed to cut loose was all— unwind all the way down and in her own way. She could surely understand that.

'Hey. You wanna go out—just the two of us?'

'Go out? Tonight?'

'Sure.'

'Okay, where?'

'I don't know, anywhere. We'll have a really exquisite meal and get as drunk as skunks on exceptional French wine.'

The idea surprised and suddenly tempted Jane, their eyes met, a plan forming—

'Oh—' she said, remembering the meeting she'd arranged with Hugo in the morning. It now seemed like she would be making it and if so she needed to keep a clear head.

'I can't. Not till this thing's settled.'

107

'Oh, all right,'

'But hopefully tomorrow night, if *you're* still free—I'd love to.'

Zoe smiled, hid her brief disappointment, and rejected the idea of suggesting a quiet meal somewhere. Going out with Jane was an experience best enjoyed with alcohol, bright lights, and distractions—like a school prom, it could be heavenly, hilarious, or horrible.

'We'll keep the taxi waiting whilst we're getting all made up,' said Jane, 'sipping Champagne and choosing high heels. We'll tell the driver to make a tour of the very finest hotels. We'll really push the boat out.'

She looked at Jane grinning and pedalling away with her hair sweat-matted across her face and her head bobbing to and fro like a balloon on a stick. That certain old school perkiness had blown right through her again and it was difficult to pin-point or ignore.

'What's gotten into you?' said Zoe.

'What? Sorry? Oh, I don't know. You know, you know . . .'

'No, no. Not at all—I do not know.'

'It's, you know, just that now is . . . is one of those times in the year. You understand—it's in between the seasons?' She looked at Zoe as if they were making some great connection. All Zoe knew was that Jaen had been working too hard, it was damn hot and not the time to be having a Crescent City meltdown.

'I bet,' Jane continued, 'all over town people are telling the boss to stick the job where the sun don't shine or they're just hitting the road, taking off round the world, jacking it all in and eloping.' She suddenly stopped pedalling and slid off the bike. 'I don't do any of that, of course—I have, well, I just have . . . *reactions*.' She grabbed up her towel and buried her face in it.

Zoe had the oddest feeling she was suddenly crying, or hiding a smirk. When Jane's face reappeared, Zoe could see it was more composed, distant and solemn.

'I see a streetcar ticket in a gust of wind and I get it. I understand it wants to be a leaf—a beautiful, dying autumn leaf, just for one second.'

Zoe now thought Jane, who again had a mystical far away look, had definitely lost the plot. She was about to make some joke about Jane laying off the Mogadon when the last hour suddenly played itself back to her in a series of frozen stills:

Jane in the steam room talking of courtship and romance.

Her wet lips when she said the word 'commitment'.

Jane's theatrical pose: '*Bam-you got me!*'

The penny dropped. A familiar, well worn penny.

'You've not been to bed with Hugo, have you?'

108

'Hugo!'

'Who then?'

'What ever are you saying?'

But Jane's face told Zoe that she was right on the money.

'I mean,' Zoe continued, 'It's not as if your life is filled with hundreds of young, virile men—'. Her voice trailed off as a new penny slipped into the slot. This one was bright, freshly minted and this one struck home and played.

'It ain't Easy, is it?'

Jane said nothing: She didn't have to, the simple mention of his name flashed a beam of light across the inside of her eyes that told Zoe all she needed to know—and a whole lot more.

'You've got a crush on the maid, haven't you?'

'No, no. Zoe. Don't be so ridiculous.'

'There's nothing ridiculous about it.'

'I admit, he's interesting. Anybody has to concede that. And he's always so incredibly up-beat.'

'Up beat?'

'Yes. Don't you find that intriguing.'

Zoe shook her head, mockingly, at her own blindness.

'My God. You *do* have a crush on him?'

'Don't be absurd, I hardly know the man.'

'He's got a great ass,' Zoe jibed.

'Yes,' agreed Jane, but with the tone of a Senior House Doctor at the patient's bedside, 'and the most perfect little strawberry nevus to the inner groin.'

'What? Perfect little - what's going on here?'

They both burst out giggling, like two schoolgirls.

'A few days ago, he was coming out of the shower, his towel kind of—' she tossed her hand away, giggling, remembering.

Zoe stood wide-eyed.

'You know, he's got . . . well a . . . '

'A what? Tell me what he's got?'

'Well, from what I remember. Which, I admit, may not be the most reliable source. A really nice . . . '

Zoe guessed what Jane was getting at and wiggled her index finger. Jane shook her head and flapped her whole hand around like a fresh caught fish. Both girls erupted.

'Jesus Christ,' said Zoe, when she'd recovered, 'I've been walking round with my head in the sink.'

SCRATCH

E asy was on top of her again. This girl was screwed up, mad as a box of spiders, but hot. She knew what to do under the cotton, she was built to be horizontal, or occasionally, whenever either of them fancied a change of scenery, up gloriously on all fours.

He'd got himself all fired up with the scent of her. It filled his hog-nostrils, flooding his bull-mouth and stallion-throat with her heat, flesh, and flavour.

'Hey, hey,' she whispered, pulling his head up to join her, 'Calm down, boy. Calm down. Where's the God damn fire?'

He'd calmed himself and began again slowly. Beth rested back on the pillows, tuned in again and began to receive.

7, 8, 8, 8, 7, 8, 8 . . . the numbers flicked up behind her eyelids.

Most guys never got further than a five. It started at one, or two if she was lucky, and crept up till they got off or she hit the limit, decided to cut her losses, take her fun, and collect.

With Easy it had been different. That day they first met she had a big fat three flash up behind her eyes when she stood watching him at the doorway. She'd immediately dismissed the idea as anything serious. When he cooked that first sit down meal for the girls and spewed his guts out, she saw this series of long, slow-burn fours. There had been something about him that night; raw, honest, and pure. She remembered being cruel to him just because of his easy rating. And finally, when she came home drunk with the jilted john and found him in the front room, it was just big, bright fives . . .

8, 8, 8, 8 . . . 9—

Here we go. She sank her fingers into his thick curls again and prised his head away from her.

'Let me have you,' she said in a rasp. 'Let me have you.'

'Calm down, girl, calm down,' he now repeated, 'Where's the god damn fire!' He took her hands and held them by her side, firmly to the mattress. 'You're just simmering is all,' and he dropped his big dog head back below.

She was quickly into solid nine territory. The colors building in her, the needle edging its way into the red. Her hands now hovered above his head, ready to prise him away, her legs were sprung wide like a bear trap, set to clamp him and suffocate them both in a thrashing frenzy.

10, 10, 10, 10!

He was suddenly in her, swinging to and fro with all the abandonment of Negro choir, and exploded into her warmth. His arms clamped to her shoulders, his face buried in her neck. She was lost in higher numbers, charting new territory. She felt his hardness breaking and they clung to each other, swirling, hands and limbs sliding over each other.

After a moment, Easy rolled to the side and released a huge outward breath.

'Wow', he said, 'that time I just 'bout almost did it!'

Beth slammed him in the ribs. The blow was a little too violent, harsh, and jarred with the intimacy. He played a little roughhouse with her, sneaking little sideways glances to work out her mood. Although the sex had been great for Easy, their little afternoon secret was turning into something more profound for Beth. He closed his eyelids just as her gaze came to seek him out. She found him; eyes shut, peacefully smiling.

*   *   *   *   *

The Laundromat was clammy, damp, and busy. Poorer students from the University mingled seamlessly with the flotsam and jetsom of Algiers. Mama-Lek left Easy folding the girls' clothes into a basket. He'd been acting odd that morning, strange and more distant than she'd noticed before. When she returned he was stood holding a pair of lacy knickers, his mind on some distant planet.

'Whaah?' Said Mama-Lek, 'You find natty mahk?'

He snapped-to, shot Mama-Lek a guilty look, and stuffed the knickers into the basket. The penny dropped; she got the whole story in one.

'No!'

'What?' He smiled and the cat was out of the bag, across the floor, and crawling up onto Mama-Lek's shoulder.

'Easy Bad-boy. Bad-bad-boy.'

'What are you talking about. I . . . we . . . ' he thought about lying to her, making up some great story, but for some reason he just didn't want to. 'It just kind of happened.'

'Uh-huh,' she shook her head, slowly, 'juskina-happen, juskina-happen, what? Like World War Two, juskina-happen?'

'Hey,' said Easy, 'To be honest—if anything, I was seduced.'

Mama-Lek frowned, not understanding this strange word.

'Wassat? Sedooss.'

'You know,' said easy, 'she came on to me.'

Mama-Lek looked at him for a full second: 'Paaaaaaaaah!' she roared, throwing their head back and calling up to the cheap hardboard tiles on the ceiling. 'He was sedoose!'

This was the best joke she'd heard in weeks, and Mama-Lek heard a lot of good jokes. She slapped her knees, opened one of the large industrial dryers and shouted into the chamber as if it was the home of the gods and they were all in attendance and eagerly listening.

'He was sedoose. He was sedoose.'

She strolled off now, with that funny little bole of hers, laughing, slapping her sides. As her chuckling rolled off into the midst of the machines, Easy held his hands up, coming to accept his not insubstantial part in the happening.

*   *   *   *   *

'It is worse than I thought, Jane.' His voice was firm and steady like a doctor delivering the terminal prognosis. Her hand gripped the receiver, knuckles glowing white in her reflection in the dressing mirror.

Hugo had called her three minutes before when she just got out of the bathroom, and now she stood wrapped in a towel in the dead centre of the vast bedroom.

'They have closed ranks on us.'

'But we expected that,' she said, 'didn't we?'

'Yes, and I said they'd come after you, but I didn't expect anything like this.'

112

'Like what?'

'These tactics. They've gone straight to the Dean,' he said, pausing for emphasis, 'They're citing some archaic article of intra-faculty conduct.'

'And has he sided with them?'

'That's difficult to say at this stage. He has requested you turn in your notes and findings and a comprehensive list of all those connected with your research.'

'Why do they want that?'

'It's just routine.'

'"A comprehensive list" of what?'

'They're just trying to scare us, Jane; the thesis is complete. The integrity is beyond question . . .' his voice trailed off, leaving Jane in an eerie vacuum.

'It appears,' said Jane quietly, 'they don't agree.'

He let that hang there a significant moment: 'Look, *I* know how you work, your methods, you're a consummate professional. I certainly wouldn't take you on, not on integrity, ethics, or anything else.'

'I'm not quite sure what you're getting at Hugo.'

'Don't you see? This just shows how desperate they are. They're hoping you've tripped up.'

'Well, I've cut no corners and I can substantiate every last detail. They can have it all, Hugo, because I know I've been thorough. Go on, yes, let them have it, and watch them choke on it.'

'Good, good. That's the spirit. But hang on, there's more.'

'What now?'

'They've started a whispering campaign.'

'Against the faculty?'

'No, Jane . . . ' his hesitancy said it all, and she sank to the bed, already knowing what he was about to say: 'It's against you, personally.'

She slumped back and looked up at the ceiling.

'They're suggesting certain elements of your personal life may be clouding your judgement on this.'

'Elements, Hugo. Elements?'

He spoke now with great difficulty, a caution, and a weakness in his voice. She could imagine him winding the telephone flex around his finger. 'Your . . . sexual behaviour.'

'My sex—, he voice caught in her throat, 'My sexual behaviour! But that's a ridiculous. *Ohmylord*, I'm . . . I . . . '

'I know, I know—' he cut in, 'it's just so awful.'

'Hugo—'

'The cheap bastards!'

113

'Hugo, you ask them to name one, just one single incident or indiscretion over my entire academic career. They won't be able to. It's impeachable!'

A silence followed as she let this go over. 'How could they?' She thought 'How bloody could they?'

'You know what hurts, Hugo? You know what really gets me about all this? This work has been my life. My everything. I haven't even had a god damned boyfriend for the past eight years!'

'Unfortunately,' he said, in that low, even voice, 'that's pretty much their argument.'

Jane felt a little dam burst somewhere deep and distant inside. It was quite the oddest sensation. She was silent, waiting for its impact, some reverberation, collateral damage, chaos. There was nothing but cool spreading sensation, gathering at the top of her stomach.

'They're trying to discredit you,' he went on, 'saying you're a man-hater and the History Department being the last male bastion, blah, blah, blah.' The floodwaters began to reach her. Rushing adrenaline, overtaking her senses, rendering her powerless. 'They say you're jealous and vengeful and that might be influencing your impartiality. Even your discovery, the Last Eunuch, they're twisting it all to their advantage.'

Jane now lay flat out on the bed, pole-axed, broadsided, totally defeated.

'Jane? Are you there?'

She tried to speak but could not. A deep breath started from her, stuttered, stuck, and finally released itself in a low wavering gasp.

'I understand this is a bombshell but remember, truth is on our side.' She felt like laughing suddenly, screaming her rage back down the phone, showing just how much all this meant to her. 'You're a brilliant academic, and after all, you're in the right.'

She wanted to come back at that: of course she was in the right. What he meant to say was that she could very well be some bitter, dried-up, spinster in waiting but that shouldn't really matter!

'Hugo,' she said, shakily, 'this is so bloody unfair.'

'I know, Jane, I know. It's a terrible thing being done, and by some pretty despicable people, but the question is, Jane, the question is what do you propose to do about it?'

She sat up and was met by a dishevelled reflection in the bedside mirror. Tears of pure anger rolled down her cheeks. She wasn't crying in the normal way, she was way beyond that.

'You know, Hugo,' she said honestly, 'I haven't the faintest bloody idea.' She wished she could cry, have a proper sobbing, snotty, snivel, saw

114

her sleeve across her nose like a schoolchild and wait for someone to come along and make it all better.

'Well, I have,' barked Hugo, coming to life, 'Thanksgiving Ball is next week. The whole Faculty will be there.'

'So?'

'So, you make damn sure you're out in public for all to see,' he said. 'You go right up in their faces, looking fabulous. You show them you're not some bitter, little nobody. You show them you're someone to be reckoned with, a red-blooded, fire-eating, cat-fighting, scratch your damn eyes out woman. You get right in there, right amongst them and you blow all their crap clean out of the water!'

Jane looked out of the window at the night sky and the full, fat moon. The confidence was back in his voice. She could feel the truth to what he said but this was just so far out of her league.

'Oh, hell, Hugo,' she whispered, 'you're so totally right.'

DEAD

It was maybe 10 after 11, with the sun bright through the slats and painting ladders across the polished wood floors. Easy sat working the brush across the tip of the shoe. He liked polishing shoes, it reminded him of the days cleaning the workers boots on the farm. Polishing girls shoes, however, was a completely different business. They were just so dainty, little curved panels of leather, strips, straps, buckles, bows, and tassels. No wide flanks to blast, heat up, and work your elbow across. Still, it kept his body busy, and his mind occupied.

Across the room, Beth sat watching his every move. His concentration fascinated her; how could a fully-grown man with such honourable bed skills be so easily occupied with a pile of shoes, a small tin of wax, and a wooden handled brush?

He hummed that little tune of his, the 'Plastic Jesus' tune. It wasn't quite blue grass, and it wasn't quite Hillbilly. Beth recognised it from the movie 'Cool Hand Luke'. Maybe he did too and wasn't half the Huckleberry he was making out to be.

'*I don't care if it rains or freezes,*' she sang in a low whisper, '*Long as I got my plastic Jesus, Riding on the dashboard of my car . . .*'

He looked across at her, smiling, her feet curled underneath like a cat. Her eyes had the hungry look in them again. He avoided her direct stare, did not want to be drawn in, not so soon. He pretended to check the time on his watch, then packed the brushes and polish pots away in the box and got to his feet.

116

Beth dropped a cushion on the floor and looked him in the eye.
'What time is it?'
'Eh?'
'You just checked your watch didn't you? What time is it?'
He had to look again: 'Gone eleven,' he said, ' I'm getting behind.'
'Be a little minstrel and fix a tired girl some java.'

Easy hesitated then went to the kitchen. They were back into their master-servant routine, at least for the time being. He could handle that, and wondered whether she would be as nimble, hop-scotching between the two worlds.

On route he picked up the silk cushion and punched it back into shape and tossed it on the sofa. Beth took his frustration as a small victory. She could hear him spooning the coffee beans into the grinder and fetching her favourite mug from the hook under the cupboard and place it on the worktop.

'Don't forget my favourite mug.'

He said nothing. She couldn't quite figure out why she was being this cruel. In truth, it didn't give her as much satisfaction as she'd expected. Something existed in the sheer power of it that tickled her, and that fact that he stood for it.

She heard the rattle of the fridge door and thought to repeat exactly how she liked her milk but before she could speak the high-pitched growling of the coffee grinder kicked in. Instead, she plucked a magazine from the coffee table, flicked through the pages and dropped it on the floor where the cushion had landed.

Easy took a quick glance at the back of Beth's head as he slipped on his jacket. What he felt towards her was a curious thing, frustration for sure and something approaching resentment, simmering away over a hot flame of devious sexual adventure. It wasn't lust, not in that pure carefree, abandoned way. When he was inside her now he always kept a part of him anchored to the reality of what was happening; an eye on the door handle, one hand on the shore, if you will.

He saw the magazine, went to pick it up and, as he did so, unfathomably, gave Beth a little peck on the cheek. He was as astonished by the action as she was and they were both at a loss for words. He noticed that predatory look was suddenly gone from her eyes and the thought flashed across his mind that maybe this was the only way to shake her off; to act like he was head over heels with her, make a great big fool of himself, get down on one knee, and scare the living daylight out of her.

He leaned in front of her and set the magazine down neatly on the coffee table. Her legs drew back from him, and he felt her hand slip up confidently between his legs and rest against his inner thigh. It was warm and needy. His groin did not react. He fought back the temptation to check his wristwatch again.

'Gimme time to reload, eh?'

'Little guys down there mixing up a fresh batch, huh?'

He smiled, and then noticed a change come over her mood as she got up to fetch the coffee.

'When you're out,' she said, in a cool, professional tone, 'don't forget to buy some more condoms.'

'Sure,' he said, but what he really wanted to say was, 'Goddamn right, I won't, you crazy, mixed up circus Gypsy!'

'Get those ones with the . . . ' she knelt up and whispered the words into his ear. He felt her hot, sticky breath on the side of his head like static electricity.

Still no reaction down in the engine room; ears always got a twitch in the right direction.

'Beth, don't you think we could, you know . . . cool it a bit?'

'Cool it a bit? What the hell does that mean?'

'Look,' he said, keeping his voice small and open 'I don't know how this started. I . . . I was just, you know, being nice.'

'You still are.'

'I didn't think we'd really end up . . . ' he trailed off, 'You were drunk. I was rusty. I just figured you needed someone to hold you.'

'Maybe I still do?'

'Don't suppose there's any mileage in you considering me as one of your regular one-night-*paramours*?'

She looked at him as she poured the coffee. She kept on looking and pouring, his request bouncing around inside her head. The guy wanted out. Or was he just scared. Like she was maybe. Time for a little honesty, she thought. Why not try him on some of his own medicine: 'You were until the morning,' she said. 'I never, ever, ever did mornings. Up and out before sunrise that was my one big rule.' she smiled, scooped two heaped spoonfuls of brown sugar into a coffee, took a little noisy sip of the hot brew then smiled: 'But we broke that all to pieces, didn't we?'

Easy just smiled back, each of her words going off in his head like a flashbulb, illuminating the new reality.

'Now I know what I've been missing,' she said with an uncommon finality.

The phone began to ring. Easy went to pick it up on autopilot, but then stopped, there was one thing he needed to work out with her.

'What about Zoe and Jane?'

Beth smiled, she knew now she had him exactly where she wanted him: 'We'll make a pact—I won't tell them, if you don't make me.' She was grinning like the cat who got the cream; he turned away and picked up the phone.

'Easy? Is that you?'

He recognised Zoe's voice. She sounded confident, businesslike, and terribly self-important.

'Sure,' he said, 'who else answers the phone round here?'

'Did you get my supplements yet?' He could hear the newsroom behind her, imagined dozens of reporters with creased shirts, and little press cards stuck in their trilby hat bands, moving through a thick haze of tobacco smoke.

'I was just on my way to pick them up.'

'Good,' she said, 'while you're out, I need you to do me a big favor.'

'Sure.'

'Grab a pencil.'

Easy scrabbled around for a pencil in the telephone stand. He felt Beth standing behind him, she began to run her hands down his back and grabs his ass.

'Yow! Got one,' he said, 'Fire away.'

As he took down the message, Beth began to whisper her little sing-song in his free ear.

'You can buy 'em Phosphorescent, Glow in the dark, they're pink'n'pleasant, Take 'em with you when you're travelling far . . . '

*   *   *   *   *

Easy walked down to Napoleon and rode the streetcar up as far as South Broad. He got off just before the Expressway and walked the two blocks to the Times Picayune. He had expected some grand imposing building with a Golden Era façade, steam pluming out the basement windows from some deafening hell-like rolling press. He'd imagined stoop-backed printers in shirtsleeves scurrying back and forth and cigar chewing, waistcoat popping editors kicking doors off their hinges and screaming *'Hold the front page!'*

Instead, he suddenly found himself in an industrial wasteland. The lot was sandwiched between the elevated section of South Broad, the 8-lane

119

freeway and a disused railroad that curled right round the site and stopped at an old half-step loading platform. The whole joint looked unkempt, derelict, and uncared for. The perimeter fence was a cheap chain-link affair, busted, sagging, and gaping open: like a mackerel net beyond repair. Rusty oil barrels and discarded railway sleepers jostled for space along the trackside.

He rounded the building and waited at the edge of the parking lot in the shade of a half dead elm, and tried very hard not to look like a hustler. A couple of street jockeys soon appeared, and one of them he remembered from his days in Algiers. The guy was an Irishman, the peaceful type, okay, but always thoroughly soaked. Easy wanted to skip across the street to avoid a confrontation but something inside him—some link with what had gone before—kept him rooted like the elm.

It wasn't until much later, that he realised what a risk he was taking. If Zoe had come out on time and seen him back-slapping these bums, he would have had a fair deal of explaining to make up.

As they shuffled towards him, sizing him up, he remembered one autumn evening, down by the river, in a little cardboard camp. This guy, this Irishman, Roary, had sung a whole string of beautiful songs about the old homeland—his Emerald Isle. He got the whole crowd going, and a few of the old boys with tears in their eyes. He'd kept it up, pounding them with song after song, with that rich, cracked baritone, and not a rebel song amongst them.

They spotted him now and were trying to place him—or make him for a tap or a *roll-over*. Easy relaxed; he would remind old Roary of that night he sang. They would swap tales and reminisce about the guys, who was still knocking around, who was doing a bit, who had *gone*, and who was *gone-along*. But in the event the guy didn't make Easy at all; his Irish eyes were a milky blue wash.

'Got a dollar for a coffee, fellah?' was all he grunted and when the Easy couldn't respond, he just shuffled off with his companion to the damp shadows under the L.

Easy felt a motion inside; a sea-swell in his guts. It wasn't in his thoughts so it wasn't in his life. Easy as that. The whole two years on the lam shrugged off in a second like a wet overcoat. Was he really, that simply, free of it?

'There you are!'

She was suddenly with him, Zoe, clipping across the parking lot on those scissor legs. He gave her a little wave as she closed him down. He noticed urgency in her movements, like she was too busy for this and had made up her mind to keep it brief. But she kept right on coming, flung her arms around him, and docked a big, wet, puckered smacker full on his lips.

All Easy could do was smile, and hope he'd remembered to brush his teeth.

Zoe linked arms with him and led him away across the car park.

'So,' said Easy, 'This is the Times Picayune?'

She heard both the eagerness and disappointment in his voice; like he'd expected something more of the place, and perhaps a guided tour of the printing presses from her.

'Yep. It's a complete toilet.'

'Must be fun to work there though. You know, deadlines, breaking news, front page scoops! Ain't that exciting?'

'Not till two-fifteen, it ain't!'

She stopped him again, spun him round so that he faced the expressway and gave him another overly dramatic hug. Her body was firm and strong and the contact, welcome though it was, lasted a second or two too long. He suddenly got the impression she was looking back at the offices.

'What's this for exactly?'

'Just for being there. And for not being an asshole when I was an asshole to you.'

'Hey, no problem. Really.'

She squeezed him one last time and then broke off and they continued walking.

'So, what's the plan? Or are we gonna just walk down the railroad track, hugging every 30 feet?'

She laughed, flicked her dreds like a girl without dreds would do in a shampoo commercial and said: 'Didn't I tell you? We're going shopping.'

They both saw the streetcar come into view and she suddenly took off and started running towards it. She was manic, everything was happening at teenage speed. Easy shrugged and went after her but before he got into his stride, he stopped and looked around himself suddenly, as if he were a bit-player in someone else's movie. Glancing back at the Times Picayune, he saw a tall, immaculately dressed black guy of about 30, staring right down at him from a top floor window. Although they must have been over one hundred feet apart, they exchanged an intense look, and the guy smiled and continued to watched Zoe running away.

Easy was waiting for someone to shout 'Cut!'

*　　　*　　　*　　　*　　　*

121

He'd never quite understood the boutiques on magazine. Funny little half-baked shops, oversized goldfish bowls with mannequins, tailors dummies, and life-sized polystyrene figurines jammed into the window display. The show was always changing, updating and outdoing itself.

When he passed on a midweek morning, shop girls would be unceremoniously stripping the models out of last week's fashion must have, and busily packing every inch of sidewalk realty with intricately crafted ensembles. Sales-banners for daily discounts, seasonal promotions, and unbelievable *NEVER BEFORE, NEVER AGAIN* reductions, fought for every inch of your attention.

He found them overwhelming, unfathomable, and somewhat intimidating. Why did women find these places so irresistible? What was it in their deep psyche that drove them into these finicky little emporiums? The mere challenge of getting through the door without demolishing some elaborate display and making a great show of himself was enough to put him off the idea of exploring their many mysteries.

Being in here with a girl, on the other hand, was something entirely different. And a girl like Zoe, who knew her way around these places and was clearly on a mission. Now he had a ticket, a defined role to perform, and a raison d'être. And Zoe, to him at least, shopped like a man. She wasn't looking at every last thing on display; she strode down the tight aisle and homed in on one or two pieces. She new her exact size and didn't need to take two or three of each item. It was grab and go shopping.

As he waited outside the changing room, he observed the others adhering to that strict intricate female shopping code; the rules, by-laws, and mores: A woman would wait, quietly—but with massive presence—for another woman to finish flicking through a rack of clothing that she intended to search. Maybe, whilst projecting this colossal intensity, she'd glance around her, pick up something else, examine it, check the price, stall for time, and trying to outwit her rival. Often she'd appear genuinely interested in the new item, only to drop it, toss it aside, or stuff it back onto the shelf, the instant her target rack became free.

The second woman, having skilfully ignored the immense angst of the first and moved freely on, would now feel ousted, and hover around and be drawn back to the rack, just to keep her eye on the first woman. She too now, as a ruse, would pick up some nearby trinket, turn it over, examine it, check the price, and all the time projecting authority and judging her opponent's every progress along the rack, torturing herself in the certain knowledge that she must have skipped past a genuine bargain, a hidden designer treasure, a chiffon Picasso.

And so it went on.

Zoe had been the exact opposite. She moved so quickly through the merchandise that Easy lost her altogether and didn't even know what she'd snatched up or into which changing room she'd vanished.

The cubicle curtains swayed gently, being nudged occasionally from various movements inside. The women worked seriously and quietly; he heard no rustle of clothing, fastening of zips, shuffling of feet, grunts or groans. A curtain would finally swish back and a woman would step into view, shoot him a scolding look, inspect herself and disappear—swish.

Zoe's curtain hung still, she made no sound. She glided from the cubicle in a fitted, knee-length, midnight-blue dress, and presented herself, to herself, in the full-length mirror.

'Well, ain't that the berries!'

His words brought her out of the zone and she looked at him, blankly. He nodded in an over exaggerated doggy way and Zoe looked at herself again then, without comment, stepped back into the changing room.

'So,' said Easy, through the curtain, 'What'd the guy do to get this lucky?'

'What?'

'How'd he get on your radar?'

'Who?'

'The black dude from work.'

' . . . '

'That's who you're getting dolly-dolled up for, ain't it?'

'Chance?'

'I don't know the man. Black dude. Handsome son. Well groomed feller of about 30.'

' . . . '

'What's he got that some other guys don't got?'

'He's got perfect pecs, a truly great ass and his teeth are flawless and go, like, right round his whole head.'

The curtain swished back again and Zoe emerged in an elegant, dark satin dress. It neither clung to her sexily nor hung from her shoulders with style. She dismissed it immediately and turned to Easy: 'Plus, he graduated with 1st Class honors from Oxford University, was top of his MBA class at Harvard Business School, and is the youngest ever senior editor in the Times 173 year history.'

'Always knew I shoulda listened a li'l at school.'

She raised an eyebrow and stepped out of sight. This time, however, she never pulled the curtain across fully and from his vantage Easy could see her reflection in the full-length mirror. He moved to reach for the curtain but as he did so Zoe shrugged the satin dress from her shoulders and stood facing her other reflection. She wore a black g-string, and her skin glowed white under the halogen downlight. Her body was pale and tightly formed and the skeleton showed under the skin, strong, angular, and graceful.

She raised a soft pale breast with the flat of her hand and let it drop. She repeated the action twice more as she studied herself in the mirror. Each time the breast bounced and settled, the white hairs round her nipple, caught the harsh, sterile light.

Easy felt the blood suddenly pitch into his loins. His penis twitched, then began to flood. He broke off his gaze and looked back out at the crammed boutique and the other dull, desperate shoppers. He'd focus on anything to keep his mind from thinking about that nipple. He could feel the flanks of his penis unfurling, and pushing against his shorts.

He heard the curtain zip back and Zoe appeared now in a short, tight, fire-engine-red dress. It was made of wool and clung to her with the effect of dampness, softening her angles, filling out her natural curves.

She knew instantly this was the dress. It didn't feel right when she first put it on and now she knew why. It hugged her hips so closely. Not too tightly, or restricting, but she'd have to stand tall and hold herself with good posture to pull this off. The top, undone, sagged forward making her small breasts droop. She could already feel the shape of it around her; knew it would gather her up and in and make her behave.

She met eyes with Easy in the mirror. His face was pleasantly symmetrical but he had on one of his most curious looks: sparkly, peculiar, fascinating, weird.

'Could you zip me into this?'

Easy said nothing and just stared at Zoe's naked back with that bare thin arm, twisted up behind her, offering him the zip. It struck him as oddly sexual and he felt another jab in the groin. If he took a calculated step, he reasoned, his cock would manoeuvre itself, either find room to expand or get comfortable and hopefully subside. She had turned round now to read his expression properly. He had to do something.

'Easy?'

His smile wasn't working right, was coming out curled up and lopsided. As she turned back to the mirror, he used the opportunity and moved in behind her. The move did nothing to ease his congestion, his penis strained against the arrangement of cotton and denim, but it held him in place.

His hands fumbled on the zip and he felt the warmth of her smooth, sculpted back against his knuckles.

124

Another surge . . .

As he began to zip her up, the smell came off her skin and rose round his face.

Thump . . .

He was standing very close behind her now, concentrating on the zip, ignoring the pressure in his loins. Her small, perfect shoulders were a red haze before him. He focused in the reflection and saw her neat, perfect breasts cupped in the bright fabric. He felt the urge to slip his arms around her then and lift those breasts, feel their weight through the tickly cloth on his hot palms.

She could see him staring at the reflection of her tits. He looked kind of vacant and starved. The dress was either working wonders or miracles. Both were fine by her.

'What do you think?'

He said nothing. Zoe was pleased by the effect but wanted confirmation, some unequivocal detail, a remark, a comment, a sign.

'Easy?'

Nothing. His inability to respond could mean anything.

She chose her moment and deliberately backed into him, nudging her tightly wrapped behind firmly into his crotch . . . and felt some-thing move.

'Oooh . . . ' said Easy in a weak, uncertain breath.

They both looked at each other, shocked and amused, but some-how not quite embarrassed: a comical, curious moment passed where neither of them knew quite what to do next.

'So, can I assume you like this one?'

'Yeah—,' said Easy, then cleared his throat. 'That would sure be a dress to buy.'

*   *   *   *   *

They rode the streetcar back to the Expressway. Easy carried the bags from the boutique, swinging them like he was in some Gap commercial for carefree summer living. Zoe forced the pace but got more relaxed and cosied-up to him as they approached the news-paper. It never occurred to him to ask why she hadn't just asked to meet on Magazine. That would have been easier but she'd been using that extremely determined voice of hers so he went with it.

As they rounded the building and made across the carpark, Chance appeared; Easy saw him slide out of a dainty little sparkly sportscar, Zoe saw him emerge from a sleek, graphite BMW Z3.

They all arrived at the door together and the open, smiley, high-eyebrowed look on Chance's face made for introductions.

'Hi Chance. You haven't met, have you? This is Easy.'

'Easy, Chance.'

The men shook hands, sizing each other's grip, pumping each other's biceps in some junior congressmen contest.

'Thanks for today,' said Zoe, cutting in as soon as they'd let each other go, and this time planting a little intimate kiss to the corner of his mouth. He could feel Chance's eyes on him, soaking up the whole play.

She left Easy with the boutique bags and Chance opened the door for her. As she swept by him and disappeared into the building, Chance gave Easy a little wink.

He wasn't quite sure how to take it so winked back and said: 'Chance. You got a li'l ketchup on your shirt.'

Chance looked down the front of his shirt and saw beyond and below that his zipper was undone. He flashed a look back at Easy, but he'd already turned and was strolling away across the lot, whistling to himself a happy little tune.

DOGHOUSE

J ane had been sitting looking at the sheet of paper for over thirty minutes and the list still contained one single entry. Since Hugo's telephone call, she'd worried herself sick over whom to ask to accompany her to the Faculty Ball. Despite the serious professional accusations being levelled at her, her mind would only and could only concentrate and fixate on this single, unrelated detail. It seemed the whole event now hung in the balance of this trivial piece of business.

This is why she hated politics.

'My God', she thought, it's the senior prom nightmare all over again. And what a total disaster that had turned out to be . . .

She remembered taking the advice of a strict, practical, but well-meaning aunt; her mother's sister, Gillian, a frightfully bright, serious, and deeply plain woman: 'Make a list of ten boys who you like the look of. Don't be shy; just make the list. Dating's a numbers game, trust me on this.' She'd handed Jane a sheet of scented paper and a fountain pen, and promptly left the room.

Jane had agonised over the first three names—she couldn't imagine ever having the courage to actually go up to any of these boy and open her mouth—never mind ask them to be her Prom date. However, once she made up her mind who was first, the other medal positions weren't quite so hard. Numbers four, five, and six were quite straightforward and the rest she just filled out with boys from her science class without much thought at all.

'Finished?'

'Yes—'

'Let me look.' She took the paper from Jane and proceeded to cross out the first three names. 'There,' she said, uncommonly pleased with herself, 'Now, just start at number four and work your way down the list.'

'What about the first three?'

'Forget them, dear. Nothing but heartbreak and humiliation awaits you with either of those boys. Trust me on this.' She folded her arms emphatically. 'You will begin with number four, speak clearly and confidently and ask as if you expect the boy to accept and accept gladly.'

'Right.'

'Be positive and be very specific; do not say: "Have you got a date for the Prom yet?" No, no, no. Say: "Will you come to my house at 8pm on Saturday night with flowers and chocolates and take me to the Prom?" It's concrete, tangible, something they can see themselves doing, and they will accept. You see, boys think in pictures, they are just like small men, really. Never forget that, Jane, and you won't go far wrong.'

'But what if he says "no"?'

'Then you say "next" and move on down the list. Don't get hung up on the whys or the wherefores. Just thank the boy, say you'll see them at the Prom, and put a line through his name. It's a numbers game, some will, some won't, so what, someone's waiting—trust me on this.'

She was right; Fraser Sames was her number ten. By the time she asked him she was too far beyond caring to worry about what anyone would think of her and came over as confident and assertive. That, in the end, was to be her salvation.

Fraser was a farm boy; strong, happy, with lively blue eyes darting beneath a heavy, wide forehead. He didn't mind she'd already asked his brother Joshua (her number 5) and his best friend Samuel Dejoie (her lucky number 7) and had witnessed them both turning her down flat.

'Yuh got pluck.' He said, when he accepted, 'That's why Ah'm acceptin'. Yuh got pluck.'

The Prom night itself was a calamity. Fraser was already a little squiffy when he picked her up from the house and was so drunk by the time the dinner was over, he had to be carried outside and laid out on the cool grass in the fresh air. She watched over him out of a sense of duty and both Joshua and Samual Dejoie brought her drinks each time they came outside for air.

At least she didn't have to deal with him trying to kiss her or putting those huge, beefy hands up her skirts. She'd survived the ordeal; secured a date—by the skin of her teeth—and got through the Prom night intact.

By all accounts it was a disaster, but a welcome one. She'd made it and all thanks to the list. Aunt Gillian had been right to ask for Jane's trust—dating was a numbers game, although Jane often wondered why her Aunt had never followed her own advice and found herself a husband.

For a time, staring at her clean sheet of paper, Jane had thought seriously about buying a third guest ticket and taking along Zoe *and* Beth. That would have been something, a marvellous distraction, and no one would think she was sleeping with both girls, and if they did, would probably still think better of her. But she rejected the idea, the smoke screen was too thin, and her career was trying to survive a blizzard. Also, if Beth got out of hand—which was not only possible but highly probable—the potential for serious irreparable damage was simply too great.

She could imagine Clements now, got up in his Tuxedo, black dickie, and dandy waistcoat, flirting with Zoe over champagne and canapés (to his wife's utter displeasure). And Hugo, with Beth jiggling in his lap, and giggling loudly right through the after dinner speeches.

It might be fun but the Faculty would still shrug them all off as a bunch of lesbians and misandrists by Monday morning coffee. It may be a marvellous distraction, yes—but only from the essential, pitiful fact that Jane, at age 32, still couldn't get a proper date.

Jane had now been sitting looking at the same sheet of paper for over thirty-five minutes and the list still contained one single entry:

No. 10—Easy.

She ran through a little scenario in her head, remembering Aunt Gillian's rule—

'Be positive, be specific, and ask as if you expect to receive.'

She'd wait till they were alone in the kitchen. When Zoe was at work and Beth still in bed: Neutral territory, where he'd feel comfortable and at ease.

'Oh, Easy,' she'd say, in a light, non-committal way, 'I've bought you an invite to the Faculty Ball next Saturday. It'll be my treat—a little thank you for all your wonderful help with my thesis?'

She'd crafted the sentence carefully so as there was no possibly way it could be misconstrued.

'Will you take me . . . ?' had connotations she hadn't thought of before. 'I want you . . . ' and 'I *would like* you . . . ' were similarly edited out so as not to convey the wrong impression. She simply stated the facts: A Ball. Next Saturday. As a Thank You.

Once she was happy with the wording she relaxed and began to think about what she was really about to do—to go out on a real live date with

129

a real live man. Yes, admittedly, the circumstances were a little contrived and the moment overshadowed by bigger events but it was still, most definitely, a *date* by any terms applied.

Hugo would be pleased. For Jane and for his part in suggesting the idea. Yes—it was working out. She could see the look on Clements' face as she walked—no—glided into the ballroom on Easy's arm.

She just needed Easy to agree and play his part.

In the event, the moment came sooner than she'd anticipated when, bright and early the very next morning, Easy unexpectedly brought her breakfast in bed.

She didn't realise the opportunity at first: Sitting up, fixing her hair, and making a few pleasantries whilst he set the antique wicker tray across her lap.

As he leaned across, she caught a whiff of strong manly scent from his body—not odour, not sweat, just his natural skin-oil and the mildest hint of soap. She was inches from his unshaven neck, noted how his Adam's apple raked up and back sending the little hairs off in all directions. It struck her suddenly that she really was about to ask this man to spend an evening out with her—on her own, and although her confidence was high, the words just wouldn't come, and the moment passed.

She ate silently, awaiting his return, and her prayers were answered twenty minutes later when she heard him bounding up the stairs and rap gently on her door.

'Ah, Easy,' she said, searching for that light, non-committal tone, 'The thing of it is . . .' she began. 'I've got, well, a small favor to ask. You see, I've got—no, I've bought you an invite to the Faculty Ball . . . next Saturday and, well, you simply must be my escort. My date. There!'

He looked at her and waited for more. She too, knew she had neglected to deliver the prepared qualifying sentence, the modifier she worked so hard on to place the invite in context.

'It won't cost you any money!' No—that wasn't it.

'Right.'

'I'll pay for everything!' No, no, no. 'It'll be my treat—a little thank you for all your help with my thesis?' Finally.

He thought for a second or two then said:

'Is it gonna be like a proper Black Tie affair?'

'Oh, yes, Black Tie, Champagne, the works.'

'With like Top Hats and Tails?'

'Yes, only almost certainly without the Top Hats.'

He stood thinking about the offer, his eyes distant and blank.

'Will I have to do anything?'

130

'Do anything. Whatever do you mean?'

'I don't know, Jane. I've never been to a Fancy Ball before at a University. Will I have to sound clever? Like I got an education?'

'Good heavens no, no. Just be yourself.' They both thought about this for a split second. 'Well, you know, within reason. We'll have to get you fitted out of course but don't worry about the cost. I'll take care of that.'

He was lost in thought again, his weight on one foot, his eyes staring out the big bay window.

'I'd be honored, Jane. Honored.'

And with that he smiled, bowed, and left the room, never once turning his back to her.

Jane took a piece of toast, bit into it, and munched as she contemplated her actions. A rush of joy suddenly shot up her chest and she gasped, breathed in toast crumbs and began a coughing fit.

She'd done it.

*   *   *   *   *

Easy skipped down the stairs with the breakfast tray. It was turning into a helluva week—first, the shopping trip and *the incident* with Zoe. (That's how he preferred to think about it when the memories recalled themselves—*the incident*). Now, Jane had invited him to his first ever Biggity Black-Tie event on the Tulane Campus. Life was running along these completely new grooves and he didn't know whether to jump for joy, laugh out loud, or curl up in a ball and sit in the corner.

He swung himself round the Newell post and tiptoed past Beth's door but she was waiting for him and stepped out, like a large, round troll, and blocked his path.

They stared at each other and as he went to speak she quickly put her fingertips to his lips.

'Shshshsh.'

Beth lowered herself to her knees and ducked under the breakfast tray.

Oh, one helluva week . . .

ROLL

'Hook, line, and sinker,' announced Zoe when she got in from work. Beth and Zoe were in the kitchen with a bottle of chilled white open on the countertop between them. Easy could tell by the speed they were drinking there was little need to return the bottle to the fridge. He was busy cleaning the windows through in the living room, sitting out on the sill with his legs dangling inside and polishing the big antique panes to a shine. The process involved old newspaper and vinegar and caused an intolerable high-pitched squeak.

'Do you have to do that now?' shouted Beth; keen to learn each and every detail of Zoe's latest exploit. He pretended he could only partially hear them, smiled and gave them the thumbs up.

'So,' continued Beth, 'How'd he play it?'

'Well, you know,' said Zoe, enjoying having something to relay at last, 'Just, like, so typically Chance.' She reached for the wine and topped up both their glasses. 'First, he asks a dozen damn questions about my assignment; he likes my work, apparently, yeah, for real, thinks I'll go *far*, blah-de-blah-de-blah, the whole crap. I just let him talk and put on this face like *I'm having great fucking sex on a regular basis and couldn't give a cow's ass about the job.*

Zoe pulled the face. Beth laughed, harshly.

'So then he cuts in with all this detail about his grandmother's funeral up in Solitude. How practically everyone she ever knew turned up to pay their respects and how the men had to jump right down in the hole and help dig out the grave!'

Beth raised her eyebrows.

'So I'm switchin' to the *I understand you too have a rich emotional life but I've just can't wait to get back home for a portion*—' Zoe changed to the new exaggerated expression.

'What is that—a vacant frown?'

'They're distant cousins.' The girls chinked glasses and Zoe noticed Easy looking at her through the glass. 'Anyway, he's back over in two minutes with the old coffee and Danish routine. So, I dig out the *Hey, my man hasn't gotten me breakfast since he moved in—he's too busy rubbing baby oil into my ass!*'

The girls roared and Easy ducked back through the window and into the room. Zoe and Beth fell silent as he came to the sink and washed his hands. He took his time over the task, working the soapsuds vigorously between his fingers, smelling to see that he'd removed every last trace of vinegar—

'Easy!' Beth finally interrupted, 'Do you mind? We're trying to have a private conversation.'

'Oops . . . '

'Sorry,' said Zoe.

'Yeah, run along to the store, buy something nice for later on,' added Beth, and when he got what she meant and clocked her, she winked back at him. He dried his hands and left, feeling their eyes on him as he went.

'So,' resumed Beth, toping the glasses up again, 'You think he's in the bag?'

'Well, for what it's worth, he booked Casamento's.' She didn't over play it, but this was her little bit of proof, evidence of his commitment, an action which she could easily verify just by calling the restaurant—which was exactly what she did the minute Chance left her desk: 'Yes ma'am, a cosy table for two at 8.30, is there a problem?' 'No problem at all.'

Beth blew a cool, sustained whistle.

'I just threw together this—,' she pulled another comical face—'*Food, yeah, before I met this guy I used to eat every day*, just to keep him on his toes.'

The chinked glasses again and drank to that. As Beth sipped her wine studied Zoe's face, something was niggling her.

'So, you're all set?'

'Yessir.'

'Feeling good about it?'

'Yeah, sure, why do you ask?'

'Only, to be honest, you don't look that up for it.'

'Really?'

'Yeah, really—you look kinda, I don't know, in between the set pieces, I'm getting these little glimpses.'

'Glimpses? Jesus Beth. Glimpses of what?'

'Uncertainty.'

Zoe said nothing, half folded her arms and held her glass just under her mouth: 'Oh, shit. You know. With everything that's happened with Chance over the years. I think I'm gonna miss the chase.'

At that moment Easy came striding back in wearing his cowboy boots. He fetched the canvas bag from under the sink and plucked the shopping list from the fridge door. He looked at Beth then Zoe, zipped up his windcheater and left. After a moment, they heard the front door close.

'Does he know?'

'What?'

'The pivotal role he played in your romantic pursuit?'

'I don't know.'

'Well, you know what they say, Zoe—be kind to dumb animals.'

      *   *   *   *   *

Easy walked along Magazine towards the Whole Foods at Arabella Station. Either, he thought, life is one cool trip, or these girls are making some kind of fool out of me.

He didn't want to get dragged in, what man does? But then he remembered Beth down in the hall, those things she could do, then the soft whiteness of the skin on Zoe's back . . . *the incident, the incident . . .* and then the image of him, all got up in a fine penguin suit, with Lady Jane on his arm. It was all too much to think about at once.

He saw a pile of leaves drifted against a garden fence and kicked out at it in frustration. The dry leaves exploded into the sky, swarming, scattering, and blowing all over the street.

'Wow,' he said, calming and letting the smile open up his face, 'Ain't that the ding!'

      *   *   *   *   *

Jane sat in front of the mirror and drew the brush through her hair. The pair of invitations stood on the dressing table, the light playing on the embossed gold lettering.

Now that Easy had accepted the invitation her thoughts had turned to the actual night itself. When Fraser Sames had agreed to take her to the Prom she couldn't recall giving the matter another serious thought. When she overheard the other girls speculating about how far they'd go and what they were and were not prepared to do, it came as a quiet shock.

There had appeared to be an awful lot of rules, most of them in contradiction, about what was and what wasn't expected of the girl. One thing, however, was certain—the date had *rights* and *privileges*. Whether he was aware of these, or chose to exercise them, was entirely another matter but they were real, they existed, these rights, only when pressed, no-one could tell Jane precisely what they were and she dared not seek counsel from the older girls, nor even from Aunt Gillian.

In her own mind, however, Jane was quite clear. Fraser, being fully aware of his lowly position on her wish list, would not presume to entertain lofty thoughts of sexual conquest, if he ever entertained such thoughts at all. If on the other hand, he behaved himself, treated her with respect, and made a gallant, charming effort to win her affections, then she agreed beforehand, before the heat of battle, to let herself be persuaded to meet his lips, briefly, and for once kiss only, at the end of the last slow dance.

In the event however, Fraser was overwhelmed and passed out drunk, and the moment was lost. It wasn't much of a loss; their pairing never rising much above a running joke for the others, and the ordeal was quickly behind Jane. And she felt certain that it was the sheer weight of expectation that drove Fraser to such swift and decisive inebriation. The anticipation experienced in the girls' camp in the run up to the Prom was apparently being matched, dream for dream, boast for boast, and hope for hope amongst the boys.

And so as she leaned over and turned off her bedside lamp, her thoughts turned to Easy, and what hopes and expectations might be going through his mind in the run up to the Faculty Ball.

Did he presume rights? Certainly not, she'd made the grounds of the invitation quite clear. They were there with a job to do—an academic career to save.

But, on the other hand, they were consenting adults and part of the act would require them, in appearance at least, to be on some intimate terms. And if he behaved himself, treated her with respect, and made a gallant charming effort, who knows, she might be persuaded . . .

*   *   *   *   *

135

The bar was packed. Beth worked the sea of faces crowding the counter; she had this very special way of dealing with customers on a busy night, it could easily be described as an offended, indignant manner. She wasn't actually disrespectful, but quite obviously hostile. To the majority—the crowd en mass—she was plain rude, but then when she was dealing with the individual, focusing on the person, she was alert, and attentive, and nothing else mattered, and then she was gone.

With the cosy little clique at the end of the bar she was a completely different person; playful, good-humored, exuberant, and all this in full view of the crowd. And they stood for it, somehow. Took it as part of the act and were glad to be finally served.

'Seven & Seven, Vodka Cranberry, and three Dewars on the rocks—*with soda back*!' came the call. She wouldn't even flinch, pretend she hadn't heard the order and turn away in a kind of disgust, like she was stocktaking after hours and the only person in the joint.

But the drinks would be fix and mixed, trayed-up and passed over the counter with such speed and gusto that the glasses slid around and the mixers bubbled and it was a brave or drunken man who didn't step clear or duck.

'Thirty six bucks, without the tip,' she'd bawl back wearily, and she'd palm the dough and toss it in the register.

She kept the banter going of course, the place wouldn't have stayed open otherwise, and encouraged the staff to do the same, but it wasn't just for business—you'd be sacked for even thinking *Have a nice day*—the joint was for real.

'Bourbon,' came the call, 'Neat, any kind.'

'We only got one kind! Six bucks, without the tip.'

He was an Aussie, a backpacker, a big, fresh, unspoilt slab of man, the type of guy she homed in on most every night of the week. And he was looking over at her with undisguised lust—

'It's Donnie,' interrupted one of her waitresses holding out the cordless. She turned from the wide, tanned face, and took the call.

'Hey, Lady E, I just got your message. Did I hear you right or do you wanna think it over till the weekend?'

'No, Donnie, I don't want to think it over till the weekend. Just tell me what do I owe you, right now?'

'Right now, it's Four Thou, give or take a sawbuck, what's on your mind?'

'Lick your pencil, loverboy, 'cos here it comes.'

She slipped out her credit card and started to read out her number. In the mirror behind the optics she could see the backpacker, squeezed in by the ice-maker, sipping his bourbon and looking at her body. She flicked her hair over to one side and put all her curves on the one foot— hourglasses weren't in it.

It felt good to be getting rid of Donnie—paying him off, cutting him out like a bad growth.

'Is that it? We're through?'

'Sure, Donnie. Goodbye.'

'So long—'

'Goodbye.' She said it politely, meant it from the bottom of her heart and felt it go over. She hung up and turned round—

'Two Southern Comfort and a Single Malt!'

She turned away as if not hearing and fetched the ice. She was aware of the backpacker's eyes on her. She could feel his big generous smile, almost see his teeth glowing. He was just waiting for that flash of eye contact and in the end she couldn't avoid him.

'I hate to be forward, lady, but I just got here and every where in town is, like, totally full up or a complete rip-off. I just wondered if you knew anywhere I could crash? Just, you know, for one night?' And with that he shot her a wonderfully unambiguous smile.

He had the genuine outdoor look; real natural. Yesterday, this guy was on the other side of the world, he'd made this journey to be right in front of her and ask her if she knew anywhere he could sleep that night. He could have been any man or everyman on the planet.

'Nice try, honey, but I don't think so.'

*   *   *   *   *

Since purchasing the small, fire-engine-red dress, an irrational fear had grown in Zoe that its appeal and effectiveness were all some Magazine boutique store ruse. A funhouse mirror deception. A trick of the light, and she'd simply bought the best dress of a bad selection, and out of desperation had convinced herself it was the real thing.

It was either that or the other distraction; something which she hadn't fully processed even yet. That strange smile, which she couldn't quite determine was a wonderful openness or just plain vacancy.

And then the contact; the heat of him down there, coming right through their clothing. She had backed into him deliberately. *Accidentally on purpose.* She'd wanted confirmation, validation, more of whatever emotion it was that was playing around with those strange, offbeat features.

That contact had set something off in her. An alarm bell. Distant but distinct, a firetruck, but definitely heading her way.

Standing before her bedroom mirror she realised she was wrong about the dress: it still looked and felt amazing. It transformed her, emotionally, psychologically, and physically. She became the desirable predator.

Her narrow hips and flat stomach leapt back from the mirror, the form turning, twisting, drawing itself in until her shape became *super*natural, alien, but even more desirable.

Her face was all she really recognised, these lips, these incredible cheekbones, the wide flat eyes—alive only when she smiled. What was really going on behind them? She could not fathom. She was not, it seemed, party to her own dark secrets. Clearly, she didn't trust herself.

She put the thermometer in her mouth, under her tongue, and seeing her reflection, abruptly turned away.

Neither did she see herself bending back the small safety pin and driving the point through the centre of the packets of wrapped condoms, one after another after another.

She withdrew the thermometer—39.2°. Perfect. She didn't need to verify the number against the ovulation chart, knew she was slap in the middle of the crimson red target window, but she did it anyway; that deep part of her, the other Zoe, still not taking any chances.

She now saw her reflection grinning back at her in cold detachment, as if it were trying to prove something to the real Zoe.

She applied lip-gloss to those thin, perfect, calculating lips, stood back and checked herself all over. Her breasts still sagged slightly—they would until the dress was zipped and the trap was sprung.

SNIFF

A t first she didn't register the car horn. The noise was too high-pitched, aggressive, and forceful. Also, not being part of her plan, the sound was being actively screened out by her subconscious. Its insistency however began to finally infiltrate her awareness. She checked the condoms were in the little inside pouch of her handbag, walked down the first floor hallway and eased the curtain back to look out to the street.

Chance's gleaming Z3 sat kerbside, purring. Headlights on full, a slight trail rising from the exhaust. 'Please don't toot,' she prayed, 'please don't be the man who toots.'

She could see through the passenger window to his lower chest, stomach, and legs. He was immaculately dressed in a charcoal gray pinstripe suite. His favorite Oswald Boateng. His hand rested on the manual shift, two inches of pure white cuff reaching passed the sleeve, a platinum cufflink.

'Please don't toot,' Zoe whispered.

The hand moved away to the steering wheel. The car horn blared, impatiently. Her head dipped and she sensed her shoulders just at that moment loosening, easing, freeing themselves of some unknown tension.

*   *   *   *   *

Jane lay chin deep in the bubble-bath with her eyes calmly closed and the scent of hot lavender, black lime, and pomegranate licking around her nostrils. The water, almost scalding, cocooned her and swam in boiling currents around her thighs as she gently sank her knees, relaxed, and let them rise again.

She'd gathered all her mousy bob into a throw-away shower-cap and the tiny bubbles clung to her neck and shoulders and popped.

She could only feel these sounds as she had decadently brought her mp3 player in with her and was listening to Ondrej Lenard conducting Tchaikovsky's Piano Concerto No.1 in Bb- on her noise equalling head-phones.

She accompanied Ondrej with an antique Bakelite back scrubber and twitching nods of the head. Her sensory envelope completed with images of black velvet, royal purple cumberbands, and microscopic close-ups of the thick close-shaven stubble on Easy's Adam's apple.

*   *   *   *   *

Easy lay on his cot bed reading the Smithsonian Encyclopaedia of American History (*Children's Edition, 1973*). It was pretty heavy on the moon landings, and he got to wondering what had happened to all that euphoria.

He heard footsteps in the hall outside his door and looked up to see the round, brass, door handle rotating slowly and silently. The door swung slowly wide and Zoe stepped in quietly. She wore the red woollen dress and an uncertain expression; animal and fox-like.

She looked around the tiny space and he remembered the last time they were up here together, on that first day when she and Beth had showed him the room.

'Man, that dress,' he said, 'You'd make the Pope kick the pew!'

His words seemed to have no effect on her. She took another step inside, those gazelle hips, jutting forward, pushing against the wool.

'What are you doing?' Her voice came mellow and dreamlike.

'Just cramming my MBA,' he smiled and spun the book to the foot of the bed.

Now she smiled. Fine, maybe he'd find out sometime soon what she had on her mind. She took a quick breath and seemed about to say something when—*PARP*—the car horn blasted again.

'Hey. Is that our hot date?' She nodded. 'Seems pretty keen to get at it.'

'Not keen enough, however, to ring the damn doorbell.'

The looked at each other a long moment and he was aware of this void between them; vast, uncomfortable, expanding.

Zoe stood hovering, almost levitating in the stunning red dress and he just lay there in his blue jeans and a tee-shirt. He suddenly wanted to leap across that void. Close down this space between them. But what would he do when he got there? Hold her, kiss her . . . those painted lips, her face looked perfect, he wanted to brush his lips over those cheekbones.

Zoe's cell rang muffled in her handbag. It didn't startle either of them, but pulled this odd moment into focus. She took a little half step backward, putting her weight on the other heel and he thought she was going to open the clip and answer the call. She didn't; didn't make any attempt at all—just stared down at Easy.

'Oh, shit,' he whispered. 'You ain't gonna get that?'

'What would I say?'

'That he should get off his ass . . . and ring the damn doorbell like a gentleman.'

The phone continued to ring. They continued to look at each other.

Zoe now half turned from Easy and lifted her hair up from the nape of her neck. Easy could see the dress was only half zipped. That triangle of smooth white skin. His hands pressed themselves into the mattress, raising his weight off the bed, he realised what he was doing and hesitated. Zoe cocked her head round to look at him.

The phone had stopped ringing and the silence was whole and complete. Their eyes were locked into each other now, the void between them gone.

The doorbell now rang. A loud, shrill, distant sound.

In one easy movement, he rose off the bed, kicked the door shut and slipped his wicked arms around that wicked waist.

*   *   *   *   *

Zoe went to the bathroom and turned on the shower. She could still smell him on her skin. Kissing him had reminded her of kissing boys at high school; those eternal explorations in the dark corners of community halls, where your jaws ground away on automatic, your tongues fought little eager duels, and all you had to do was remember to breathe, keep tabs on where his hands were going, and not giggle as hot, tickly shots of breath jetted up your nostrils.

She tested the heat of the water—not too hot—and stepped under the stream.

She wasn't dirty but wanted to be fresh. The sex had been good, much better than she had imagined. He was natural, gave himself over

141

completely, then retreated into his shell, regrouped, wasn't clingy or needy. She liked that.

He'd gone down between her legs and she had done the same to him. She wanted to check him over, smell he was clean, as if that meant anything. It struck her as sad, comic and shocking that after all the checking, research, and background detail she'd amassed on Chance, just because he couldn't ring a doorbell she was fucking the home-help.

As she washed herself she thought back to that silent awkward moment, just prior to making love—when you know it is definitely about to happen—and he reaches for the condoms, and you slide up the bed, ready.

That moment hadn't even occurred.

She'd wondered now where her mind was precisely at that second. While they were kissing and undressing, she'd planned it all out; if he reached for *his* bedside drawer, or maybe that old suitcase, she'd been ready and get to her handbag first and use her own supply. But they never skipped a beat, or batted an eyelid, he was kissing her then he was simply inside her and they made love.

Collusion was suspected second time round, when they once again blew right through the awkward impasse. By the third, after they'd held each other in their arms for over two hours without saying a solitary word, it was confirmed.

*   *   *   *   *

As she left the bathroom, Beth was waiting, silently, leaning against her bedroom door. Zoe didn't see her straight away and her face showed the surprise.

'Good night, I take it?'

'Yes,' she said, smiling, not wanting to talk, scared she'd put her foot in a bear trap. 'It was really nice.'

'D'you get the baffoes?'

'What?' Zoe really didn't want to get into it.

'The baffoes—Casamentos is famous for them.'

'Oh.' She refastened the towel around her hair and continued to move on down the corridor. 'We didn't quite get as far as the restaurant.' She reached for her door, smiled, and turned the handle.

'What—that's it? No low-down? No post-coital?'

'I'm tired, Beth. We'll talk later, yeah? I promise.'

'Yeah, you go put your feet up . . . like, high.'

Beth grinned, rolled off the door jam and went back into her room.

Zoe went into her room and began to get dressed. She calmed a little but realised she'd have to invent some seriously juicy detail to keep Beth happy and keep her from finding out what really went on.

Baffoes!

*   *   *   *   *

Mama-Lek held the dryer door wide open and shouted her high-pitched voice into the cavernous drum: 'He was sedoose. He was sedoose *two-time*!' She slammed the door, turned, smiled at Easy—and then cuffed him up the back of the head.

'Hey, I said this was different. I'm 'fessin' up. This time I, like, definitely made a move too.'

'You mada move too,' she said mockingly, 'Wha—self-defence!'

Man, he thought, once this old girl got you on the hook, you were cooked: 'I mean, I was complicit.'

'Comp-*lee-ceet*. Big word for takin' 'vantage of this crazy ho'monal freak. Wha's you problem? No have 'nuff bump-fuzzies with voodoo-mama?'

'What? Bump-fuzzies!' he said unable to prevent the image pop into his head. 'Oh, no! Jeez. Anyway, this isn't nothing like what Beth and I do.'

'No! How so? I gotta meet *dis* chick.'

'I mean this is like, for real.'

'Oh, you in love her?'

'No, Jesus H. I mean, this is for a purpose. You know, for her baby.'

'Oh, you jus heppin her for make baby.' She deftly threw a pair of tightly rolled sports socks at him: 'Dumb-ass, cun'ty-hick. Be you dumb-ass baby too. You fink 'bout dat?'

Easy had: A baby, his baby, after all this time. The thought never failed to make him smile. And with a classy, independent, working woman like Zoe. By any terms, this was a serious result.

Mama-Lek looked at his big, grinning, dumb-ass features: 'Hey,' she said, flashing her eyes at him in a mock seduction, 'you wanna come wuk my house?' She sidled over to him and pretended to ruck up against him like a little dog on heat.

'Okay, Mama-Lek, take it easy.'

'Wha—you get picky? C'mon loverboy, defend yo-seff!'

143

WAG

L unch had been stressful. Zoe had expected the Spanish Inquisition from Beth and she hadn't been disappointed. She wanted to know every detail of the date and it took the last of Zoe's storytelling, imagination, and energy to flesh out a convincing blow-by-blow account and satisfy her curiosity.

She decided early on to stick as close to the truth as possible. Keep it simple. Lies were slippery things, alive, cunning. The truth had chronology and a kind of built-in simplicity. Her descriptions of the flirting, foreplay, and distinct lack of pillow talk were honest, vivid, and persuasive. She simply swapped out Chance, wrote Easy into her scenario and worked around the changes. She realised, in fact, during the telling that this was pretty much what had happened in reality. And the trade, substitution, or exchange itself—if that's how it could be described—was still just too incredible a thing for her to even try to explain in any remotely accurate way.

Beth believed Zoe had discovered a different side to Chance and was intrigued. She saw utterly no resemblance to her own little trysts with Easy but was genuinely surprised Chance had been so damned romantic and, moreover, committed.

Zoe steered clear of all but the most basic descriptions of the restaurant, Chance's club, and his luxury apartment. She could invent it, but it didn't ring true, and after all, what was the point? Beth wanted a different type of detail; the emotional nitty-gritty, and she had that, plenty of that, so that's what she stuck to.

She found it surprisingly easy to talk about the sex, and convey the appropriate thrill, wonder, and self-satisfied afterglow. Also, she realised, as the story built layer upon layer, that her fictitious relationship with Chance—and specifically the next date with him—would provide the perfect cover for her next liaison with Easy. Maintaining the façade for now would be quite simple, effortlessly plausible, and somehow under the current circumstances, perfectly reasonable. The bigger the lie, it seemed, the more readily it was believed.

In the taxi home, however, when Beth quizzed and questioned Zoe again about her plan to get pregnant, fault lines in the story began to show.

'He does know, doesn't he?'

'Sure,' Zoe said but thinking of Easy.

'Well,' said Beth, 'That really does take the biscuit. All this time he's been dogging around the office and now, just like that, his granny dies and he wants a kid!'

Zoe didn't react to her irreverent tone and just smiled. 'Enough, Beth, eh? I feel like I'm on the grand final of Twenty Questions.'

'Okay, okay. I'm only kidding is all—kidding and damn confused.'

'Well, don't be. And anyway, I've said plenty, you haven't said a damn word about your latest exploit.' With that, it was Beth's turn to tighten up and Zoe realised she'd been missing the trick of counter pressure through the whole lunch. 'Come on, girl—dish the dirt.'

'There's really nothing to say.'

'What! I've just poured my heart out over the best part of two bottles of Sancerre and you've got *nothing to say*?'

'Well, it's complicated—'

'And me going for a child—' she paused, for effect, 'is what? Sportsnews?'

'I didn't mean that . . . God, I'm—'

Zoe felt sure Beth was actually going to say the word 'sorry'. It would have been a first, a seismic shift in their internecine rapport—but it never came. Beth just looked down and shook her head instead.

Zoe pressed on now, piling the questions up on Beth. Not because she really wanted to know about her latest jock-quest, but because it kept the spotlight off of her. She realised, also, with some relief, that her apparent, honest outpouring throughout the lunch had earned her some genuine breathing space to work out her next move. And she sensed a change in Beth, who normally had no problems elucidating the most depraved sexual episodes. It wasn't her reticence; this was more of a hesitation—almost a vulnerability—like perhaps she was finally needing more out of a relationship.

Beth asked the driver to pull over on Magazine, five blocks short of home. She didn't want to be having this conversation in the house.

'What are you doing?'

'Let's walk,' she said, getting out and paying the fare, 'I could do with some air.'

Zoe knew it was just an excuse to change the subject: Fat chance. She nipped away at her for the full five blocks and Beth got more and more snappy with every step they took towards the house.

'Just let it go, Zoe, will you?'

'But I don't see the big deal—either you are seeing the same guy again or you're not.'

'Well then I am. But he don't smoke no goddamned pipe!'

They entered the house and Beth hoped that was the end of it. She wanted to fetch herself a drink and go to her room.

Zoe felt cheated but this was masking a deeper concern: Although she'd lied her ass off right through lunch, her emotions had been real, it had been exhausting, and now she felt she deserved some honesty and openness in return. But underneath this, she genuinely hoped Beth had finally met some one worth seeing again. Someone who could get through that iron hull and melt that heart. She was happy and wanted others to have whatever it took to make them happy too.

'So who was it then?' she pressed, 'Who have you been seeing?'

'Look, you can't possibly know him, so why bang on?' She turned away and entered the living room, where Jane was sat opening mail and Easy was preparing food in the kitchen area.

'Just give me a name. So I'll know next time who we're talking about.'

Beth shook her head, Zoe thought it was over and although frustrated was just deciding to let it go when Beth, almost to herself, added: 'It's just some new guy.'

'Whoa,' Zoe pounced, 'Some *new guy*.'

'Yeah, so what?'

'That's great. New Guy. *New* Guy! Because *New Guy* is like one huge step closer to *boyfriend*.'

Beth stiffened at that, caught like a rabbit. 'Oh, girl,' she said, trying to affect nonchalance, 'you're beginning to sound like Sister Jane.'

'Don't bring me into it,' barked Jane.

'But *New Guy* means,' continued Zoe, 'like, you're still seeing him?'

Beth was working very hard not to look in Easy's direction but equally she wanted to see how he was taking this. Her body was stiff, her movements awkward, and she really had nothing to say.

'Ha!' Screamed Zoe. 'It's true.'

'I might, so what?'

'There is life between Playgirl and Hormone Replacement Therapy.' Zoe threw her arms wide: 'Beth's discovered romance.'

Beth could feel Easy's eyes upon her now. She suddenly felt acutely alone, exposed, and weak. Zoe and Jane had never seen her like this before and for a split second she seemed about to cave in and cry.

'Lord, Beth,' said Jane, 'Are you alright?' She spoke softly and with feeling but it came over slightly sarcastic.

'What the hell is it to you?' she spat back.

Jane rose, walked to the door then turned and said: 'Because if you're going to start acting like a normal human being, I'd like, if at all possible, to support you.'

Touché . . .

Jane left. Beth slumped into the sofa—in about thirty seconds she'd ask Easy to fix her a drink. Zoe sat at the table, watching the back of Beth's head, trying to figure out whether this was a great or terrible day.

Easy hummed his little 'Plastic Jesus' tune.

*   *   *   *   *

'What's gotten into you, Chicken?' His voice was mellow and rich and he had a sparkle at the corners of his eyes.

Zoe was lying in bed when the call came through her computer. Since he'd learned to Skype, her Dad had been crazy about it, he used it all the time and it had breathed a new life into him and their long distance relationship.

'What are you talking about?' she lied, but she couldn't deny the deep, peaceful glow of serenity she was giving off, even on the two-inch screenshot.

'You quit that paper? Got promoted? What?' As he spoke, Easy entered from the hallway. He knew to keep behind the laptop, out of frame, and came to the bottom of the bed, and held up two little pairs of baby booties—one pair pink and one pair blue.

Zoe smiled: 'You're seeing things, pop. I'm just the same old me.'

'Well, I like what I see, baby.'

147

She smiled at both men and Easy shook the blue booties and raised his eyebrows. 'Look, Dad, I'll call you later, okay. I'm gonna be late for a shoot.'

'Zoe, baby—whatever you're doing—just keep on doing it, okay.'

She flushed a little: 'I'll call you, dad, later today.'

'You know what,' he said knowingly, with a big generous smile, 'somehow, I don't hope you do.'

She cut the call, climbed over the laptop and kissed Easy. He dangled both pairs of booties again: 'Seemed to make sense at the time.'

'How long we got?'

'Beth's stock-taking and Jane's at a fitting for her ball gown.'

They smiled at each other and began to undress.

*   *   *   *   *

The night was hot and quiet and a colossal moon hung high, bright, and silent over the city. Zoe stood gazing up at its sheer fullness in awe. Its Silver Mountains shone in noiseless brilliance and every desert lowland from the Sea of Showers to the Sea of Crises were clear, dark, and achingly mystical.

She could never remember a moon so enormously detailed, captivating, and perfect and for a split second she completely forgot what had driven her out to the back yard at this hour—then she felt the grit falling from her grasp and her primal, selfish plan snapped back into focus. She gathered a little more grit, took aim, and threw it up at the tiny dormer window.

The tiny stones showered down on the shingle, bounced, and scattered away. Surely he must have heard that . . .

Easy registered the tick-tick-dance of grit and got off the bed to open the window. He saw Zoe alone in the darkness, the bright oval of her face gazing eagerly up at him and he gestured calmly down to her. Zoe understood and tiptoed off quietly to wait in the tool shed.

Easy closed the window and turned back to the room where Beth sat on his bed drinking her vodka and looking at herself in the tiny wardrobe mirror.

'Christ!' she whispered, 'Someone should invent a mirror with a conscience.'

She had slipped into one of her moods immediately after her orgasm. The sex had been brief, lusty, energetic, but unsatisfying. She was sure that he hadn't come, although he'd pretended to, and she was left to

148

conclude, with that horrible sinking feeling, that he was gradually, but undoubtedly going off her.

'Come off it,' he said brightly, 'You've got a figure that could stop a coal barge . . . ' he hesitated, read her look, and added, 'and the watch in the pilot's pocket.'

She smiled but it drained away as she met her reflection again.

He hadn't been fair to her: He'd thought about Zoe whilst they'd had sex. Thought about her, wanted to feel that body, its strength, vigour, and purpose, instead of Beth's. He didn't have any trouble getting an erection, he still found Beth attractive, sexy, animalistic, but he hadn't been able to ejaculate. Part of him was thinking about meeting up with Zoe at midnight and as he ran lap after lap, steadily getting exhausted, he just couldn't get himself down the back straight.

They'd had to be quiet. Zoe and Jane were in bed, so when he couldn't take it anymore he pretended to come, intimately, keeping restraint, holding himself back, a big goddamned Act. He'd thought he'd been quite convincing but now realised she'd seen right through it.

'When I've been with you,' she said softly, still looking at herself, 'I look at myself and I can really see me—with all my paint and wrinkles—like I've just ran into an old friend.'

Easy pulled on a fresh t-shirt, and sat down next to her on the bed: 'And how does that make you feel?'

'In a word—Mortal.'

'Hell, Betty. At times, you can be the real plummet-pie.' He rose, tucked his t-shirt into his jeans, made those grunts and gestures that he hoped would get her to shift herself.

'You're all right. But you gotta look after yourself better. Start eating good, exercise a li'l, lay off the booze.'

He took her empty glass from her and helped her up.

'Like you, you mean?'

'Just keep it simple, is all—If *you* don't start loving you, who can?'

He slapped his stomach and struck a few body-builder poses in the mirror. He knew she'd giggle and jollying-up someone else always made him feel great.

'Man,' she said, joking, but with an honesty that made him laugh, 'how can a guy be so good looking with just one head?'

Easy threw her on the bed, gave her a big kiss, then dragged her up rolled her out the door.

'Go to bed. Say your prayers. Let me sleep. I got chores.'

'Tomorrow,' she whispered, slinking away down the stairs.

I'LL BE YOUR DOG

*   *   *   *   *

The tool shed was warm and dark. Although it was silent, he knew she was there; he could taste her in the electric air as he stepped in.

'Where are you?' he whispered.

Zoe unlocked her cell phone and the screen cast her in soft blue light. She sat on the floor with her legs stretched out across a cosy pile of American quilts. She looked like a statue in marble, a modern mother-earth goddess.

'What kept you?'

He said nothing and just looked at her. She opened her gown to reveal her breasts and stomach.

That body.

He closed in and lay down with her, kissing her stomach and breasts and neck and lips. Her skin was warm and smooth, fresh from the tub.

She could taste the fresh toothpaste on his tongue, and smell soap on his skin. The last few times they'd had sex, she'd initiated—grabbing him when the house was empty, leading him up to her room. The shed had been his idea, for times when the others were at home. If they were disturbed, she could hide quickly, and he'd pretend to be sorting screws into jellyjars.

She noticed, since the first time, he'd cleaned away the tools and cobwebs and had fixed up and hung two candle lanterns. He'd also brought out the pile of fresh linen, which they'd keep in a tea chest. She liked that he was in for the long haul and was making the effort.

GROOM

'**W**ell, give the dog a bone,' said Beth as she and Zoe watched on in surprise. Jane strode up and back, modelling an elegant black velvet balldress. It clung stylishly, cut on the bias, to accentuate her youthful waist and neat, frank hips. She wore tight, white, elbow length gloves and a beautiful crimson-lined dolman. Her body waved and spun to and fro in its very best impersonation of Scarlett O'Hara.

Easy, sporting a hired wingtip shirt and dickie-bow tie, stood in astonished admiration, running her up and down, like she was some prize-winning French-Trotter.

'You got it down, lady.'

'Why, thank you, kind *sah*,' she replied wallowing in her new found grace. In truth, Jane looked fabulous, chic, pleasing, and stylish, but she still retained an edge of fragility, a brittleness, as if one word could deflate or shatter her and make her give it all up in an instant.

At first, Beth couldn't quite handle the balldress as anything other than an absurd joke, but as Jane grew in confidence and the possibility grew real that she might survive the first five minutes, she became more openly savage.

Zoe, for her part, perceived no threat in the arrangement and was deeply happy for Jane, in the way that one can be for a niece or God-daughter on a first big date.

'Well, whadayaknow,' bawled Beth, 'it's a woman all along.'

Jane ignored her, and ran her gloved-palms across her teenage midriff and turned to watch admiringly as Easy slipped on his jet black tuxedo jacket.

'God,' he hissed, 'I shoulda got into this dressing up game years back. I've got the shape for it, I reckon.'

'Very handsome,' said Zoe, with a genuineness that drove a fresh spike into Beth.

'Very handsome,' agreed Jane.

'Nice outfit,' said Beth, 'What—you lease it from Critter Kingdom?'

Easy smiled, turned to her, unfazed: 'Nope. I found it on the back seat of the Tchoupitoulas streetcar! Just my size, ain't it?'

Beth laughed cruelly but the mock stuck in her throat. 'He looks like Desperate Dan.'

'Well—' said Jane, 'You'd know desperate, wouldn't you?'

'Screw you!'

Then the doorbell RANG the end of the round and Jane peered out to the street: 'That's us.'

'I feel great,' said Easy, enjoying one last look at himself in the mirror.

'You look it,' smiled Zoe, 'Really. You both do.'

'Hey,' grinned Easy, 'do you think they'll call our names out as we walk in?'

Jane frowned: 'Maybe.'

'I've always wanted that to happen,' he squeezed her hand then twitched like he'd been hit by a pebble: 'Diggity ding! I almost forgot.'

He rushed to the kitchen, pulled open a drawer and returned brandishing a medium sized, coral corsage. He began to pin it on to Jane's dress, above the right breast. She was utterly flattered.

'I did a bit of book looking on etiquette. This flower is all part of it. It's called a courage.'

'Corsage,' corrected Jane.

'Oh, right—'

'Freakshow,' hissed Beth.

'I'd like to see you at a ball, Betty,' replied Easy, 'fanning yourself with a dinner plate.'

'Go on, you two' interrupted Zoe, 'get going.'

'Hang on a minute.' Easy slipped his arm around Jane's waist and pulled her in towards him: 'Let's do this thing right. There, look it.'

Jane now saw their tight reflections in the full-length mirror—immaculate, avid, suddenly sophisticated. Beth could take no more and stomped away to the kitchen and the comfort of the refrigerator.

'I feel magical.'

152

'Well, it's a magical night.'

She turned to him, took in their closeness: 'You're giving off something . . . an aura.'

'It's my aftershave.'

'No, it's . . . it smells like apples. Apples and fresh rust.'

It meant nothing to Easy: 'It must be how I smell.'

They returned to their reflections.

'Look at us,' said Jane. 'We're like a couple of Kingfishers. Look at our markings.'

He grabbed her then and they danced, hulking, amateur but confident. Easy led the way and that's all that mattered. The little flourish began to work on Zoe, drawing out some itch close enough to be called jealousy: 'He'll drive off if you don't hurry.'

'Don't worry about us,' laughed Easy, 'We could turn up a day late looking like this.'

The bell rang again, filling the hall with a magnetic pull. Easy and Jane danced out through the door and down the corridor.

Beth and Zoe were left with each other, separated by the counter top, listening as they door opened, bounced and slammed shut like a gaol-cell.

Beth showed Zoe the Vodka bottle. She shook her head and looked around to find where she'd set down her cranberry Monavie.

Beth filled a highball with ice and poured herself a small liver scar's worth of sparkling silent vodka.

'Hey—I got one. What do you call that soft bit at the end of a guy's pecker?'

Zoe thought, disinterested, and shrugged.

'The girlfriend!'

Zoe's laugh came out more like a *humph*: 'Drink your damn vodka, Beth.'

Beth rattled the bottle back into the door of the icebox as Zoe gathered and plumped the cushions, and got herself comfortable on the couch.

The night could go one of two ways: they could have a girlie-chat, which would get way too detailed, tricky, and uncomfortable for either of them to actually enjoy. Or, they could try and find something good on the T.V., a movie, a comedy hour, anything to get them through the evening without admitting that they suddenly, and apparently, had very little in common.

Beth flipped through the first dozen channels without success. Zoe sat beside her flicking through the T.V. guide.

'What do you fancy?' asked Beth.

153

'Nothing heavy. Nothing real.'

Beth skipped over the sports stations, live medical shows and weird body programmes. A slight nervous, unease began to build in each of them. She hit on a third-rate, derivative dance contest, which promised forty minutes of mind-numbing escape, but as soon as the first couple began their routine, the man's tight ass turned Beth's thoughts immediately back to Easy and Jane.

'You have a go,' she said and passed the remote to Zoe as she got up to refill her glass.

*   *   *   *   *

To Easy, Tulane Campus represented a mystical otherworld. A biosphere populated by a different kind of human being; not only the educated, but the educable. It was real—more than real—hyper-vivid, super-vital, and alive. Not just a tangible reality, like the house, work, and sex, but an aspiring, minutely considered, cleansed reality: Somehow whole, interconnected, and full of endless theoretical possibilities.

He felt strangely optimistic.

It's was a candy store of thinking, all Gob-Stoppers, Sherbert Dips, and Boston Baked Beans ('How did they reach the books on top?'), laid out in a perfect mini-city, somehow separated from the garbage strewn, wind-swept, über-reality of the street, mindfully ring-fenced in the invisible barbed-wire of Academia.

He sensed money too, but now it didn't matter, it was too opulent and abundant to be the focus of anything.

True wealth, he assumed.

They reached the ballroom building, golden light pouring from the tall, gracious windows, splashing the lawns in soft yellow pools. Music, laughter, and the eternal tinkle-chink of crystal. Chandeliers, champagne, and chauffeur's key-fobs.

The waiter, buttoned into a scarlet-red tunic greeted them, tipped, and listened with due intent.

Easy and Jane step into the main ballroom.

'Miss. Jane Grayson and Mr. Easy, Esq.,' he announced and a sizeable chunk of the hall fell quiet. Jane saw Hugo, mingling with a dignified, but stiff group of historians and wives. The group looked up with a mix of amusement and curiosity, and then continued with their chitter-chatter.

Easy slipped the waiter some money. Jane didn't see how much; the Waiter pocketed the bills and slipped away effortlessly.

'Ain't you always wanted to come in like that?' he beamed.

She nodded, slid her gloved palm over his lapel: 'Thank you,' she said in a whisper.

'Pleasure. What d'you want we do now?'

Jane was incredibly glad he'd agreed to come with her. It was paying off and it was going to be all right. She looked around with a growing confidence and noticed the History wives shooting volleys of nasty little arrows.

'Champagne,' she announced and Easy led the way.

Having ordered and taken possession of two chilled flutes of Champagne, Easy tried to pay the barman and learned he was at his first ever free bar. Abundance and opulence and no one lying drunk in their own vomit in the corner.

Class.

They toasted one another then Jane and Easy threw back their first flutes of Champagne. The second, third, and fourth followed swiftly and Easy sneezed with such astonishing volume and violence after each glug that it was only made believable by its perfect repetition.

'Are you okay?'

'Hell, yeah, I think so. What's in this stuff, anyways?'

'Wine. Wine and bubbles.'

'It works—in quantity. You 'bout ready for a dance?'

She hesitated, felt the fear and decided to go for it anyway. He made her feel different, out of herself, not confident exactly, not safe, but otherhow, different, as if she was wearing fancy dress.

Easy led her confidently, tracing the rim of the other dancers. They swooned past Hugo and the clique and she registered their animosity and picked up on the haywire of confusion. It was working. Hugo, smiled, the master tactician, the play-maker, match-maker . . . had she just thought that?

No mind. Push on, fold into this man, this wide, healthful chest, flute in hand, feet in time. Spin and swoon, gliding away.

She caught Hugo's eyes again, just once, for a split second but it might as well have lasted aeons. The clarity of his bright mood, shining amidst the dull, parched faces of Clements and the clique. Keep your enemies closest. They were confounded and would break up and disintegrate now. The fragments would gravitate towards Hugo. Seek his opinion and guidance, peel off Clements and orbit his new sun, until Clements too, alone, distanced, and dark, would find him out and beg place at his rim. A new Pluto.

Jane slipped and almost fell off her high heels. A shriek—gay, bursting with abandon, escaped, rushed from her and was born. Easy caught her toppling back, stepping out of herself and they folded away into each other and the shadows off the dance floor.

More Champagne followed, followed by more sneezing. At a corner table, overrun with discarded drinks, half empty bottles, and party debris, they found themselves, loose-limbed, excitable, and thoroughly soaked in sweat and each other's company.

'Did I tell you I was a Virgo?'

Easy shook his head in sympathy and understanding then perked up with a thought.

'I didn't think you got women Virgos?'

'What?' She looked at him, waiting for the other half of the joke; he stared at her, solemn and quite serious.

'Anyway,' he picked up, 'I thought you said you didn't believe in star signs?'

'I don't,' Jane said, 'I mean, how can anybody really, you know . . . such twaddle.'

Easy gave her a wide-eyed look: 'Man, are you kidding, I love that stuff . . .'

'Really?'

'Sure. I eat that stuff up.' He sat up straight and fixed her in the eye. As he spoke she began to notice just how drunk he was. Little glimpses of oblivion beckoning through his increasingly childish enthusiasm. 'When I lived in Baton Rouge a buddy of mine, PeeWee, was across the river in Port Allen. One day, I'm walking over Horace Wilkinson bridge and I suddenly realise—wow—what a miracle it is.'

'What?'

'That I can actually find his place at all!' He half stood, reached between his legs, and pulled his chair up close to the table. 'See, we're ninety-three million miles from the Sun?' He gave her a wide-eyed look like this might have been news to her.

'I'm aware of that,' she said, adding, 'Yes,' when her voice came out sounding vague and non-committal.

Easy now snatched up and arranged various items from the table: Empty Champagne flutes, cake plates, and half-full ashtrays became the sun, planets, and moons of our own solar system.

'Well, it kind of goes like this—once you know that magic number, the ninety-three million, you can work out our Orbit.' He circled his half-full flute around the heavy stellar ashtray. 'First off, you double the ninety three million to get the Orbit's width.' Then you multiply that number—

one hundred and eighty-six million—by this funny number called Pi!' He gave her the eyebrows again. 'Don't look at me,' he said, tucking his chin in and curling out his lower lip, 'it was some academician who sucked that one out of his thumb. And that ain't the half of it—this number, this Pi, is the only number no one has ever pinned down. That's right! They know it's over three and under four but when they try to nail it—to give it the exactitude behind the decimal point—it just keeps on going, shifting around on them and hiding out in its own little infinity. Which is kind of crazy when you really shine your light on it—there being this infinity right there in between good old number three and four.' He fixed Jane brightly with his head cocked slightly to one side, the bar lights shone in his eyes. 'Stick with me here now, sister, 'cos this next little ditty really dills the pickle!'

Jane laughed. Easy shuffled in his seat and took a deep breath—

'The Orbit works out about six-hundred-million miles. That means the Earth is tearing through space at over one-and-a-half million miles a day. Can you imagine? I walk over Horace Wilkinson and PeeWee's apartment is one and a half *million* miles away from where it was yesterday. But then so is the Bridge, and the Mississippi, and everything else—even crazy old me!' He paused, trying to get his head round this whole deal again. 'I guess that's what Albert was trying to tell us 'bout relativity.' He smiled to himself. 'Plus a librarian once told me the good Earth is spinning—which I already knew—but not at a thousand miles an hour!' He considered draining off his Champagne, but, deciding against it, set his flute down and rubbed the tops of his head vigorously with his formed fist. The hair stood up, pointing clean up to the stars. 'I nearly fell in the drink thinking about it!' He slapped his knees and rubbed his hands together. 'Then PeeWee tells me when the moon goes around us it pulls the surface of the Earth up towards it like a big water-balloon. It only moves about ten feet but still, these Puerto Rican guys live right above PeeWee and you wouldn't wanna knock on their door by mistake.'

He lit the candle on the table, thrust a cold coffee cup and saucer into Jane's hands and grabbed up a couple of shot glasses. 'Then I read in a book that the other planets make us wobble as we swoosh past each other and our Sun—which is, as you know, just a star up close—is pulled about by other stars in the very same way . . . and, and, and our whole galaxy is pulled about by other galaxies! And all the time we're every*thing*one*of*us zooming away from this Big Bang that supposedly got the whole show started.'

His eyes burned, Jane was captivated. He was a Shaman, a Seanachaí, the false prophet, Akhenaten incarnate.

'And, thankfully,' Easy said, 'someone clever billygoat can break the whole wonderworld of it down into these twelve easily understandable Star Signs.' Easy blew out the candle and held up the flutes: 'Of course I believe it. Now, what do you wanna do more of first—dancing or sneezing?'

Jane sat for a moment, charmed and mesmerized: 'Sneezing.'

*   *   *   *   *

The Champagne had begun to run low behind the bar. Bottles of thinner, sweeter, decidedly cheaper wine were now being passed off in the calculated hope that everyone was too tight to notice. Or, if like Easy, they did notice, they were too tight to complain.

'I'm not drinking that,' announced Jane, to the barman. ' I asked for a glass of Champagne.' She was fierce and fiery and suddenly sober, but it all melted away like a snowflake on your fingertip when she sipped the real wine and thanked the barman.

They whirled around the floor under the glitter ball. The dancers had thinned out a little, and the bar and tables were crowded, loud, and busy. She knew she was being watched, could sense the low electric intensity each time she was in clear view of Clements, but she soon lost herself to the music, the rhythm, Easy's confident, muscular lead, and the slow, firm grip of the alcohol.

'You want some air?'

Her cheek was scrunched on his shoulder. The suit fabric smelled hot and clean, of Borax and soda-crystals. She imagined Easy's neat, spicy odour working through from the other side. She didn't care. What had he asked? She couldn't actually open her eyes with ease and so just laughed.

'C'mon,' she heard him say, decisively.

They staggered off, pushing through the silhouettes, she could feel the noise and colours zipping past, her heels struck the ground noisily. Then a blast of cool, night air. Soothing her cheeks, licking her neck, sharp in her nostrils. Their feet crunching over the courtyard gravel. Unsteady now in the heels, she clung to him. His step was firm and assured. Their arms fast around each other like Siamese twins.

She noticed he held a full bottle, must have swiped it on the way out. It hung loosely from his hand and he swigged from it occasionally.

She placed her head on his shoulder again. Felt his arm slip down her back, rest and hold at her hip. She found her hands and clasped them together, secure around him, the easy sway of his gait. Safe.

'You okay?'
'Mmm . . . '
'You sure?'
' . . . '
'Jane?'
'I need to sit down.'
'You need to keep walking. Get some of this good night air into your bloodstream, baby.'

They walked on like that for a while. Crunch, crunch, out of the courtyard, across the campus, their steps in time. Her calves grew cold, a shiver ran up her back, and she stopped and opened her eyes.

'What's up?'
'I need to tinkle.'
'Oh, okay.' He looked away, back towards the buildings.
'Like now.'
'Right, right now.' She shoved off him and headed for the dense blackness of the trees. Easy looked around, suddenly alone, silent. Then a crashing sound came through branches: 'Oh, Lordie.'

He went after her.
'You okay? I'm coming.'

*   *   *   *   *

The neat stream of pale urine dived and bubbled into the water in a small, thunderous staccato. Zoe curled her wrist to manoeuvre the tiny fabric window into the jet . . . momentarily exploding it, sending warm rivulets scattering minutely over the back of her hand.

She looked at the pencil—blank, of course—and balanced it on the lip of the sink. She wiped, pulled up her panties and jeans and rinsed her hands under the faucet.

Still blank.

She couldn't face herself in the mirror. Couldn't physically command her neck muscles to lift her head and meet her own gaze. What was she going to see? Her eyes seemed willing, but rebellious, they kept low but found her shadow falling across the basin. The shape commanded, demanded her attention. This was her. This was *she*. This is the shape of her shadow seconds before she might know she was pregnant.

Still blank.

A few strands of hair were misbehaving, escaping the shadowmass and digging out across the tiled wall. Her shadowhand gathered them in.

Still blank.

A sudden glimpse of her reflection . . . the pull was too great and she abruptly faced the detail of herself. The reality of the moment.

Still blank . . . no. A shadow, a faint blue blemish. A darkening band of tone, strengthening, emerging, becoming.

Her reflection: its eyes clear, brilliant, and foreign. The skin (her skin), the cheekbones (her cheekbones), her lips, vivid, alive, somehow irreversibly new and different.

The distinct strip of navy blue.

Certainty.

The limits of confirmation blurring, changing already.

Minutely studied.

Vivid.

Unmistakable.

Pregnant.

*   *   *   *   *

The branches spread out in dense blankets against the sky. Jane leaned back against the huge ancient tree, drew in the heady familiar scent and watched Easy drink from the bottle.

'Mmmm. That smell.'

'Pine,' he said.

'Cedar, silly. Where did you say you grew up?'

'Pisgah,' he grinned, remembering.

'Bless you,' she said, using his old joke. 'Where on Earth is *Pisgah*?'

'Halfway between McLain and Citronelle.'

'That's Alabama!'

'Citronelle is, I guess, Pisgah's right on the state line but Louisiana all the way.'

'What was that like—growing up out there?'

'Compared to what? It was just like any place. And it was all I knew.' He took another high sip of the wine. 'I remember a lot of chores, splitting logs, plucking chickens, and a three-mile walk to the schoolhouse.'

'What did you do for fun?'

'Split logs, pluck chickens, walk three-miles to the schoolhouse.' He chuckled. 'Naw, we did a lot of fishing, rough-housing, making camp, whatever.'

'Boy's own stuff, huh?'

160

'I guess. There'd be a dance maybe. Or a family wedding. Cook-ups most Friday nights when the men came home, and the Chicken Drop every Saturday at the Spendthrift Bar and Grill.'

'What in the good Lord's name a Chicken Drop?'

'Hell, girl. Where you been all your life? You really don't know what a Chicken Drop is?'

'No sir.'

'It's a Louisiana Institution. First everybody gets drunk, women included. Then by about five in the afternoon you head down to the Spendthrift. Herb, the owner, charges everybody a dollar but for that you're also buying a numbered floor tile in the dancehall.'

'Why?'

'That's what I'm trying to telling you—for the Chicken Drop. Once all the tickets are sold, you pile in and after a few more kegs of beer, Herb appears with this chicken called Lucky—'

'A chicken called Lucky?'

'Well—it's a different chicken every week but it's *always* called Lucky.'

'Why?'

'Because he ain't yet in the deep fat fryer.'

Jane explodes.

'Then after a bit of introduction and ceremony, Herb blows straight up Lucky's ass—'

'Why does he do that?'

'Custom, I guess. But we all think Herb kinda likes it. Then he throws Lucky up in the air and he lands on the floor and tears about in the spotlights, squawking, and clucking with all the kids chasing behind. It's a blast, a pandemonium, a real hootenanny, and this carries on until Lucky decides or otherwise to take a poop.'

'And whoever has the tile where it poops is the winner?'

'Yep. And they scoop the jackpot. Then we drag the tables out and eat.'

'In the same room?'

'Sure. It's the country. You get used to poop. Poop's everywhere.'

'What happens to Lucky?'

'Ah, then he ain't so lucky.' He made a deep, sizzling sound.

'He weren't that Lucky anyway. Not with the kids chasing him and the spotlights and Herb blowing up his derrière.'

'Yeah, I guess it seems kinda strange. Maybe that's why in Pisgah we don't kiss when we greet.'

Jane laughs again.

'You know what I miss most though, about being a kid? The . . . ' he clicked his fingers, recalling the word, 'the intimacy of it.' He turned and

161

stood along side her, leaned himself against the trunk. 'I remember going back to school one morning, after a long hot summer and my favorite T-shirt—the one I'd been wearing the whole damn year—was suddenly *pastel.*'

'Pastel!'

He nodded: 'The little man hormones were kicking in at the school yard and somehow colors—especially *pastel* colors—now mattered a whole great deal. That closeness we had began to slip away and you quit wrastlin' each other and it turned into a kickin' and punchin' game instead,' he smiled and flattened his misshapen nose.

'Boys.'

'It ain't just boys, sure, something dark gets going around that age for us but we're all changing so fast. I remember how some of the girls you'd seen only six weeks before the holidays had just suddenly grown up— "Hey boys, Bessie Allen's got *ta-tahs*."'

Jane laughed and jabbed him in the ribs, playfully. He offered her the bottle, she refused and he took a long drink then set the bottle down.

'Hey,' she said, 'you didn't sneeze.' This seemed as much news to Easy. She took up the bottle and took another sip. She was sobering up and cooling down fast. 'The bubbles are going. We need another.'

'You sure?' he asked, making to get up.

'Sure,' she said, but tell me another story first.

'What about?'

'Pisgah—you're first girlfriend.'

'I remember fooling around with this girl, Eulalie Babin, she weren't no girlfriend, we were practically cousins. She was pretty though and a brave little thing. Used to ring chickens' necks as soon as throw 'em hayseed. One of the older girls dared me to put my hand up Eulalie's skirt one Sunday after church and when I did I 'bout jumped clean out my bib and tucker. Eulalie had hair, a little wiry clump of it like rolling tobacco. She slapped me so hard. The older girls laughed. Man, I ran so fast. I took clean off and threw myself in the river.'

He laughed out loud and the moonlight dappled his face. He noticed how intently she was looking at him. 'That was the end of me and Eulalie.' He got up, 'I'll go get that champagne.'

'Technically . . .' said Jane, then stopped and cleared her throat, 'Technically, I'm still a virgin.'

He stopped and turned to her: 'Technically?'

'The last time I did anything remotely . . .' she fluttered her hand in the air vaguely before her, 'was at a Future Farmers of America dance. That was over eight years ago, behind a hay-loft. I—well, nothing, really . . . I dare say it wouldn't count in a junior school playground. The boy just . . . well, to be honest he just ruined a good dress.'

'Okay.'

'That was pastel too, if I recollect.'

They grinned at each other, then she put her hands together behind her back, cleared her throat and looked him in the eye: 'Are you going to kiss me?'

'Yes, ma'am, I think I will.'

'Any time soon, do you think?'

'Right 'bout now, I should say.'

They embraced, slowly, tenderly. Their lips touching carefully, parting, touching again, searching each other out. That first kiss had plenty of that *first-love*, school-kid *honesty* about it, and afterwards, when they lay on the soft bed of fallen cedar loam, and he held her in his arms, Easy was astonished that he hadn't entertained a single thought about Zoe or Beth.

PEDIGREE

Mama-Lek walked up and back, transferring a service wash from one of the battered old sud-tubs to the tall chrome dryers. Half the time she listened to Easy, who sat cross-legged on the end of a row of three preformed plastic chairs bolted to the bare brickwork wall. The other half of the time, when she was loaded down and hidden behind great armfuls of washing, he tried to remember what he had told her and keep his story straight.

'So, really,' he continued brightly, summing up, concluding, 'it's like just this raw, physical, rough-house deal with the Betty. A fight, a mud-wrestle, no-holds barred. With Zoe it's a more kinda focussed, deliberate, baby-making arrangement—charts, thermometers, timetables, recuperation times, the works. And then it's just like this wonderful, light, happy, whispery, holdy-handy deal with Jane—like we're schoolkids, or Freshman at college, or something—'

'Yeah, 'cept you do the ding-dong wif all fee of dem!'

'Well, yeah. But, you know, Mama-Lek, we're all grown-ups—mature, reasonably intelligent, consenting adults, and I've got this feeling that, you know, this is all gonna kinda work itself out just fine.'

Mama-Lek opened her favourite dryer, the one with the direct line to the Gods, and walked off.

'Tok to da dryer. Mama-Lek no liss'nin'.'

*   *   *   *   *

Beth plucked a pear from the fruit bowl with her thumb and forefinger and held it by its stalk like a small dead rat.

'This pear is rotten.'

Easy thrust his hands into the greasy, soapy water as he washed up last night's dishes. He was tired, hung-over, a little the frayed at the edges—and looked it.

'Did you hear me?'

He didn't answer her. What was there he could say about a rotten pear at this time and in morning?

'What's the point of having fruit in a bowl if it's left to go rotten?'

'Don't ask me, Betty. I fill the bowl. I thought that was my job. Now you want me to what—be fruit quality monitor?'

She noted the new tone in his voice, a frustration, and let the rotten pear drop back into the bowl with a sickening splat. She moved off around the room and ran her finger along the top of the window ledge, shelves, and CD player.

Easy came through drying his hands. He scooped out the offending pear, wiped off the other fruit, and carried the pulpy mess to the trashcan.

'And look at this dust. It's disgusting. You used to dust, remember?'

'It's on my list.'

'*It's on my list, It's on my list*. Where does your time goes these days?' He said nothing—just stood there, frozen with his brain aching and rattling inside his skull. Beth walked over to him and got right up in his face. 'I asked you a question?' She barked, but still he said nothing.

'Don't tell me—*list writing*.' She was pleased with her little joke and it diluted the poison, briefly. She took in a quick breath, was about to say something equally witty and bitter but stopped, as finally registering him up close. He stared down at her, waiting.

'Jesus. Look at you. You could shave once in a while, couldn't you?' He turned away from her and went back into the kitchen. She followed tight behind him: 'And get a haircut. We pay you, don't we?' He spun and faced her and she almost walked right into him: 'There's no need to slop around like some damn caveman.'

He grabbed her by the arms and pressed his mouth down over hers. She resisted but her lips betrayed her, puckering on autopilot. After a couple of workings of his jaw, he felt a change in her body, but not the usual softening, a stiffening, a retreat within, so he broke free.

Beth wiped her mouth on her sleeve: 'Uh,' she groaned, 'Dog breath.' And with that she turned and walked away.

165

*   *   *   *   *

He tried to avoid Beth for the rest of the day, but it wasn't easy. She'd dig him out where ever he was hiding, give him a chore to do, let him know she wasn't satisfied with the laundry, his yard work, or point out some tidemark on the bathtub that only she could see. He'd leave her lying on the sofa, watching TV, but then turn on the landing and find her sat on the stairs, waiting silently, like Deputy Dog: 'You dropped this,' she'd say, holding up some sock or pillow slip, 'Get with it, boy.'

He found sanctuary in Jane's room, taking his time sweeping the Egyptian rug, wiping down the window frames, vacuuming the dust out of the cracks in the old chestnut floorboards.

Jane came and went, didn't seem to mind him being there at all, just busied herself with a great pile of travel magazines in her usual thorough, organized manner, until finally, when he brought her up a cup of coffee she said quite calmly:

'Would you like to come with me to Zanzibar in October?'

'Zanzibar! Sure, is that on the other side of Pensacola?'

She spun the magazine, holding it up to show him a double page spread.

'Tan-*zane*-ia?'

'Tanzania,' she corrected, 'It's in East Africa.'

'Okay, sure,' he said, 'Let me just finish up here and I'll get my windcheater.'

She laughed and looked at the magazine herself again.

'Would you really just come with me?'

'Sure, why not—Zanzibar sounds cool. I bet they've got lots of cool stuff to do that we don't got in Louisiana.'

'Have you ever been on safari?'

'Girl, I ain't never been on a surfboard, but I don't let that stop me.'

'Tanzania's a great place to see the big five.'

'I'm on it—I loved that band—got everything they put out on vinyl.'

'Stop it—the Safari big-five—You know, elephant, lion, rhino, leopard, and . . . ' she suddenly drew a blank.

'Monkey?'

'No, it's—wait up,' she scanned the magazine.

'Giraffe?'

'No, no—'

'Snake?'

166

'Easy.'

'Crocodile, penguin, Chihuahua, turtle dove!'

'Cape Buffalo!'

'Cape Buffalo? Are you sure that's in the big five?'

Jane showed him the magazine again.

'Jeez—that's one ugly steer. I think I'd rather see a giraffe up close before a Cape Buffalo. What else they got in Tasmania?'

'Tanzania.'

'Right.'

'The landscape is just breathtaking. Mount Kilimanjaro, Mount Meru, the Ruvu river, the Rufiji. We could travel. Explore. Live. There's a whole lot more to Africa than safaris.'

'Let's do it.'

'We could go see the tribes, the real people. The Sukuma, the Makinde. The Maasai are amazing. We could live right there with them, find out what they do, and just do that.'

'Cool. I could learn to speak the lingo, hunt with a spear, and make a fancy shield out of buffalo hide.'

'Sure—' she said, not knowing if he was kidding, 'probably not buffalo, but sure. And then, when we've had enough, we could just pack up and move on. I've always dreamed of going to Kathmandu.'

'Kathmandu! That sounds even more the *ding* than Zanzibar. I never knew they were so close?'

'Zanzibar and Kathmandu?'

'Guess not, huh. Geography weren't never my specialized subject.' He had a thought: 'Hey, how long we gonna go on this trip?'

'I don't know. Does it matter? The first thing we have to do is work out where we want to go. Time will take care of itself.'

'Sure, only anything more than two weeks and the girls would, like, starve to death.'

She gave him a funny look just then, studied his face intently for some sign, then said ominously: 'Let me handle Beth and Zoe.'

*   *   *   *   *

He'd never been photographed before. Not like this. Sure, he'd had his picture taken growing up; rag-headed, scabby-kneed, and grinning wildly. At weddings; roughed into a straggled line by some uncle in a creased suit brandishing the complicated, crowd silencing contraption. The wait, the jostling, the endless smiles pasted on everyone's mug. Then "click", and that walk-away moment, when the group disintegrated and is lost forever.

And he remembered once, an old-style snake-oil salesman turning up one summer to the school-house. Conning Miss Ruttlehedge into a group photograph. She'd regretted her moment of weakness, spent the next four weekends riding out and visit the parents, his included, and mouth-whipping them into stumping up a dollar to pay for the print. They'd caved in at the end and the picture balanced proudly but unframed on the kitchen mantelpiece until it curled up, faded, and died of old age.

This time it was different—this was him deliberately having his picture taken, on his own. He was complicit, buying into the whole deal, and incredibly conscious of the finite moment.

Zoe had started snapping him a week or so back; as he stepped into her room with breakfast, or with his arms deep in the sink, or raking the leaves in the yard. He didn't like it much, thought she was taking a pretty serious risk, what with how things were and all. He liked the photos even less. The word she used to describe them was *candid*. The word he'd used was *humiliating*, so she'd agreed to shoot him for real and now here they were.

'Where do you want to go?' she said.

'I don't know. I thought you might have some idea.'

'Where do you like most in the whole world?'

'My bed,' he said genuinely, 'but not with a camera present.'

'Where else?'

'How about the docks?'

'What—take a ride on the Natchez? Too obvious.'

'The Quarter?'

'Likewise.'

'How about City Park?'

'How 'bout Tangiers?'

He nodded, considerately, and tried not to swallow his tongue down whole. She was homing in on him. Wasn't she?

'Can be pretty rough over there.'

'You know it well?'

'Some. I don't know if I'd take my fancy camera over that way without giving it some thought.'

They headed for City Park to get warmed up. She with her camera in an old shoulder bag and he with a few shirts, vests and his windcheater stuffed in a knapsack.

He didn't know what to expect and couldn't get any real conversation going on the streetcar. He kicked something off—the weather, the bus driver's ears, the neighborhood, but she wouldn't sit still. She kept popping up, changing seats, kneeling over him and shooting off the camera. He was embarrassed, looked for some clue in the eyes of the other commuters, some connection, some sympathy. All he saw was more embarrassment. He wanted her to tell him what to do, but when she did, he felt even worse: 'Just relax. Think of something that makes you smile. Makes you laugh. Makes you cry.'

'Which one?'

'Any one.' He couldn't do, couldn't just turn it on. His face muscles wouldn't co-operate and felt numb or stiff or lumpy. 'But not all three together.'

He buried his face in his arms. This was nothing and it was too much. He'd expected her to be goods at this—to be able to put him at his ease. Instead, she just clicked away at any dumb thing he did.

'Look,' she said, 'we've covered shy, bashful, lost, and care-in-the community. How about something a little lighter?' He wished she'd shut up now. 'How about you just smile at me?'

He smiled—his cheeks winching up like a busted blind.

'Okay, scratch that. Just look out the window. Further towards me, fine, just hold that . . . ' she came forwards and mussed his hair, turned his chin a touch to the right.

'Jesus! Your like a waxwork.'

His temper bubbled up from nowhere and his eyes flicked to her—Click, click, click.

'Don't stop.'

'Don't stop what?' He said, 'I didn't do anything.'

It went on like this, even as they stepped off the streetcar and when they entered City Park. She'd be off first, into the open ahead of him, ready to capture him as he hit the sidewalk, or came through the gates.

The park cheered him up, or calmed him down, or distracted him. Whichever, it seemed to work for Zoe and she crouched and pivoted, bent and angled herself into various contortions while she worked the shutter, holding her breath and grunting these little half grunts with each new image.

He liked the way the willow branches held themselves, like a time-lapse firework, falling even as they climbed, and always dropping, finally diving at the water. And the chestnut trees, their massive jutting boughs, sailing out, low and assured, over the dark green mirror water.

They reached the old bridge and automatically stepped onto it. He stopped halfway towards the island, turned and rested his palms on the stone wall and looked out over the lake. He listened to hear the distant camera click. It didn't—instead he was sure he heard Zoe laughing.

'What is that? Your audition for American Way? Get real.'

Infuriating—he boiled inside.

Click, click, click.

He passed a small sandstone statue a little further along. It stood right at the water's edge, between two mature green ash, shaded in their dapple-light. A female form, naïve and naked, kneeling wide-legged on a rough-hewn block. Her back arched upwards, her face skywards, jawbone catching the light, her arms raised above her head, holding up a bundle, a swaddled baby, an offering, a burden.

A third ash had been recently felled. The stump still shone corn yellow against the vivid green moss. He looked down on the disc, the age-rings of tree life, outer bark, inner bark, cambium, sapwood, heart.

Zoe was now close to him, static electricity over his shoulder, the quick coldness of her shadow.

She held something out for him. Ridiculous and unnatural, a stick of gum, a band-aid, no . . . he took the thing. Let his fingers wrap around it. Unreal, nose-nudging at the limits of his consciousness like a baby shark, seeking a chink, a gap, a fold, the hidden entrance to his mind-labyrinth.

A pregnancy stick.

Click, click, click.

His eyes zoomed in on the window, the wide dull by unmistakable blue marker.

Click, click, click.

Seismic.

Click.

Easy felt something soft and hot exploding in the crater of his chest.

Click, click, click.

His head rose, then dropped and his hand reached out for her.

Click, click, click, click, click.

BREED

A peaceful, solemn stillness infused the Health Club that night. An uncommon tranquillity, almost a hush. The single female predator was elsewhere, applying war-paint, lying in wait, hunting, but elsewhere.

Zoe and Jane sat side by side on the gym equipment. Lame cheerleaders missing out on the big game. Unpicked substitutes, left on the hockey bench.

They could have been related, not sisters perhaps, but close cousins. Equally tall, smooth skinned, and slim; Jane's pliability matching Zoe's lean strength.

They sat, snug, for now, in each other's silence, happy in their own thoughts. Yes—the time would come to be open, and clear the stale air at the house, plant the truth squarely before the others and let the matter live.

What would be the harm?

Zoe was utterly pregnant. Jane was utterly in love. And they were both content to sit and watch their fuses slow-burn towards the inevitable detonation.

Jane rose, finally: 'Fancy the steam room?'

Zoe shook her head. The gym was warm enough—98°; perfect; incubation: 'Maybe later. Still no news from the faculty then?'

171

'Fuck 'em!' said Jane, cheerfully but with force. Zoe laughed and opened her eyes again. 'They can stuff their Professorship up their collectively retentive sphincter.'

'You don't mean that.'

'Don't I? Who wants to spend the rest of their life digging and dusting dirt and rocks. Poking around tombs and graveyards? Really, what was I doing all those years?' Zoe peered at her all the harder. 'I've been thinking. I might take some time off—A year's sabbatical. Sod it—maybe two.'

Zoe straightened and leaned forward just enough to get in Jane's vision. 'But what about your research? Won't—I don't know—won't someone else come along and make your discoveries?'

'Good Lord, Zoe. It's not a yard sale. Besides, I'm not entirely sure it's what I really want to do anymore.'

'Really!'

Jane thought before responding, calmly and evenly: 'Yes. I thought I might try my hand at travel writing.'

'That's a bit sudden, isn't it?'

'Well, I've always loved travel and writing. Why not combine the two?'

'But you spend all that time, all that intensity, that focus on your career, and then you just . . . ' she faltered, and her voice fell almost to a whisper as she realised the hypocrisy of what she was saying, 'swap ships.'

Jane looked at Zoe. She couldn't know already. She couldn't have guessed about her and Easy—they'd been so discreet, so proper about meeting, and apart from the night of the ball, and a further encounter, when the other girls were out at work, so terribly decent.

Zoe looked at Jane—her familiar, blank, innocent face, that delicate upturn to her nose. Impish and elfin, yet thoroughly good, trusted, and un-wicked. An adult girl's face—still young but almost asexual.

Almost? Yet some new awareness seemed to have made itself known to Jane, acquainted itself with those virgin features. It swelled and widened her cheekbones, plumped her lips, steadied and deepened the set of the eyes. Some new understanding, a confidence gained by exact knowledge.

'What's brought this on, exactly?' Zoe said, coldly.

'Nothing. Nothing—' said Jane, backtracking, 'it's just one of my dying leaf moments.'

She couldn't possibly just tell her now, like this—just come blurting out with it. The shame. The agony.

Zoe looked up at her again. Jane seemed to be inspecting the concrete wall—making deep sense of the smooth grey patterns.

Zoe spoke now, of other matters; her father's affair with a new "62" year-old widower: 'And I bet the old bitch isn't a day under 70!'

Jane smiled, glad the moment had passed and then instantly wishing she'd taken the opportunity to unburden herself.

'Life goes on, Zoe.'

'Not for my dad. It's . . . unwholesome. No, disrespectful to my mother.'

'Your mother's memory.'

'Well, yes. I suppose. Look, don't stick up for him. He's an old goat, and that's all there is too it.'

'I'm just saying. Maybe what you mean is he's being disrespectful to you?'

Zoe's eyes widened some at that. She lowered her head an inch and composed herself like a boxer defending his chin. She looked long and hard at Jane, trying to figure out what had gotten into her. Jane stood up well under the withering look, and even managed a little shudder of defiance. After a moment Zoe said: 'Maybe you're right.'

Jane once again irrationally thought—she knows. But this time it came with more than a mild twinge of approval. Zoe knows; has deciphered it, worked it out. Easy and I. She knows. Understands we're two peas in a pod, far removed from her world but made for one another. She can see what links us—the odd chains of bondage, of reciprocated love, of true romance.

She placed a warm, wet hand on Zoe's knee and said: 'How long have you known?'

Zoe stared at the soft, firm hand on her leg. She could already hear the echoes of a series of far away concussions. Like the distant witness to an Atom bomb. Numb, expectant, knowing, already doomed.

'I'm sorry,' said Jane, and with a gentle, studied squeeze on releasing the knee, 'It just happened.'

She looked at Zoe, tried to make eye contact, willed her to look up and give her some clue that it was all right. But it was too soon, of course, simply too much of a shock.

'You must think the worst of me,' she said, emptily, building a bridge of reason word by word out into the void between them. 'I understand, but believe me, Zoe, non of this was planned.' And then a rush of guiltless emotion, for that very lack of planning, and the night and the days that followed. 'I'm as surprised as anybody. After all, as you well know, I have hitherto had rather strained relationships with the help.'

Zoe spoke then, finally, but so softly that Jane did not hear: 'Oh, Jane . . . '

'I know, I know,' said Jane, filling the terrible void, giving a lead to the moment.

'Oh, God . . . '

'And I know you're probably thinking I'm just some frigid old ice-queen who's finally had the *damn good horsing* everybody said she needed—and maybe so, that's probably true, yes—but it happened and while it's still happening I'm . . . I'm . . . Well, to continue the euphemism, I'm staying in the saddle.'

Zoe stood. Then her legs buckled and sat down again. She looked at Jane, but seeing the even greater hope and fire in her eyes than she'd heard in the voice, looked down again at her feet.

'Zoe?'

She raised her hand to stop Jane but still could not speak. She could not trust herself to begin. Did not know where to start or how it would end.

'You're upset with me. I'm sorry. I suppose I've let you down . . . '

Zoe rose again, and this time stepped away, out of Jane's field of love and innocence and potency. She could breath now. She could think too, and would, she knew, very shortly be able to speak.

'I know this messes up what we've got at the house, but we're adults, Zoe, we can work it out.' She got up now too, and stood mirroring Zoe, hands at her sides, her shoulders open.

'Easy and I are going to take off . . . let you and Beth get used to the idea.' Zoe shrank, folded her arms around breasts and stomach, but still said nothing. 'And if you want to move out then that's okay too. Don't worry about the rent, or anything, and I'll pay back your bond as soon as I can but don't, you know, just don't make any rash—'

'Stop!' said Zoe, in a crisp, harsh voice. Then she breathed and spoke with more control and less mania: 'Just stop, okay. This . . . this is, like, totally insane.' She came toward Jane, fixed her dead in the eye and said: 'It's foolish, Jane. We . . . you hardly know this man.'

'No,' said Jane, 'you're wrong—'

'Stop!'

'Stop what?' Jane asked, 'I'm considering having some time off, that's all.'

Zoe broke away, picked up her towel and covered herself.

'No, you're not. What you're saying. You're really talking about something else. Something a lot, lot more than that.'

'No.'

174

'Yes, Jane, admit it. You're talking about going away for a year or two! Then you're talking about taking Easy with you. No. No, no, no! It's madness. Sheer madness. You really don't know this man—you don't—and you're just throwing, throwing away your whole career.'

'You're wrong—I do know him. I do. It's you who doesn't know him, Zoe.'

Zoe felt herself drifting into an odd dream-state. She knew she should be paying attention but those aftershocks were now impacting on her, reverberating inside, shaking her very core. She could hear Jane talking, more conciliatory and considered: 'This isn't just an infatuation . . . If you only knew the way his mind works . . . You'll see . . . There's never been anyone more right, more perfect, for me.'

She could divine what was coming next, the 'I love him' moment. She had to stop that from coming, just had to.

'Lord, Zoe. One minute you're scudding along, planning out your life, giving it this damn infinitesimal structure and worrying about every little detail. The next, *boosh*, all you care about is how to survive the next five minutes before you can reasonable lie down with him and do it again—'

'Zoe! Really—'

'Has he agreed to go with you?' she interrupted, now firing on all cylinders.

'Sorry?'

'On this trip. Have you discussed it, planned it, set dates, booked it?'

'No, no—'

'Well, thank God!'

'But it'll be no big deal for him. You watch.'

'Jane!'

'He's just so totally different from anybody else.'

'Listen to me—'

'And all I'm going to do is *not* end it. All I'm going to do is keep in there and see what happens. What so bad in that?'

Zoe came at her again now, with more force, and a look too close to hysteria.

'You can't. Okay. You just can't. Wait. You must. You need to stop and just wait.'

'But . . . that's exactly what I am doing.'

'No. No. Taking this year out—no. It will put you both under pressure.' She had no idea where she was heading with this and suddenly a chink of light appeared. 'Tremendous pressure. It's . . . it's forced, Jane. It's way too sudden, too rash, too hasty—It's won't last if you begin like this, Jane, and, and it's just not *you*.'

175

Her words, this time, seemed to register, to make some small impact on Jane. Serious work still needed to be done but this was the time for that effort.

'Look, Jane, we've been good friends for how long? Seven, eight years? Now, I wouldn't say this if I didn't care for you. If I didn't care for you, I'd let you run off happily, trotting away over the sunset and into some certain misery. But, seriously, if you value my opinion as a friend then hear what I'm saying. Take my advice and, please God, wait.'

With that Zoe sat again and waited for a response. Jane, now leaning against the cool, concrete wall for support, managed to lift her head and look at Zoe. The face was impassive, lost, then she managed a brief, unfathomable smile. She heaved herself off the wall and joined Zoe on the bench.

Zoe kept her gaze straight ahead. She couldn't give in on this; there existed no other acceptable option than complete compliance. She felt Jane's cool arm slip around the small of her back.

'I hear you,' she began, 'Okay, okay? I hear you. I know I'm crap at this. Why wouldn't I be? And I'm touched you care enough to stand your ground like that. And make me listen.' It was still in the balance—Zoe kept her whole body unnaturally still, frozen like a statue, fixed like a radio receiver, tuned only to one narrow frequency. 'I'll take my time. I promise.' She rested her head on Zoe's shoulder: 'I'll wait.'

SCENT

Beth sniffed around in Jane's room. She'd never done this before—not to Jane, she'd never had occasion to. Zoe; sure, and every other flatmate she'd ever lived with. She'd been through Zoe's junk a hundred times, but there'd never been much interest or reason to *dig up* Jane. With her it really was all on the surface—what you saw was exactly what you got, like an advert for a contraceptive—no, more like a crepe bandage, or a knee-strap.

Jane's transparency or lack of depth had bugged Beth when she first moved in to the house. Jane had been without doubt the dullest, most uninspiring, and tediously dreary person she'd ever met—even the divorced, alcoholic losers who hit on Beth at the bar snuck to the restroom once in a while to jack-off.

Beth had studied Jane, waiting to discover the one big weakness—booze, Valium, sleeping pills, pornography, serial-murder—but nothing. She couldn't even imagine Jane masturbating—never mind catching her at it. With Jane somehow self-sex just didn't seem necessary or even worthwhile, whereas Beth offed herself frequently, several times a day, whether she'd just been with a man *or not*, and sometimes because she'd just been with a man *or not*.

She remembered once, getting fixated with Jane's obvious lack of vice, and taking a sneak-peek at her while she took her usual long, ritualised, old-fashioned bath. I mean, thought Beth, what woman takes a bath these day unless they're washing the kids or planning a little self-love.

177

She crept silently with her chair from the bedroom and stood up on it to peer in through the half-light at the top of the bathroom door. The dirt and steam hindered her view but equally helped obscure her. She'd seen something new. Not the envisaged leg-parted, finger-probing, top lip curling pose, but Jane—be-headphoned, eyes calmly closed, brows dancing with the shape of the music, and with a lemon-yellow face flannel laid carefully over her privates!

What was that about? Was she getting chilly down there? Ashamed to look at herself, or half expecting firemen to brake the door down and wanting to look her best?

Lately, however, Beth had noticed a definite change in Jane. An unspecified casting off of that irritating girlishness, a certain maturing. She couldn't place it but sensed its echo and opposite, its inverse shape as it were, in the cooling of her own relationship with Easy.

She pulled a pillow off the bed and smelled at it—mothballs, duckdown, and oil—faint, familiar, persistent. She drew back the bed quilts to inspect the sheets. Jesus, who still had quilts? Her grandmother didn't even have quilts. The sheets were gone. She didn't know what that meant at first. The bed was made without the sheets. Her eyes scanned the room and stopped at the wicker snake-charmer basket. It contained panties, lose pastel socks, a single crumpled sheet. She drew it out and smelled it in big careless fistfuls.

Bingo. That faint, oily musk. Mixed with other odours but still unmistakable. Her heart skipped a beat and dropped, plummeted like it was going to fall through her stomach.

*   *   *   *   *

Scuffing silently along, minding their own business, making slow certain progress towards some great specific meteorological meeting over Arkansas, Louisiana clouds fascinated Easy. He stood, staring chronically at these passing giants, as the damp washing grew cold and heavy in his hands. He counted and timed the vapoury tendrils, vanishing, reforming, making their way into the darkening massiveness of the north. He loved Louisiana clouds.

The fly-screen creaked, calling him from his trance, and he saw Beth at the back door with the bedsheet trailing from her hand.

He knew immediately what she was thinking. This was it. Not the end, but the beginning of the end. He could barely look at her, found it impossible to meet her eye. He shoved his face in her direction and by

178

sheer force of will finally took on the looming gaze. Her eyes were veined and brilliant, and now that she had him zeroed, she spoke as if they were sharing the pillow and not twenty feet apart.

'So, you're doing all three of us?'

She let this hang there, gave it time to transmit and sink in—as if this stuff never moved at the speed of sound.

Easy dropped his head, studied the wet fabric in his hands, and let it fall back to the basket.

'Answer me, damn you.' She came closer now and he could feel the shockwaves of her anger; huge, raw, and bloody. He bristled, readied himself, and as she approached found himself giving a half-arsed affable shrug. Beth slapped him full across the face.

'Don't you dare!'

Oh god. This was it. But what can you say? What can you do about it? It's all over bar the shouting.

'What were you thinking?'

He thought about an answer—decided that he hadn't really been thinking—shrugged again and got slapped again. Ouch! She had some bite in that palm of hers, he could imagine her doling out the licks to the drunks at the Dead Pirate, but what could you do but grin like an idiot?

'Don't you dare. Look at me. I'm crying. *Me!* I haven't cried since nineteen-*goddamed*-eighty-*fucking*-nine, you rat bastard!'

He allowed the pause to grow. Fought hard not to make any inane gestures. The shrug was clearly not going over.

'You . . . you Goddamned man.'

She drummed her fists against his face and chest and he took it for a while then batted her arms away and grabbed her wrist.

'What—you want me to say I'm sorry?' She stared up at him. He was looking hard at her mouth. The uneven wetness of the lower lip. 'What do you want form me?' But before she could say another word, he kissed her.

*   *   *   *   *

Jane and Zoe took a taxi back home from the gym and sat in silence. The moon was a thin crescent, just strong enough to model the clouds. Nonsensically, Zoe wished she'd brought her mountain bike to beat the traffic. Wished she were already home to see him first and get her story in, her version of it at least, her indignation, her retaliation, her plea.

Jane sat mesmerised by the streetlights zipping up the Taxi's windscreen, her mouth a firm slit, her eyes on some future conversation.

As they approached the house on Magazine, Zoe dug around in her bag for money. Jane broke from her reverie, tapped the driver on the shoulder with a neatly folded bill and was out the door.

As Zoe took the steps in one quiet bound, Jane already had her keys turning in the door. Neither woman noticed the house was in darkness. Zoe wanted to scream out his name but that was wrong. She turned on the hallway light and looked up the stairs.

'Easy?' called Jane in a flat, businesslike tone.

'Beth!' called Zoe, betraying an unexpected tightness in her vocal cords. Both women moved through to the lounge. The light snapped on violently, revealing the room cold, quiet, and empty.

Zoe returned to the hallway and looked again up the very centre of the stairwell. A light, dim and faint, picked out the banisters at the very top of the house: 'Easy.'

Jane shivered, pulled her coat around her, and noticed the back door was lying open an inch or two. She quickly closed it, then opened it again and stuck her head out into the yard. 'Hello.'

Zoe reached the attic floor quickly. She saw the yellow bar of light under the door. 'Easy,' she hissed, but there was no reply. She put her hand on the doorknob and felt the weak drag of nausea against her stomach wall. She imagined him, stretched out on his cot bed, barefooted in blue jeans, asleep, with a hardback of Moby Dick, for some reason, laid open across his chest. All manner of urges and longings jumped up inside her, racing in her bloodstream like foolish, determined salmon.

Jane looked towards the tool-shed. Its cracked, dull window pane flickered light across the yard; bedsheets swayed pale and silently, slow as tide water. A basket, lay upended in the gravel, begging attention.

Jane stepped forward, her foot landing in a crunch—deafening, and sensed clear up to her knee. She'd never make it.

Zoe left her nausea on the attic floor with Easy's empty room. She skitted, navy-style, down the stairs, gripped by some unknown panic: 'Jane!'

The window pane fluttered with moth shadows. Jane froze—her warm breath escaping around her. Noises, shuffling, regular, and interrupted, then a gasp—animal, hungry, desperate, human.

She placed her finger on the thin edge of the pinewood door and swung it open. The earthy, fetid air met her as she stepped in.

Her eyes, partially adapted, opened further to the darkness. She read a jumble of feet—squirming, fat, pink trotter-like. Then a lunge of thigh, lean muscled, contoured in the mustard light. A curved swathe of plump, white flesh. Pale hairy forearms, hands sunk deep in the quilts.

Easy suddenly stopped and gazed down at his hands like a crazed murderer. Then, inexplicably, he turned, and saw Jane. She felt a terrible urge to say his name. Just announce it, to make the moment real, to pin it in time and place. Not to scream or screech it from the pit of her guts. Just to say it and hear it.

'Don't . . . ' Beth roared, breathless, into the blankets, 'Don't stop!'

The quick sound of Zoe's feet scudding across the gravel saved Jane from certain, crushing death. She turned and fled and they collided in the narrow opening.

'What's the matter?' Jane said nothing and rushed to the house. Zoe looked into the darkness and met the scene—

Beth sat, gathering the quilts up around her.

'Get out!' she screamed, sending Zoe stumbling back. She looked again—Easy's stood up and faced her.

'Easy?' she whispered.

'Get out!' Beth shouted, burying her face in the blankets. 'Get out, out, get out.'

*   *   *   *   *

Jane sat wide-legged and slumped on the sofa, her arms flopped across her like a cloth-doll. One of her buttocks had forced apart the seat cushions when she'd collapsed on to the sofa, and there she remained, wedged, lopsided, and demolished.

Beth, dressed in a T-shirt, her lower half wrapped in a thin quilt sat propped at the worktop, her black Medusa head supported on clenched fists. She looked coiled, unreachable, distant, and dangerous.

Zoe stood with her feet shoulder-width apart at the other end of the room, arms folded across her stomach, waiting by the doorway that led out to the hall.

The three sat quietly beneath the humming 100-Watt bulb, their stares triangulated, and claiming every unmapped inch of the room.

In the silence, they could hear Easy, way up at the top of the house, sliding open drawers, closing the wardrobe door, creaking the cot springs, snapping shut the locks on his battered old suitcase.

He came down the steps steadily, heavily, and finally appeared in the doorway. He set down his suitcase stepped right into the crossfire and took a sharp, noisy breath to speak . . .

Easy searched the girls' faces quickly. Neither one of them looked back at him, and he felt both emboldened and terribly lost. He waited a long moment, staring at a patch of carpet, then looked at them each again: Beth, who he'd been locked into just moments before seemed now as distant and obscure as that bright curve of moon. Zoe stood glowing, poised, her shoulders against the wall, but balanced, ready to flip off and to run for her life. She seemed to meet his stare for a moment but her look just bounced off his shoulder and rested on the bookshelf. Jane sitting battered, drooped, and wilting, like a dead swan, was his biggest regret— these other two were big enough and brute enough to handle themselves, but Jane—that was just a wonderful mistake.

'Wow—' he said finally, 'Ain't that the *ding*?' and with that he walked to the door, picked up his case, and left . . .

The door, when they heard it close, didn't slam or bounce, but closed very quietly, so that it registered, but didn't disturb. It was the way a first-time father would close the door on his baby's nursery; the way the Latino Toyboy slipped from the cuckold's Sunday morning kitchen; the way the undertaker locks up shop.

Jane broke first, dredging her useless limbs from the jaws of the sofa and lumbering, staggering across the room, leaking life like a shot deer.

Zoe caught her as she fell: 'Jane, wait, wait!' The words worked upon her like acid, whip-marks, and salts.

'Wait!' she spat, throatily, savagely, 'Wait? How could you, Zoe? How . . . how . . . ' She collapsed in Zoe's arms, sapped, rung out, all her focus on the moaning, and the thrashing but unable to resist Zoe's arms and her rocking.

Beth slouched off the stool and came padding to the centre of the room to get a good look at them. She had half a mind to run and flop across the top of them, to complete the heap. But instead, she tightened the quilt around her and said: 'And she's pregnant, Jane.' Then she laughed at herself. 'Yep. She's having the freak's baby.'

DOWN

The bar was packed and business was brisk—New Orleans loves a convention. Fat, gleaming faces shoved hundred dollar bills over the counter. They served themselves, 'Coming Thru!' ass and elbows out, pork-sausage fingers pronging the tumblers away to the table; they went at it from lunch till four in the morning. Spring Break for low-ranking, brain-dead, cubicle dwellers.

Beth sat alone watching the entropy of alcohol-fuelled fun, and ignoring the subtle-less stares from her staff. She was needed, but useless. She forgot orders, over-changed, and couldn't add up—her cocktail magic failed.

A reeking drunk, thoroughly soused in cheap liquor woke and peeled his papery cheek of the hot varnished bartop. He sucked his chops a few times then pulled focus and saw Beth looking back at him . . .

'Smile, cher, it might never happen.'

Beth's hand shot out involuntarily and landed in a precisely formed fist smack on the drunk's snouzer. He reeled, fell backwards clean out of his chair and landed at the bottom of the stool on his neck. After a frozen second, he rolled over onto his knees and came up slow and steady and with his dukes a-ready. A big cheer went up and Beth stood surprised, with her hand over her mouth. She didn't know whether to rush round to him, flee, or say sorry. Instead she turned slowly and walked to her office.

*   *   *   *   *

Jane finally got out of bed, strip-washed, pulled on yesterday's clothes and hauled herself around the park. The sky was pale, overcast, and a dirty white. She scuffled her feet through the damp, dead leaves. Their colours not the vibrant autumn palette she needed but a putrefying, rotting, melancholic brown.

Children rode on the swings, their cries muted and despondent, told of deathly internecine conflicts, their mothers were absurdly young and unusually pale. Even the blades of grass seemed cramped, too tightly packed, and struggling for light and life. She welled up, every pallid shade was seen through seeped tears, and made her want to collapse.

But she couldn't, wouldn't. A conversation was missing and was required. An obligatory scene. A vital episode had yet to be played out. But it was coming.

*   *   *   *   *

Zoe turned her space into a darkroom and locked herself away. She'd been crying a lot this last week, sobbing, snivelling, teary over small matters. The triggers could not be remembered later. Just the crying, and always with the dull dragging ache at the wall of her stomach.

She set up her baths, measured out her chemicals, set herself tiny tasks, rewarded herself regularly with tea and chocolate. But it was not good.

She developed the prints. Calmly, methodically, precisely, for there was no other way, and this task served her well . . . while it lasted.

She saw his mug face forming in the emulsion, his goof-ball looks, his buck teeth, his temple veins, his beauty. And she wept.

*   *   *   *   *

The house, so perfectly recovered and charming, now suffered an insurgency, a coup, a collapse from within. Tulip petals curled, died, dropped, and chased themselves around the dining table. Pollen drifts clogged the console. Curtains hooks turned brittle, perished and disintegrated. Rancid dishes filled the sink. Mold grew and multiplied. Mushrooms sprung fully formed overnight in pots and cups and take-out cartons. Dead bumblebees rolled along the windowsills like tumbleweed. Trash-sacks huddled like biker-gangs on the stairs. The drains choked

184

and cemented. Sash cords snapped, hinges sprung loose, keys spun vainly in their locks, lightbulbs vanished, faucets coughed dust.

*   *   *   *   *

Jane was dragging and leaking a sack of trash across the floor when it hit her—a week had helically unwound and Zoe and Beth were sitting together on the sofa watching a game-show in the dark—This very room, though Jane, had travelled 10 million miles through space since it last held Easy.

She saw this vast column of dark identical rooms, blue lit by television, one after the other, stretching off into the night, reaching back into the solar system. And in one of those rooms, 10 millions miles away stood Easy, flushed, silent, and looking down at her crumpled form on the sofa.

The moment seemed unbearably far away, and yet painfully real, and everything else utterly unimportant. She gave up, dropped the trash, left it oozing out in the middle of the room, and went to her room. The TV crowd laughed and cheered her exit, their applause drifting out across the airwaves forever.

*   *   *   *   *

Beth was lying across her bed, listless, horny, and drunk. She had a bottle of Vodka and a dry glass. Her eyes focused on a thing half sticking out from beneath the bed—a plastic basin, the base settled with vomit.

She heard a ringing somewhere down below. A comedy ringing, like a fire alarm in an old black and white movie. Recognizable but unfamiliar—their telephone. She jumped up, crashed over, got back up again and made for the door.

In the corridor, Zoe slammed into her like a speed-skater. They both rolled along the carpet and scrambled to their feet. She got the look in Zoe's eye. Her hangover evaporated.

She rushed after her down the stairs, Zoe sweeping bags off the steps with huge kicks.

The telephone still rang . . .

They burst into the living room and saw Jane sitting at the table with the telephone placed before her.

Beth and Zoe stopped.

The telephone rang . . .

185

'Answer it,' said Zoe. Jane just looked at them, panting, making little hops from foot to foot.

'It might be someone,' said Beth.

Jane just sat with her arms folded, staring at the telephone.

'Answer it!' said Beth, but Jane still did not move.

The telephone made a short ring—like a fullstop. Beth snatched the receiver off the cradle and put it to her ear. The line was dead.

Jane looked at her, mockingly: 'It might be someone?'

*   *   *   *   *

Easy hung up the receiver and looked off down the row of broken 'phone booths. Having found two quarters, a dime, and then a working payphone all in the space of thirty seconds, he'd taken it as a sign and immediately called the house. He'd really thought his luck was in; money aside, finding a working public 'phone in New Orleans these days was rare—as rare as hen teeth.

A depression was settling in on him, dulling his flesh, numbing his bones, readying him, preparing him for winter on the streets. It struck him as disappointing that his body, his nature, knew enough to start making these definite decisions without bothering to consult him.

The week was soon over, seemed to have passed quickly, but each day had dragged, the hours racked up, but the minutes crawled slowly around the clock-face. He felt stretched, distant, and outside of things.

At first he thought often about the girls. The girls and the house. He missed them. He missed the duty and structure of his life. Thinking about Betty, Zoe, or Jane made his chest tighten in a death grip, the individual chest muscles twining, tiring, aching. Thinking about the house put him at ease, made him close to happy. The house, he concluded, he had not betrayed. You could not easily cuckold a three-storey flat-board Victorian, and if you did, it forgave you. A thorough sweep, scrub, and mopping and you were absolved.

Sleeping rough was easy. He was strong, healthy, and well-fed. The cold hadn't got into his bones, that would take another couple of weeks—or one freak cloudless night, when the heat just fled from you, rose like alcohol vapour and was lost to the stars.

He scuffed along the street, heading for the river. Water made him calm, drew him out of himself, proved beyond doubt that the world was still turning, that life was still going on.

186

Looking at the dark muddy swirls in the Mississippi made him think of Zoe. The whirlpools, the pull, the dragging danger. The banks were Jane, contoured, complex, allowing, safe. The water never made him think of Beth.

On the Southside, teenagers hung out on every corner, smoking, and shooting hoop. They'd bounce the ball off his back, his legs, shoulders, his head, whatever. They all seemed to play the same game, like they'd just invented it, and they seemed to get a lot of fun out of it too.

Easy didn't mind. After the first couple of times he didn't even defend himself, or act surprised. The teenagers laughed, hard, harsh, and desperate—overloaded, wide mouthed laughs. Time was closing in on them too and he pitied them right back.

He found a good dry spot under the bleachers at Behrman Park. He made no effort to talk to other rough sleepers and they left him and his little suitcase alone.

Sleep came easily and he thought less and less of the girls, and more and more of the house. He wondered if they were treating it well. Hoped they would but knew deep down it was impossible.

He walked variously around the Shopping Centres at McArthur, Village Aurora, and Cypress Plaza. From the first few days, whilst his clothes were still clean, he could make out to be someone, a shop assistant, a teller, a working person going about his business.

The suitcase was a giveaway—not for the real people but the security guards. They made him for a bum the second time he showed up carrying it and would square on to him at twenty yards and click their walkie-talkies. Maybe it was all in his mind but he wasn't going to dump the suitcase—it was all he had.

One morning, over in Terrytown, he saw an old guy loaded down with these yellow boxes. They were cardboard, overfilled, collapsing in on themselves. He went to help, smiling at the old guy, understanding the burden. But the old man just looked at him with frightened eyes, told him to "Back-off", and struggled across the street to avoid him. He was acquiring the look.

Later that same day, in a half-dream about Beth and window cleaning, Easy narrowly missed colliding with a lithe, slippery young woman on the empty sidewalk.

'Sorry,' said Easy, smiling.

'Say what?'

He turned and found himself looking into the eyes of a dart-eyed, pinch-faced, crack whore. She teetered on dirty, 4-inch platform sneakers, and stood winking and blinking and looking between him and his little suitcase. Something about the way the light dappled her skin took Easy back to a hot summer's day . . . a beautiful girl . . . a dropped purse. Eons had passed.

Her pimp now appeared, tall, wide-shouldered and narrow hipped, reminded Easy of someone. He shoved Easy aside as he passed and started right on it, arguing with the hooker. Easy understood the play: he was meant to get drawn in, defend the girl, and get subsequently rolled.

He turned and walked away, fast, fearful, and for no reason at all suddenly remembered a perfect little girl with her perfect little kitten and a crisp hundred-dollar bill.

That night, outside the V. N. Liquor Store on Behrman Highway, Easy stood facing an old ginger mongrel. It cowered by a busted down chain-link fence—looking lost and scared and, like Easy, had been drawn in from the gathering dark by the brash neon lights. Out of habit he reached to comfort the dog but it snapped and nearly bit his hand. He saw now, thankfully, that the dog was tethered to the fence, and it jumped and growled and barked and slobbered at him.

After a moment, the dog's owner came out of the liquor store, bearded, black-toothed, bagged bottles clutched to his guts. He calmed the dog, shot a disgusted look at Easy and waited for words.

'Sorry, I thought he was lost.'

'Nope. He ain't lost,' said the man into his beard and stood up to face Easy. Easy backed away, the tension killing him, eating him alive. He wasn't scared but incomprehensibly overwhelmed by the moment. He strode off into the darkness, in search of shelter.

The following morning Easy realised why he'd come south of the river. He watched the old lady unloading the machine, lost inside its chrome cavern. Her eyes hidden in plump wrinkles, her thick, bandy legs, her freckled fists of laundry.

He stood by the window and looked in, his face flat and impassive, but ready to smile the second she saw him. When she did, he couldn't do it. His face refused to work, and the muscles set themselves into a silent rictus. She looked right through him at first. Saw the man, the tramp, the rough sleeper, but not Easy.

In recognition, her shoulders dipped, her head tipped an inch, and she softened. Seeing a woman again somehow made the hammer strike. Finally. Fatally. A realisation of what he had done? Mama-Lek opened the door creakily and spoke in a soft voice: 'Bad dog.'

He cried a lot that afternoon. Big sobs of it, snivels, sniffles, deep keening and at one time an unholy wailing. It felt completely right to be doing this in the Laundromat, disproportionate but apt.

While he whimpered and howled, she stripped him of his filthy clothes and agreed to lend him the fourteen dollars for a service wash. He thanked her, bawling, stood like an infant in a borrowed bath sheet.

He recovered, at length, then blubbered some more. Mopped his soaked face, gathered his breath, and grizzled and gibbled anew. Finally, Mama-Lek drew a line under the nonsense and brought him a pint of tea—green, bitter, and smarting—in a chipped tin mug.

'Thank you,' he said.

'Yeah,' she said. ' You smell bedda now, aw-white.'

LEASH

Zoe ran through her reasons for going back to work: 1. Money, 2. Pin–down maternity package, 3. Social interaction with people she hadn't slept around on. Her reasons for staying home and pretending to be sick: 1. Work now seemed utterly pointless, 2. The girls hadn't yet cleared the air (by that she meant they hadn't screamed at each other, had an unholy cat fight, or crept into each other's rooms after midnight with blunt instruments or sharpened blades), 3. There would be a strong possibility of bumping into Chance . . . and 4. There would be an outside possibility of sharing the elevator to the news-room . . .

'So I tell them,' said Billie, in her best Cajun accent, 'Dem people in N'Orlins don't care *how* you live your life. They want to *know*, but they don't *care*—'

Zoe grinned and wished she had stayed at home.

* * * * *

Beth saw a great deal of merit in putting in the hours at the Dead Pirate. It took her mind off Easy, gave her a noteworthy sense of direction through this turbulent post-partum chapter, and allowed her ample opportunity to become royally soaked and comfortably cloaked in quality, cost price liquor.

190

Beth patrolled the outer bar but remained, at all times, keenly conscious of the proximity of (and the most direct route to) her office—her inner chamber, her sanctuary.

She'd stop, mid-way collecting plate or glass, and bestow an uncharacteristically appropriate comment upon an unsuspecting and suspicious patron: 'Nice hat, George,' or, 'Hey Nancy, where did you buy those boots?' only to pivot half-way through the reply and rush for her bunkered bottle.

The waitresses, now accustomed to finding her tearful, sweary, and comprehensively nuked by mid-afternoon, would not pass comment but simply and firmly pull shut the office door, and be thankfully Beth was incapable of calling her bookie and blowing their wages.

*   *   *   *   *

Jane claimed the house. Its foot-print, its territory, its space, but not the responsibility for its upkeep. She would not lift a finger to help the others but nor would she weaken, ask them to tidy up, or ask them to leave. That, she decided one dark silent night, was just too damned obvious and above all, petty-minded.

No.

She'd grind out some new reality—a third and as yet uncertain path. Where there was no way, a way would become clear; from no-thing a thing would emerge. Of this she felt uncharacteristically sure and all that this new reality required of her was resolve, inaction, and patience. Qualities, thankfully, she had in spades.

'I'll go if you want?' said Beth, drunk, challenging, defiant. This was on about day three.

'Do as you please.'

'I will.'

'Suit yourself.'

'Pah!'

And later, on day five, in the early evening, passing Zoe outside the bathroom.

'We need to talk.'

'Right now?'

'You can't avoid me.'

'I'm not, really, I just need to pee.'

And then through the door.

'Jane. This is ridiculous.'

'What, exactly?'
'We can't . . . we need to sit down and—Jane?'
'Yes.'
'Can you hear me?'
'Yes—now, will you let me pee?'
And so it went.

*   *   *   *   *

Napoleon Wharf had changed: It was a lot dirtier than he remembered
and it seemed bigger—a whole lot more massively bigger. The gaspipes
and cranehooks seemed like parts out of a giant's toy trainset; steam
valves like merry-go-rounds, ropecoils the size of wigwams. It was
foreign and unsettling—a grown man's trip back to his infant school—
sitting in tiny chairs at miniscule desks—only this was in reverse.
Perhaps his memory was playing tricks on him.

'They taking on?' he asked the guard.
'Maybe,' said the Union man, 'what can you be?'
'Longshoreman, dunnage-stacker, shim-setter, bit of everything.'
'Stevedorin'?' he asked doubtfully.
'Sure, I'll stevedore, if there's a tub would take me.'
'You got your papers in order?'
Easy nodded and shook his suitcase, 'Even packed my toothbrush.'
'Wait there,' he said, adjusted his pants, and made back to the office.

An hour later he was in a bar. A place that specialised in fleecing
longshoreman. It smelled keenly of vomited and alcohol—rum, whisky,
whiskey, rye, and bile. Service was fierce.

'Coffee?' asked the dockhand. He wasn't the biggest, dirtiest, or even
the most senior of the group in the corner but for whatever reason he was
the one they sent over to talk Easy out of applying for the job.

'Sure. I've worked coffee. And steel, and corn syrup in little biddy 100-
gallon drums.'

'How do you feel 'bout 16-hour back to backs? Nuits blanches?'
'I feel great 'bout it.'
'What about the February sleep death?'
'Drunk or straight?'
'We're dry on water!' he barked.
'Suits me.'
'What 'bout sickness, gout, gambling?'
'You'd better look elsewhere.'

192

'Tough guy, huh?'

Easy shook his head: 'Just a working man.'

'What 'bout women trouble?'

'What of it?' said Easy, fighting the urge to turn and look over his shoulder, back at the City.

'One thing I can't 'bide is seein' a grown man pinin' out at sea.'

'You'll get no trouble from me. And I can cook some.'

The dockhand smiled, tipped his head towards the barman and held up two thick, black, crud-encrusted fingers. Two shots of grogue slid across the bar.

'We leave day after tomorrow.'

'Thanks.'

They clunked tumblers and drank.

'Your suitcase . . . '

'What of it?'

'—just walked out the door.'

Easy looked down to see his case was gone. In the doorway, he saw a rough, old docker, drunk, bearded, and bent over bundling the suitcase out of the bar.

'You know that guy?'

The dockhand shook his head: 'He's all yours.'

Easy finished his drink then went after him.

*   *   *   *   *

The Howard Tilton Memorial library wasn't quite as Beth expected— she'd envisaged oakwood panelling, polished inlaid floors, and legions of quiet, powdery librarian spinsters bent to their cataloguing.

The students, on the other hand, were exactly how she imagined. Pale, indifferent, intelligent, slim, youthful, undersexed. They buckled down to their cheap polished plywood corals with routine apathy, rising occasionally, to float off to a bookshelf, ponder, decide, select, and die a moment more. Apt training, she thought, for the cubicle work, cubicle career, cubicle life ahead.

Zoe had lost hope. This being the third library of nine they'd searched. A pattern formed, Beth to the left, she to the right, one floor at a time, blank-faces mirroring one another as they passed by empty-handed.

Beth finally found her, feet crossed on straight legs reaching under the table, arms folded across her sunken stomach. Her head balanced perfectly on her shoulders, like a pale, wigged globe, as she looked ahead

193

over the modest stack of books to a screwed up piece of paper on the coral shelf.

She returned with Zoe and they flanked Jane and made increasingly loud coughs and whinnies to break Jane's reverie. Finally, she looked up and saw them; Zoe first, understandably, but then Beth . . .

'Oh,' she said, realising instantly the reason they had searched her out, 'Okay . . . ' and she began to pack up her books.

HOUND

The girls took seats around the dining room table. The pleasantries of weather and health and outlook as such were thoroughly dealt with on the way home. Jane noticed they hadn't sat together, identically placed, since Easy cooked the first big meal. She recalled that night, her hostility building, going nowhere, and those terrible smashed-life stories. Maybe he was out there, she thought, cooking for others, telling the tale of us.

'So,' she started, 'where to begin? . . . I don't think I can lead this discussion. I'm frankly not up to it.' A heavy silence followed.

'Well,' Zoe broke first, 'The house is just dying. Look at the state of it. We need to organised.'

'Did you clean today?' asked Jane.

'Yes, but I can't do it alone. And where's the cooking roster. Who's turn is it, because I don't think it's me—'

'Quit blabbin'—both of you' said Beth, loud and flat. 'What is this? Why don't we just admit it, for God's sake—we miss the guy, we miss the sex!'

Jane bristled, Zoe controlled her body. There. It was out. The words still bouncing puppy style round the room.

'Screw convention, girls,' said Beth, 'that boy's the best damn lay I ever had.' The girls sat in silence, their position now indefensible. Beth laughed and pointed to Jane: 'He's the only lay you've ever had. And you,' she pointed to Zoe, 'you're up the god damned pole!'

Jane looked at Zoe, arms cupped around her minuscule, yet colossal pot-belly.

'I'm the one he loved,' stated Jane.

'Sure,' said Beth, 'have it that way, if it makes you feel better.'

'It's true!'

'Maybe—' said Zoe, 'but where does that leave us?'

Jane got up: 'I need to know, Zoe. Do you think he loved you?'

Zoe thought for a moment: 'No.'

'But he sure liked the idea of her,' said Beth.

'You can shut up. I know he didn't love you, Beth—you he pitied.'

Beth wasn't taking the bait: 'I don't care what you call it, sister, just bring it on back and pour it all over me.'

She lent her chair on the back legs and laughed.

'I ain't taking all the blame for this, girls. Sure, I got it started, but think on the bright side. If I hadn't, she'd have gone plumb crazy by now and you'd still be a damn virgin.'

'What? You want us to be grateful?' said Jane. 'Don't be pathetic. If we're pathetic, we're finished. If we're pathetic we're . . . we're right back where we started.'

'I, for one,' said Beth, after contemplating for a moment, 'ain't never been here before.'

'Heard that,' said Zoe.

'Oh, Lordie.'

'Question is,' said Beth, 'What are we going to do about it?'

They looked at one another for a long, terrible minute.

*   *   *   *   *

The battered chalkboard sign read—PORTSMOUTH 16, DAKAR 8, MANILLA 1. A hairless, calloused hand wiped a dusty rag across the board removing all traces of the last entry. The hand belonged to an old Port Official who sauntered back to his office where a curious fellow with a curious name sat waiting.

*   *   *   *   *

Across the river, Jane worked along the fat crescent swathe of city from St. Charles to Tchoupitoulas. She showed Easy's photo to every shop-keeper, café owner, dog walker, and unsuspecting pedestrian she came across. Easy was surprisingly well remembered, and well liked, but as the

196

day dragged on it was clear that no-one really knew him, or knew where he was, or when they'd last seen him, or where to start looking. It struck Jane as ironic and strangely typical.

In the bars, eateries, and Quarter hot spots, Beth used her contacts to put the word around. They circulated Easy's picture, stuck it prominently above the banks of CCTV monitors at the security hub, posted it behind bars on their 'Do Not Serve This Man' boards at the cash registers, and taped up fly-posters of Easy on doorways, derelict shops, vacant lots and rock venues with the words - Easy Come Home.

Zoe got to work early, strong-armed the Picayune's missing persons desk set up after Katrina to post Easy's picture on the website and put it out on the wire for the police department, homeless shelters, and even the city morgue to take a look at. She used that full-face, surprised mug he pulled out at City Park at the news of her pregnancy.

At first it seemed a big mistake to have put their 'phone numbers on the fliers—the first thirty-eight calls were from single men on the make, lawyers, various women's groups (who'd seen two different posters and were calling to tell Zoe about Beth, or Beth about Jane), and a New Orleans blogspot called SofaScene, for semi homeless singles inquiring if they had room for a partially sighted, 21-year old, drug dependant Hispanic until Easy came back.

The thirty-ninth call was from Mama-Lek. Zoe thought it was another hoax, especially when the woman demanded they come to her Laundromat with the fourteen dollars he owed her before she'd tell them where he was headed.

Eighteen minutes later, the driver of the taxi they had waved down in the street, had found the Laundromat and they had paid Mama-Lek.

'Leh me looka you,' she said hustling the women into a rough line like she was buying a goat at market. 'Oh, you da fust one, def'nit'ny,' she said to Beth. 'You na him got whole fing started. What you finkin', gul?'

'Can you just tell us where he is?' asked Zoe.

'He was righ 'bout you—miss stri'ty bid'niss.' She then turned to Jane, who'd paid the fourteen dollars and still hadn't spoken. 'You the romantic? Goofuh you,' she said and squeezed Jane's forearm gently before turning to address them all.

'He's working a boat to Manilla. Fipeens. Leaves this morning. Go, go, hurry, hurry,' And with that she shooed them out of the Laundromat.

*   *   *   *   *

Jane, Beth, and Zoe rode silently in the taxi to Napoleon Avenue. They drove down the side of the freight terminal and came to the main gates. A firm looking security guard eased out of his tiny hut and waddled towards them.

'Turn it around, folks, no civies allowed.'

'Leave this to me,' said Beth. Two minutes later they were inside the pound, cruising along passed the huge, cavernous hangers.

'Stop!' said Zoe, seeing some longshoremen at the end of their shift. She jumped out and showed the group Easy's picture.

'Sure,' said one of the men, in a deep, Louisiana baritone, 'That's the new cook on the Hisboro?'

'Where's that?'

'The Hisboro,' he drawled, pushing the sleeve of his rough coat up to expose his wristwatch. 'Sails about now.' He looked back down the row of hangers to a wall of rusting steel at the end: 'Yep—there she goes.'

The wall began, deceptively at first, to move, to slide away. They girls ran towards it. A letter appeared, massive and scanning, fists of rust pocking the white-work . . .

H – I – S . . .

The horn blasted.

- B - O - R - O

The girls arrived at the quay, breathless and frantic. They called, shouted, and finally screamed up at the passing monolith but the tanker simply slipped silently away. They stood and watched, saw it disappear in colossal silence down the Mississippi.

The women fell quiet and drew in, gravitating towards each other in a desperate, generous, three-way embrace. They had never been so close; their smells, their touch, their whimpers and sobs, familiar, yet made new and intense by proximity. It was not an entirely unpleasant place to suffer such pains and after a tentative start they wallowed in each other. An unguarded moan from one would set the others off afresh, like hysterical children, like geese, and around and around the outpouring went. At length, however, they gathered themselves, stiffened in awareness, and parted, and noticed the taxi had slipped away and gladly without collecting his fare.

*   *   *   *   *

They decided to walk the mile and a quarter back to the house. Zoe started out briskly but soon stopped and waited for Jane who had herself slowed to Beth's funereal crawl. They looked a sorry state, strung out like Arapahos, traipsing back towards the Garden District, and drew attention from residents and those driving by.

They didn't appear to be lost or in obvious distress but their sheer hopelessness was clearly projected. Each sidewalk and turn brought them closer to the house and to the realisation that life was going to be very different, and by the time they reached their block on Magazine their mood had descended still further into a despairing black fugue.

When they reached the house, however, something brought the girls up short—it was the unmistakable site, stationed like palace guards alongside a battered suitcase, of Easy's cowboy boots.

Easy himself, lay asleep on the porch, his long curved reptilian back, his legs drawn up and folded into him. The late morning sun fell across his face and he woke, very slowly, tipped his head back, and looked up at Jane, Zoe, and Beth.

They smiled down at him and he was sure it was a dream until he heard his own Louisiana voice say: 'Hey.'

STAY

Within a week the house was returned to its pristine best. Clean, bright, comfortable, and inviting but, above all, lived-in. Sun-sparkled in brilliant streams through the vinegar washed windows. Fresh-cut flowers and market fruits arranged themselves effortlessly into still-life tableaux in every bowl and vase. And you didn't just want to view, you wanted to select a fruit, button-hole a carnation, put your feet on the table and get comfortably involved.

Jane fixed breakfast at the stove, a blue and white-stripped cotton towel folded neatly over her shoulder. Toast and pancakes kept warm with the plates in the oven, eggs and bacon sizzled and spat reassuringly in the frying pan.

Zoe had ground fresh coffee, filling the kitchen with a rich, earthy aroma, and she now watched as the steam hissed and percolated through the grounds and into the waiting pot.

'I like Phoebe,' said Jane, 'for a girl, of course.'

'Ooh, yeah, Phoebe's nice. I've always liked the classics.'

Beth set the table—plates, knives, forks, napkins, salt and pepper, a jug of juice and four stout tumblers: 'How we doing on the protein?'

'Thirty seconds—' said Jane.

Beth nodded, smiled: 'I've been thinking—how do you like Tallulah or Scarlett.'

'Ooh, they're strong,' said Zoe, 'Tallulah, Tallu—*lah* . . . ' she rolled her tongue around the word, 'Scarlett, Scar—*lett*. I like *both* of them.'

In a well-practiced move, Jane killed the gas, drew the plate from the oven, slid the eggs over the toast and arranged the bacon beside the pancakes. Zoe set the coffee pot, cream, and sugar onto the tray. Beth inspected it, then carried it hence. Zoe and Jane flanked her as she left the kitchen and headed off through to the immaculate dining table.

Jane tapped of the back window and Easy appeared, back-lit in golden sunshine, smiling and bare-chested, with a huge potted palm. The girls arranged themselves at the table and began breakfast.

'Jane?' asked Beth, 'I was wondering—could I swap my Tuesday night with you?'

'When for?'

Easy entered clutching armfuls of beets, which he began to wash at the kitchen sink.

'Thursday.'

Two little worms creased across Jane's brow then straightened themselves out: 'I can swap if Zoe can give me Thursday afternoon?'

'Thursday afternoon?' said Zoe, sneaking a little cut of bacon off the breakfast plate, 'Sure. We've got the ultrasound Friday. That and counting stretch-marks is my whole week.'

'Good,' said Jane, 'Then I shall be able to make a day of it.'

'Good for us,' said Beth.

Easy entered with a bowl of beets and Beth held out a T-shirt for him to put on. He dressed and sat among them.

'Well,' he said, 'Ain't this the ding?'

The greeted him and he helped himself to breakfast.

'Hey,' he said cheerfully,' with a forkful of pancake tucked into his cheek, 'I was thinkin'. How 'bout Delphi, you know, if it's a girl?'

'Ooh, Delphi's lovely,' said Zoe, 'Delphi. Del—*phi*.'

'Delphi was where the Oracle lived,' said Jane. 'The Prophet who advised the Greeks.'

'Delphi's *strong*,' agreed Beth.

'Well,' said Jane, 'It's all about the girls today.'

Easy smiled at them. One by one, the women smiled back and continued to enjoy their breakfast . . .

Also available from Thinking Ink

Robbie McCallum

Hips, Lips
&
Fingertips

Jolyon Lax, a pickpocket and street jockey, dreams of opening London's
first ever lap-dancing club—a seductive and exclusive place, where the
celebrities and gangsters rub shoulders and even the Police
Commissioner has a regular table. But his plans threaten the established
order of strip-joints, organized crime, and prostitution and brings Jolyon
to the attention of the underworld crime bosses.

A talented and imaginative writer, McCallum leads us through the seedy
underworld of pickpockets, strippers, criminals and street hustlers in
1980's London. A story of greed, lust, ambition and betrayal. Every scene
brilliantly conceals a lie, a seduction, or a confidence trick.

Also available from Thinking Ink

Robbie McCallum

The
Fixer

A mysterious man arrives on Santa Monica beach and through his wisdom, kindness, and common sense advice attracts a following of hookers, junkies, bums, and alcoholics. He convinces his 'disciples' to give up money and develop a more enriching economy based on trust, friendship and mutual help. The community prospers and the man attracts media interest as thousands come to hear him speak. Their livelihood is threatened by the authorities when similar economies spring up over the U.S. which the I.R.S. are unable to tax.

A thought provoking, modern day fable from a versatile and highly entertaining writer. McCallum never lets his story slip into moralising or tub-thumping. Instead he relies on great dialogue and memorable characters to deliver the universal themes.

Also available from Thinking Ink

Robbie McCallum

The Road to
Marfa Lights

Sam and Toby, two goofball kids, pull an audacious scam with a Vintage Mustang to fund a road trip across Texas. On route they spring Sam's dying uncle from jail and embark on the adventure of a lifetime. Booze, girls, bar room brawls and high adventure—and none of it going to plan.

A funny, face-paced road trip from a versatile and talented writer. McCallum pulls us into the chaotic world of Sam, Toby and Uncle Billy and through a series of well-worked set pieces unveils a heart-warming story of freedom, family, and friendship.

Also available from Thinking Ink

Robbie McCallum

The
Fingerman

Eddie McConville locates and identifies petty crooks, deviants and informants wanted by the criminal fraternity. His is a uniquely specialized, highly respected, and well-paid job in the morally murky London underworld. Eddie sleeps soundly, knowing that he's only ever picked out the rotten apples, until a job goes horribly wrong and he's left with blood on his hands, a price on his head, and not a friend in the world.

A rich, detailed and highly entertaining romp through London's criminal underworld. McCallum's characters, dialogue and plotting grab you from the very first page and leave you gasping for breath at the close.

Also available from Thinking Ink

Robbie McCallum

Cape Verde:
The Now People

The Now People puts on record a Cape Verde we're quickly trading for the package flight and all-inclusive, day-glow wrist-band. Detailing the life on the 10 disparate islands and, in particular, in the wonderfully romantic city of Mindelo, McCallum captures the pirate-slave spirit of a five-hundred-year-old tradition.

A quiver-full of short stories, as balanced, welcome, and rare as a rainbow. This storyteller, whose prose is lithe and mackerel bright, treats us to a vivid, stark, and intensely moving portrait of the Cape Verdean dream.

An Extract from

Cape Verde:
Smiling Out Loud

Robbie McCallum

CHAPTER ONE

FIRST SIGHT

'**R**ed!' I whispered, as if clearing my throat and in the general direction of no-one in particular, 'Get your face set!' She heard me just as her blue-green eyes fell upon the house. Her whole face lit up, then, heeding my warning, her features quickly composed themselves into an inquisitive, studied, yet non-committal alertness.

None of the locals spotted it—we were still in with a chance.

'It's this one,' said Bubu our self-appointed guide, taking my elbow and turning me to face the enormous, double fronted, abandoned, colonial home.

'You like it?'

'Mmm . . . ' I said coolly, as if I flew three thousand miles to remote Tropical Islands and bought historic properties just like this one every other weekend. 'Shall we see inside?'

Bubu waved a hand at the elderly, straight backed, janitor, who we'd met only minutes before, and he in turn produced an enormous brass key from his trouser pocket and approached the massive wooden doors.

I looked for Red as we drew towards the entrance. Her eyes saw mine searching her out and flicked away. That meant one thing.

She'd already made her mind up that she wanted the house. Right there and then on the cobbled road she could have sold up everything we owned and handed it over gladly, willingly, and whole-heartedly, for this—as yet unseen—pile of stone and timber.

And I would have followed her, foolishly or wisely—for at that moment I really didn't know whether this was going to make or break us. Thankfully, Red did. Red always knew about buildings and houses and homes. For her it was easy. Buildings were real and three-dimensional; living, breathing spaces. They worked or they didn't work and her homes always worked brilliantly. The tiny first flat in West London, the collapsing pile, south of the river, in Brixton, and the smart Georgian Terrace in Brighton: Each move up the property ladder, a seismic shift for a humble Glaswegian tenement-renter like me, but nothing more than a signature, a coy wink, and a deft plucking of the keys for Red.

And here we were, apparently about to do it once again. Only this time in a different country, on a different continent, and in a different time-zone. Was this really going to be a step too far?

We had arrived in Cape Verde only four short days before, leaving our two children behind in the loving, capable care of their Aunt, Uncle and cousins in Lancashire. The arrangement had been quite clear—we'll look after your kids, you go and buy a nice modern flat in the sunshine with all mod cons and we'll all go on our holidays together. You could be forgiven for thinking, with the colonial pile we were falling in love with, that we were somehow overstepping the mark a little.

The house was located in the city of Mindelo, on the island of São Vicente. This was a place we had heard a lot about and we were thrilled to finally be here. Discovered in the 1460 by the Portuguese, the island had been practically left untouched until 1850 when the British saw its strategic value and turned the unusually deep and sheltered bay into the busiest port in West Africa.

And so Mindelo was born. *Mindelo*—arguable the most pleasing and enjoyable city in the whole West coast region. Even the name sounded evocative and calming, mellow, like the sound of an oboe.

Our trip had been meticulously pre-arranged. It had to be. We only had seven days including travel and this, after all, was Africa, but not only Africa—sub-Tropical island Africa; with all the usual corruption, mismanagement, and inequality, but with the added complication of being 350-miles off the coast of Senegal. That put us way out in the Atlantic—Next stop Brazil! If anything went wrong we would be stranded, and at the mercy of local hospitality.

Our meetings, day-trips, excursions, hotel bookings, and airport transfers had all been booked, bought and paid for only for the whole planning to go out the window before we'd even left the runway in Manchester. We were delayed for 4-hours due to bad weather and that was enough to see our first vital steeping stone sink without trace into the fast-flowing, every-snaking river of African business.

We settled in at the corner table of the coffee shop and decided to use the time to re-organize and gen up on the trip ahead. Cape Verde has only one decent guide book: The Bradt Guide. There's a slim chapter in the Lonely Planet's Guide to West Africa, but it doesn't merit the purchase if your not visiting the mainland.

Skimming through the book, it struck me once again that Cape Verde is a curious combination of worlds: Old yet embryonic, colonial but crumbling, Tropical yet barren, European *and* African. Every month of the year enjoys glorious sunshine but you are never without a cooling ocean breeze. The Eastern islands are flat, golden, sandy, treeless and windswept but those to the West—a mere 80 miles away—are crystal black, sheer-sided, dense, lush volcanic mountains. The difference couldn't be more startling.

The people too are as unique, complex, and varied. Poor (by Western standards) yet happy (by any standard), industrious yet relaxed, wholly inefficient and yet willing, capable, and occasionally—just when the moment requires it—genuinely inspired.

We couldn't wait to get under way and begin our adventure and were glad when we were finally called to the gate.

The five and a half hour flight passed without further mishap but instead of arriving at Sal International Airport at a leisurely, alcohol induced fugue, to be picked up and whisked on to an all inclusive resort like the rest of our fellow passengers, we were tipped out onto the baked, hot-blown runway with only 15 minutes to make our connecting flight.

In place of the scheduled meeting with the local agent to go over the connections, contacts, schedule, and "island hopping" itinerary, our official welcome and debrief consisted of half a sheet of A6, screwed into a tight ball, sailing over the heads of the Cape Verdean Customs Officials to bounce unceremoniously off my hot sweaty forehead.

'Bubu,' the smiling guide shouted, trying to sound relaxed and cheerful. 'Bubu will meet you at San Pedro.'

'San Pedro?' I called back. 'We're going to São Vicente!'

'San Pedro is the airport *in* São Vicente. Relax. Enjoy. Be careful!' and that was all we heard as we were bustled away to the departure lounge.

I carefully unwrapped the ball of paper, not wanting to lose any of the scant information held therein—it read simply "Bubu". No number, no address, no description—"Bubu".

The polite, glamorous flight crew could have doubled as a tribute band for *The Supremes*. They relieved us of our carry-on bags and the flight—a 16-seater De Havilland Dash—shot down the runway and took to the skies whilst Red and I were crawling up the aisle in search of our seat numbers. We needn't have bothered, for we were the flight's only passengers. We were heartened to learn, as the hostess handed out the boiled sweets, that they had held the flight back especially for us.

The safety announcement, delivered in French, Portuguese, Italian, Spanish, and I presumed, Cape Verdean *Crioule*, was just wrapping up as we began to dip towards our destination, São Vicente, in the North East of the Archipelago.

To describe the airport at San Pedro as tiny would have been a gross exaggeration. A single halogen floodlight lit each corner of a terminal building about the size of a regulation squash court.

Surprisingly, a large number of taxi drivers and baggage handlers milled about the interior under a single, naked 40-watt bulb. There was either *The Supremes* tribute band fan club or stiff competition for flight crew girlfriends.

We collected our single case directly from the baggage handler and headed out into the throng. A large, heavily built man of Mediterranean set, stepped forward and smiled at me, with an open, honest face.

'Robbie?' The voice was clear and deep, the accent Latino and heavily Americanized; just how I imagined a Puerto Rican might sound.

'Bubu?' I shook his warm, comfortable hand and introduced Red.

'Nice,' he said, nodding appreciatively, and bent to kiss her cheek. 'Is this really all you guys brought?'

'Traveling light,' I said and Red's eyes beamed at him 'Get this from the start, we're on a mission'.

'Okay,' he said, as if in response, 'let's go.'

4

person when you
...ne thousands of
...ed free from the
to a comfortable

...nd allowed me to
...er shoulder pack.

He led the way through the sea of hot, muscular bodies, and across a rock-strewn, dirt-floored waste ground that I realized—when I squinted into the darkness—was the airport car park. After about five yards, the wheels on my case were clogged with dirt and stones and utterly useless. If the designer had intended his luggage to double as a rock-scoop, he was to be congratulated. I dragged an impressive collection of pebbles, grit, and rubble along with me until one of the wheels suddenly gave up the game and fell off.

Whilst I was cursing, Bubu lifted the bag onto his shoulder and once again, graciously, said nothing.

In the car, a big, simple Ford pickup, sat a beautiful Cape Verdean girl. A Crioula.

If Bubu was thirty, this girl was twenty-two. She was short, curvy, and petite, with large, bright eyes, a confident smile, and teeth that just went on and on right to the back of her head where she couldn't possible need them. Unless of course, I thought oddly at the time, she was throwing her head back in laughter.

'This is Alegría.'

We said hello and climbed aboard; me riding shotgun, Red in the back with Alegría. Robbie, Red, Bubu and Alegría. It felt like a scene from a movie—some Latino Heist flick or Tropical adventure.

That first 10-minute drive into Mindelo seemed longer and more detailed than at any time since. Although Red and I were both tired and swimmy from the flights, we soon perked up, and as we crested the long rising road, the whole city and the sweep of the bay spread out before us under an ink-black star-filled canopy.

'There she is,' said Bubu, 'Mindelo.' He said *Meen-deh-lo*, playfully, with a high-pitched voice, like Speedy Gonzalez. 'So, where do you guys wanna go?'

stories that change the way you think

Thinking Ink Limited
Media House, Suite 32
Brighton BN2 3HB
United Kingdom

www.thinkinginkmedia.com

Lightning Source UK Ltd.
Milton Keynes UK
10 December 2010

164182UK00001B/6/P